THE Murder GAME

Also by Tom Hindle

A Fatal Crossing

TOM HINDLE

THE Murder GAME

C

CENTURY

1 3 5 7 9 10 8 6 4 2

Century
20 Vauxhall Bridge Road
London S W 1 V 2 S A

Century is part of the Penguin Random House group of companies
whose addresses can be found at global.penguinrandomhouse.com.

Penguin
Random House
UK

First published by Century in 2023

www.penguin.co.uk

A CIP catalogue record for this book is available from the British Library.

ISBN: 9781529902174 (hardback)
ISBN: 9781529902181 (trade paperback)

Typeset in 13.5/17 pt Fournier MT Std by Jouve (UK), Milton Keynes
Printed and bound in Great Britain by Clays Ltd, Elcograf S.p.A.

The authorised representative in the EEA is Penguin Random House Ireland,
Morrison Chambers, 32 Nassau Street, Dublin D02 Y H 68

www.greenpenguin.co.uk

For 'the Baxindles' – Mum, Neil, Harry, Tess and Connor.
With much love and many happy memories
of sunny Exmoor summers.

It's a curious thing to realise you hate someone so much you could kill them. You might imagine it to be a conscious decision. Often, it comes as more of a discovery. Like stumbling on a box of belongings you must always have had but never realised were there.

Edward Finn came to this realisation while fetching in the rack of postcards and crabbing lines that stood outside his shop. He hadn't sold one all day. A couple of ramblers had passed through, but there were no tourists to sell to on New Year's Eve. Martha often said during the winter months that she wasn't sure why he even opened.

He supposed it was the routine that kept him going. Barring his stint in the navy, during which he met, married and convinced Martha to return with him to Hamlet Wick, Edward had spent his life in the shop. The place was in his blood, just as the salt was in the sea and the bracken was on the moor.

Lingering on the cobbled pavement, he took a breath, cold air filling his lungs. In years gone by, this white-stone building had been the harbour master's office. It was perched on the seawall, the water beneath smeared a deep shade of mandarin as the sun dipped low over the crest of Exmoor. Edward felt the breeze on his face and imagined how it would once have carried the cry of gulls and the bellowing of sailors.

Of course, the fishermen were long-since gone. Now, Hamlet Wick boasted a pub, Edward's shop and half a dozen single-storey cottages. Brightly painted sailing boats bobbed on the water, and the only building to be found without a thatched roof was Hamlet Hall, the stately home that presided over the shingle beach. It was a noble old place. Run-down, admittedly, but a reminder of how the little harbour in Hamlet Wick had once made the adjoining market town of Hamlet one of the most prosperous in all of Devon. Most days, the sight of the house caused Edward to swell with pride. But in that moment, it seemed only to worsen his mood.

He'd never been one for New Year's Eve celebrations, but he was especially unhappy about what lay ahead of him on that particular evening. A murder mystery party. He didn't know what Martha had been thinking by signing them up. Murder wasn't something to be made fun of. He'd even heard there were going to be *actors* involved.

The thought of Ian Davies and Will Hooper being behind it did nothing to put Edward at ease. Ian, the latest owner of Hamlet Hall, was a decent sort. But there was something odd about Will. Nothing you could begrudge him for exactly – what he'd experienced as a boy was something no child should have to face – but it seemed to Edward that a party treating murder as a game was made all the more inappropriate by Will's involvement.

The light dwindling, Edward turned back to the shop. As he did, his eyes were caught by the stark white of the lighthouse. Set on the crest of a small hill, just short of half a mile away, it still cut as imposing a figure as it must have done two hundred years earlier. It was beautiful, but even at a distance, he could make out the terrible work that was being done to it.

Tall fences had been set up, topped with barbed wire and emblazoned with the words *Cobb Construction Ltd*. When darkness fell, floodlights would cast the tower in a harsh light, the arched backs of the diggers looming like monstrous beasts.

Edward wasn't alone in his despair over the luxury home to which it was being converted. Tragedy has a way of lingering, and he could think of little as tragic as what had happened, more than twenty years ago, in Hamlet Wick. The lighthouse should stand as a reminder of that heartbreak; a place to be respected, not bought and renovated like some old warehouse.

He was encouraged to know how many local people seemed to share that view. Last time he checked, the petition that Martha had helped him set up on the internet, protesting the development, had accrued nearly a thousand signatures – not far off the entire adult population of Hamlet. Just that afternoon, she'd said an actress with a nearby holiday home had shown support. The woman had put it on social media, or something to that effect.

And then there was Gwen Holloway, head of the local tourist board. As always, Gwen had been kind. Edward remembered the morning she came to the shop, back at the beginning of the year, and told them of her plans for the lighthouse – to preserve it as a memorial for all to see. He had approved of that idea. As far as he was concerned, when the council changed their minds and reallocated the planning permission, Gwen had been betrayed nearly as badly as he and Martha.

The final nail in the coffin had been the two break-ins at the shop. Only a bit of money was stolen and the local handyman – who had bought sweets over the counter as a boy – had fixed the lock free of charge. Still, it had been salt in the wound, and while there was little hard evidence that the construction workers were responsible, Edward felt certain they must be. Nigel Cobb had needed to bring in outsiders to carry out the work, with none of his local boys willing to be involved, and both incidents had occurred in the short space of time since they arrived. It could only have been one of them.

The council had been useless. Edward had complained several times, only to be told that the lighthouse would look magnificent when it was finished. The woman on the phone seemed to have intended it as a comfort, but it only made his resentment burn even brighter. Resentment for his disregarded pleas. And for Damien White, the man whose selfishness – whose arrogance – had descended on Hamlet Wick in the form of barbed wire and floodlights.

Edward stood there, his fingers going numb with cold as he looked at the lighthouse. Over the years, he'd often wondered how something so beautiful could mark the scene of such terrible loss. Now, as he despaired at how it was being violated, he realised that if he ever had the opportunity, he could happily kill Damien White.

Returning his attention to the shop, he saw Martha in the upstairs window, readying herself for Hamlet Hall. He knew that he had to go, however much he disapproved. He was all too aware of how rarely he agreed to an evening out. If it made Martha happy, he could bear it for one night.

He dropped his head and stepped inside, doing his best to leave all thoughts of the lighthouse, and of Damien White, at the door. But some wounds really did just run too deep.

Justin Fletcher typed furiously at his desktop computer. It was an ancient machine, whirring and rattling as if threatening to take off. On the days he resented it most, he wondered if it might be the same dusty contraption on which the *Hamlet Herald*'s stories were first written in 1845.

The office in which he sat was certainly the same, sandwiched on Hamlet's high street between a butcher's shop and a store selling fishing equipment. In the new year, he hoped his editor would finally see sense and consider a new location. It had become far too expensive for a dwindling local paper to sit on the high street – even a high street as modest as Hamlet's – but she had so far resisted. They were the beating heart of the community, she would say. They needed to be visible. Perhaps that had been true when she was his age, back in the 1980s. But right now, the *Hamlet Herald* was on its last legs.

He sat in total darkness, the window foggy with condensation and an electric heater in the corner providing bugger all in the way of actual warmth. The logo that had once been proudly inscribed on the glass was fading, the Christmas lights on the high street flickering through the specks that had peeled away.

Justin typed even more fervently, all too aware that he needed to leave soon for Hamlet Hall. The murder mystery party would make a nice feature, his editor had said. Something a little different. And if Gwen Holloway thought it worth attending, then the *Herald* ought to as well.

While Justin agreed that time with Gwen was always valuable, the thought of spending New Year's Eve in Hamlet Wick didn't fill him with enthusiasm.

A travel blogger had once written that arriving in Hamlet Wick was like arriving at the end of the world. She'd meant it in a wistful, romantic sort of way, as she described standing on the beach and gazing out at the Bristol Channel. For Justin, that was exactly the reason he loathed it. Even getting there was tedious. The little harbour clung to Hamlet by the Lane; a two-mile track so narrow that if you ran into another car coming the other way, you'd often have to reverse the best part of a hundred metres before finding a spot where you could pass without clapping wing mirrors. Dropping down to Hamlet Wick served only to remind him of how he was wasting his youth in this quiet corner of Devon. Of the busy, bustling life that a nineteen-year-old such as himself could be living somewhere else. *Anywhere* else.

Yes, reporting on the murder mystery event was a change from the local bake sales, amateur dramatics and charity raft races. But there still were a dozen other places he would rather spend New Year's Eve than in Hamlet Wick, and a dozen other ways than at a party organised by Will Hooper. It was three years since they'd been at school together, and Justin doubted his old classmate had become any more interesting as they approached their twenties. There was always a big reveal at the end of a murder mystery, wasn't there? Perhaps tonight's would be that there hadn't been a murder at all. The victim had actually done themselves in after spending an hour talking to Will.

Instead, Justin's sights for the evening would be firmly set on Damien White's project at the lighthouse. The greatest local outrage for generations. An exclusive scoop from Gwen on *that* particular topic . . . Now that would be worth writing about. It might even be the story large enough to finally earn him a place at a *real* newspaper.

This wouldn't be the first time Justin had written about the lighthouse – far from it, in fact. Reporting on the work that was taking place had become almost a daily occurrence, to the extent that, even in that particular moment, he was trying desperately to finish an article on Edward Finn's campaign to save it from Damien White. An actress with a nearby holiday home had tweeted a link to the petition, and Justin was determined to file his article on this new development before setting off for Hamlet Hall.

He sat back in his chair, swearing loudly as he struggled to think of an appropriate adjective for his final paragraph. If there'd been anyone else in the little office, he would have done so under his breath. But at this late stage in the afternoon he was completely alone, his editor having clocked off a good forty minutes earlier. She hadn't thought the actress's tweet was worth writing about, but then Justin wasn't convinced that she knew exactly how Twitter worked. She'd certainly never made any effort to help him run the *Herald*'s own pitiful account.

Deplorable. That would do. He typed it in, ignoring the Christmas lights on the high street as they blinked in his peripheral vision.

There would be free booze at Hamlet Hall. And dinner, too. However mundane Will's murder mystery game might prove, at least that was something to look forward to. He'd heard as well that a few of their old schoolmates would be seeing in the new year at The Boatyard. Will wouldn't show his face, of course, but if the party wrapped up quickly, Justin might make his way there and see if he could convince someone to buy him a drink.

He skimmed through his editorial. Considering how quickly he'd written it up, he was pleased. It contained all his usual criticisms of Damien White, with just enough embellishment of the actress's involvement in the lighthouse campaign to offer a fresh spin. He'd even managed to include a scathing line about the construction workers breaking into Edward Finn's shop. That always riled the locals. It was bad enough that White had put an end to the memorial Gwen had been planning for the lighthouse, but for the men working on his development to have upset the Finns was unforgivable.

Glancing at the time, Justin checked his emails. Failing to find what he wanted in his inbox, he tried his junk mail instead. He was looking for a name. Specifically, the name of Damien White's personal assistant. But there was nothing. If her increasingly curt deflections over the phone were anything to go by, he knew there was no chance of her granting an interview by email. Still, he checked. And each time he did, his disappointment grew.

At first, he'd felt a sense of pride in taking on Damien White, the local boy turned London property magnate. If he was honest, though, he now realised that he didn't bear any genuine resentment towards him. He knew about the lighthouse's tragic history, and the scandal White had caused by stealing the planning permission from Gwen. But he didn't see why it should matter. What mattered to Justin was the story. Writing the piece that would help him to apply for a position at a broadsheet. Or a tabloid. Even another regional. All he wanted was his ticket out.

His article finished, Justin hit send. But rather than disappearing into the ether, the words stayed where they were, staring at him defiantly as the computer froze. Silently, he cursed his editor. He'd tried several times to argue that he should be allowed to work on his own laptop. Anything, frankly, would be an improvement on this useless antique. But she remained adamant that he needed to use the *Herald*'s machines.

Swearing even more loudly than before, he thumped the monitor with his fist. It was a procedure he'd carried out so many times he was surprised he hadn't dented it. With the article finally vanishing, he turned off the computer, zipped up his coat and hurried to his feet.

Nigel Cobb had been waiting forty-five minutes for his wife.

In fairness, he was used to it. When Sylvia had first placed their enormous wicker chair in the hallway, he even wondered if it had been to provide him with a place to sit while she prepared for their next excursion. It was a theory he had long-since abandoned. She didn't care enough about his comfort for such a kindness.

One small mercy, he supposed, was that while this was a familiar routine, over the years it was one he'd found himself playing out considerably less frequently. Until recently, there'd barely been a luncheon, cocktail party or even afternoon tea in Hamlet to which Sylvia didn't procure herself an invitation. Nigel, on the other hand, had never been one for socialising. He had installed a pair of wrought-iron gates at the end of their driveway for a reason, and his ideal evening was spent firmly behind them. Preferably watching a football match, with a cold Budweiser in his hand. Sylvia had tried to convince him to drink Birra Moretti instead, claiming that it looked more civilised, but he hadn't taken to it.

Meanwhile, she engrossed herself in the outside world more than enough for both of them. Nigel was happy with that. He knew she was too.

But the evening that lay ahead of them was different. Sylvia had insisted they both attend the murder mystery party at Hamlet Hall. They were on a diplomatic mission. One to restore their place in society.

From the enormous wicker chair, Nigel surveyed the over-sized Christmas tree that filled half of the hallway, the only place in their house big enough to contain it. The tree had been positioned by the staircase, so that the tip reached over the banister and he found himself face to face with a Christmas angel every time he left his bedroom.

It would be coming down in the morning. If he'd had his way, it would never have gone up. He suspected that was why Sylvia had it delivered while he'd been out pitching – unsuccessfully – for another contract. He should make a New Year's resolution to keep a closer eye on her spending. If their efforts at Hamlet Hall were unsuccessful, he might have no choice.

When he'd first received Damien White's contract to renovate the Hamlet Wick lighthouse into a luxury mansion, Sylvia had been all too keen for him to accept. The adjoining bungalow that had once been home to the lighthouse keepers was to be a double garage, while the tower itself would contain a guest room, a lounge, a kitchen and a dining room. It would be snug, but lavish beyond belief, with only the finest designer furnishings and trimmings. The most significant part of the project was to be the very top, with the light completely removed to make space for a master bedroom that boasted a panoramic view of the Bristol Channel.

It was an enormous undertaking; the single largest job that Cobb Construction Ltd had ever been offered. When Sylvia heard the proposed fee, Nigel could almost see the new Range Rover and Caribbean holiday gleaming in her eyes. He, however, had been wary. All he could think of was the tragic history that surrounded the lighthouse, and of the local sentiment towards it.

But Damien White's offer was ultimately too much to resist. In the end, and largely at Sylvia's insistence, he had accepted.

It was the greatest mistake of his career.

Within days of the work beginning, Edward Finn had raised a petition against the project, and with it, Sylvia's luncheons and afternoon teas had quickly dried up. The *Hamlet Herald* began writing brutal editorials on a near-daily basis and the crew that Nigel had brought in had even been accused of breaking into the Finns' shop.

'This can't go on,' Sylvia had said. 'We have to do something. For the firm.'

For the firm, Nigel thought bitterly.

He didn't doubt that his wife cared about Cobb Construction Ltd. It funded every social engagement she could squeeze her way into, not to mention her monthly shopping excursions to Exeter and Bristol, the receipts for which he was too frightened to look at.

It was the word 'we' that he objected to. He was the one getting his hands dirty. He was the one who would incur the wrath of Damien White and need to grovel to restore his reputation in the community. Still, if it meant the survival of the company, it would be worth it. And if it meant that Sylvia once again attended her afternoon teas and cocktail parties – in short, if it meant getting her off his back – then it would be better still.

What Nigel hadn't understood was why she'd chosen a murder mystery party as the moment to take action. She wasn't interested in that sort of thing. And the costume she'd made him wear – the double-breasted, pinstriped suit and the black trilby – was, frankly, humiliating. But all became clear when he learned that Gwen Holloway would be there.

He had to admit, it was canny. To be in Gwen's good graces was to be in all of Hamlet's. Quite how Sylvia had found out she would be attending, though, given her current state of excommunication from her various social circles, Nigel couldn't say. In the end, he'd decided not to ask. Sylvia had her ways, and however she'd managed it, he was sure that he didn't want to know.

When she finally descended the staircase, brushing a bauble with black-gloved fingers, she looked to Nigel almost exactly as when she'd disappeared nearly an hour earlier. The same glittering dress, same feathered headband . . . All that seemed to have changed was the black feather boa now draped around her shoulders.

He didn't point this out, of course. Instead, he simply stood, fetched the keys to the Audi from inside his jacket and opened the door for her. Not a word was spoken between them as they stepped into the cold.

13

In fifteen years, only a handful of the countless functions and events Gwen Holloway had attended in Hamlet had ever made her nervous.

There was the funeral of the teenager who died in a yachting accident and whose parents had asked her to deliver the eulogy. And the open day she'd attended at the local retirement home, having just recovered from a vicious bout of the flu.

This time, it was her own husband putting her on edge.

In a seaside community that thrives on tourism, everyone vies for the attention of the head of the local tourist board. You don't marry her if you aren't prepared to shake a few hands and smile for a few photographs. Hugh knew that. He followed Gwen to every engagement without a word of complaint. Never resented her for the spotlight in which she spent her every public moment.

The murder mystery party at Hamlet Hall would be different.

When Gwen had first signed them up, she'd looked forward to it. Christmas had been lovely, but you could only turn on the Hamlet high street lights so many times before the novelty wore thin. Hearing that such a unique event was taking place in

Hamlet Wick, and on New Year's Eve . . . In the rare absence of any other engagements, she'd been keen to go, even buying a brand-new bottle-green ball gown especially.

At first, Hugh had been up for it, too. Of all the restaurants and hotels in the county to which he delivered produce from the surrounding farms, Hamlet Hall had one of the most lavish menus. He didn't often get to sample his own wares, and he was looking forward to the dinner they'd be served before the mystery began.

But his mood had been catastrophically dampened that afternoon, when Sylvia Cobb had texted Gwen to say that she and Nigel would also be there.

Of course, Gwen had known straight away that she'd have to share this with Hugh. There needed to be some ground rules in place if he was going to meet Nigel. Specifically, there was to be no discussion of Damien White, and certainly none of his project at the lighthouse.

Since that conversation, Hugh hadn't said a word. He'd disappeared into the living room and closed the door behind him, although from her seat at the kitchen table, Gwen could still clearly hear the rugby match that he was watching on the TV. Theirs was only a small home. If she planned to one day pursue her ambition of becoming Mayor, she had to cement her image now. It wasn't enough to be warm and attentive. She had to be modest too. To that end, she and Hugh lived in a renovated cottage. Beautiful but compact. Just as she needed it to be.

She couldn't blame him for the way he felt. After all, they each had their own reasons for hating Damien White. The memorial she'd planned for the lighthouse had been years in the making; years of work that he'd snuffed out in an instant, with a rumoured substantial 'donation' to the local council.

But Hugh's hatred ran so much deeper. It was primal, a cocktail of grief and rage that fizzed in his blood. He would never forgive the damage Damien had done to the Holloway family. Nor would he forget how the police let him walk away.

As long as he lived, Gwen knew her husband's fury would never leave him. It was just unfortunate that, by association, it now extended to Nigel Cobb.

She would simply have to manage Hugh's temper. She understood his pain, but she couldn't have him coming to blows with Nigel at a public function. Least of all, one that was being attended by the *Herald*.

The discovery that Justin would be there too had done nothing to soothe Gwen's nerves. He was far too interested in the lighthouse, and to hear him interrogating Nigel about how he could lower himself to work on it might just light the fuse on Hugh's frustration.

Still, Hugh had his instructions and Nigel was ultimately a timid creature. If there was drama to be found, she could bring it to heel.

She fixed a glistening string of pearls around her neck, before lifting the invitation from the table and running her fingers over the letters. *Murder at Hamlet Hall* was printed in raised gold type. The invitation had been nicely produced. If it was anything to go by – combined, for that matter, with the catering order Hugh had delivered to Hamlet Hall that morning – Ian was putting significant effort into the evening.

But then, it wasn't all Ian's doing.

Gwen's last encounter with Will Hooper had been at a school sports day event, perhaps ten years ago, where she'd been handing out the prizes. On her way there, she had wondered if she might be able to pick him out – the child from the news stories. When she arrived, she spotted him almost immediately. There was no doubt in her mind that the jumpy, nervous-looking boy who seemed so desperate to distance himself from the other children was the one everyone in Hamlet had been talking about.

It was hardly surprising. Few people would ever experience something so traumatic, and fewer still at such a young age. Nobody could deny that it might cause him to grow up a little different.

She heard the rugby cut out in the next room. Composing herself, she tucked the invitation into her handbag.

It was time to go.

Murder at Hamlet Hall

Guest list

Gwen and Hugh Holloway
Nigel and Sylvia Cobb
Edward and Martha Finn
Justin Fletcher
Lily and plus-one

Actors

Jack Marshall
Theo Bloom
Claire Foley

Staff

Ian Davies
Carl Gifford
Will Hooper

Seven o'clock

1

All at once, Will Hooper was seven years old again. He gambolled onto the beach at Hamlet Wick, plastic bucket in his hand, while his dad went in search of a ticket for the car park.

He was going to find a fossil that morning. He was sure of it. In the spring, he'd stumbled on an ammonite, barely larger than a button, but which immediately became his most prized possession. In the months that followed, he'd been so determined to find another that they'd had to visit Hamlet Wick every Saturday morning so he could comb the beach.

Buffeted by a bracing October wind, Will kept his eyes on the ground, the shale shifting and sliding beneath his feet as he made his way to the water's edge. This was where he'd found his fossil before. This was where there'd be another.

He scurried forward, moving as quickly as he dared until, without warning, a loose stone went flying and his legs disappeared from beneath him.

Picking himself back up, he wiped his hands on his trousers, brushing off salt and dust, and looked around for his bucket. It hadn't gone far. But he immediately lost interest when he saw what lay beyond it.

A few metres away, heaped by the water, was a shapeless mass of dark fabric. A dozen gulls were fussing over it, flapping their wings and squawking at each other.

Transfixed, Will took a step forward.

At the sound of his approach, the gulls looked up. One shrieked at him angrily and hopped away. He took another step and one by one the birds all lifted into the air, revealing the scene like a Polaroid pulling gradually into focus.

He heard his dad, calling out for him to stop, but he paid no notice. He was just feet away now. As the gulls dispersed, he saw a shock of matted hair, a pair of wide, unblinking eyes and a pale, outstretched hand.

Rooted to the spot, he opened his mouth, cold air filling his lungs as a piercing scream rose to his lips.

The sound of a metal pan rattling to the floor wrenched Will from the twelve-year-old memory.

With trembling hands, he took an inhaler from inside his dinner jacket, shook it vigorously and drew in a breath. He closed his eyes, taking a moment to ground himself.

He was in Hamlet Hall, standing in the narrow corridor that was tucked away at the back of the hotel. The kitchen was a few short metres to his left, the smell of roasting lamb filling his nostrils. To his right, the muffled sound of a jazz record drifted across the entrance hall from the restaurant.

His eyes still closed, he pulled on the inhaler again.

He remembered that day so vividly, sometimes he could hardly believe it had been over a decade since it had happened. But it was difficult to forget something you revisited on a daily basis.

The flashbacks came without warning, often without provocation. If ever Will allowed his mind to wander, it seemed always to go straight to that moment on the beach. The moment that had gone on to engulf his entire life. From time to time, there was something just startling enough to tug him away. In school, it might have been a teacher snapping at him for daydreaming in class. At home, his dad grasping him by the shoulder.

This time, it had been Carl, Hamlet Hall's resident chef. He'd been clattering about all evening, using his pots and pans as more of a percussive ensemble than a means to prepare dinner for the guests. Will wondered if one of them might complain about the noise, and his palms began to sweat.

When he'd first asked about staging a murder mystery night at Hamlet Hall – a conversation that had taken him several weeks to muster the courage even to broach – Ian Davies, the hotel's owner, had been deeply sceptical. But after much nervous petitioning from Will, he had finally agreed. If the party was a success, he would make a regular feature out of it. It would become an invaluable way of drawing in the locals outside of tourist season.

It was no secret that he needed the income.

As grand as it was, Hamlet Hall had never been intended as a hotel. The old manor house had stood in Hamlet Wick for three centuries, built as an ancestral home by one of the first Earls of Hamlet when the harbour had been bustling and the adjoining market town one of the finest in Devon. Outside, it still looked the part. The first impression guests would receive was of the great oak doors, ivy creeping up stone walls and broad bay windows that looked out towards the Bristol Channel. It boasted ambience; promised comfort and luxury.

But a glance at Tripadvisor suggested that, for many guests, the fantasy ended there. Much of the stonework needed restoring, the wood panelling had dulled and the rooms lacked double-glazing. There were more functional complaints too: reports of faulty coffee machines, intermittent Wi-Fi – that is, for those who managed to access it at all – and rooms' worth of furniture that badly needed replacing.

In any other profession, Will thought it might be a relief for such criticisms to only need worrying about for half the year. But for a struggling hotel, in a little-known village on England's south-west coast, the almost complete lack of business during the autumn and winter months must have been just as disheartening as the barrage of complaints during the summer.

He'd heard all about Ian's attempts to draw in the locals out of season. There had been afternoon teas. Dance parties. Film nights. As far as Will knew, none had been successful.

All Hamlet Hall could offer that *did* seem to be of any interest was the restaurant. Carl's cooking had quite the reputation among the surrounding villages, but Ian couldn't turn a profit for six months of the year solely by serving Sunday lunches. And so, in a bid to try something different, he had allowed Will to use Hamlet Hall as the venue for his murder mystery party.

When the event was first announced, the ensuing silence had been deafening. A fortnight passed without a jot of interest. Then, miraculously, there'd been registrations. Within a week, they had eight eager participants.

Suddenly enthused, Ian had thrown everything he could at the party. Champagne was being served throughout the evening. Carl had been tasked with preparing a lavish three-course dinner. Rooms were even offered at discounted rates, for any guests who might want to stay the night, although Will noticed most had overlooked that particular offer.

He, meanwhile, had done his best to anticipate every problem they might encounter during the game itself. He'd thought of contingencies for a guest not attending, for the clues proving too difficult to find or an actor forgetting the prompts and instructions that would keep the mystery on track.

One thing he hadn't counted on was Carl making so much noise in the kitchen that it risked completely shattering the atmosphere.

As Will's panic at the thought of a guest complaining increased, a door opened to his side, causing him to jump. Realising that the sudden movement had only been Ian emerging from his office did not put him at ease.

During the weeks they'd spent organising the party, Will had never seen Ian bear any expression other than a frown. Set beneath a receding ginger hairline, on a square, flushed face, the creases on his brow seemed to be fixed in place, as if they'd been etched into an angry lump of clay. But at the sight of Will hovering in the corridor, that frown became as severe as he'd ever seen it.

'I just stepped away to meet the actress,' Will explained hurriedly. 'She wanted a glass of water before she joined Jack and Theo in the lounge.'

Ian murmured something that, for the most part, was

unintelligible, although Will was fairly sure he'd caught the word 'useless' towards the end. Then he yanked the office door shut and strode into the entrance hall.

Will didn't follow straight away. Instead, he raised the inhaler a final time. Screwing his eyes shut, he breathed deeply.

He needed to be calm. To be in control.

Stuffing the inhaler back inside his dinner jacket, he hurried after Ian, shoes clicking on the tiled floor as he crossed the hall.

The music rang out even clearer as they stepped into the restaurant, Frank Sinatra's silky tones bouncing from the wood-panelled walls. Despite his growing nerves, the sight of the room caused Will to glow with pride.

He and Ian had spent the afternoon arranging the furniture, creating one long table that was now perfectly laid with sparkling glassware and gleaming cutlery. The fire was lit, crackling beneath an enormous portrait of the first Earl of Hamlet, while Will's gramophone stood proudly on an oak sideboard, beside an ornate drinks globe. Even the stag's head mounted above the door, which had been described in some of Hamlet Hall's most critical reviews as tacky, had an air of nobility to it. They'd adorned the place with a few props, too, just to drive home the evening's theme. A string of black and white tassels was draped over the sideboard, the table's ironed napkins swapped out for glittery gold serviettes. Ian had dug out a few brass candlesticks and Will had even managed to bring along an antique magnifying glass from the shop.

It didn't take long, though, for the pride to dwindle, and for his nerves to once again make themselves known.

To see people signing up had done wonders for Ian's attitude towards the party. Head of the local tourist board Gwen Holloway's attendance had been cause for celebration, while an email from the *Herald*, outlining their plans to send a reporter, had even prompted a hint of a smile.

People were interested. The fee of fifty pounds per head seemed not to have been balked at, and if all went well, the party could be replicated, with larger groups and more lavish menus. Throw in some breakfast the following morning and guests might even come from the surrounding villages, if they could be persuaded to stay the night. In short, Ian's dream of a regular, out-of-season event finally seemed on the cusp of being realised.

But when Nigel and Sylvia Cobb added their names to the guest list, Will had worried that Ian might call the entire night off.

Everyone in Hamlet knew that Nigel was working on Damien White's project at the lighthouse. Just as they all knew about Edward Finn's petition to see it cancelled and how White had effectively stolen the planning permission from Gwen. More than that, however, everyone knew what the lighthouse *meant*. It was more than a piece of history; it was the site of a wound from which many would agree Hamlet had never recovered. After it had stood derelict for more than twenty years, rusting and crumbling as it loomed over Hamlet Wick, Gwen had been the one to finally step in. To try to transform it, and create something that would honour the tragedy it represented.

That is, until Damien White had returned – until he'd snatched the place from under Gwen's nose and recruited Nigel Cobb to carry out his work. If you'd asked Will, he'd have said that having the Cobbs spend an evening with the Finns and the Holloways was like tossing dynamite onto a bonfire.

But of course, Ian wouldn't cancel. Not when this had been his first successful attempt to draw in the locals. The only option was to persevere; to keep a tight rein on the guests and do everything possible to keep the conversation away from the lighthouse.

For the time being, at least, they had remained civil. Carl had mixed a few cocktails that were supposedly popular during the roaring twenties, and the group now milled around the fireplace, sipping at Sidecars and Singapore Slings. Edward Finn was casting a poisonous glare at Nigel, who seemed to be doing all he could to pretend he hadn't noticed, but no unpleasantries had yet been exchanged. From his vantage point in the doorway, Will heard Gwen make a joke, prompting Sylvia to guffaw, all lipstick and gleaming teeth.

'Don't leave them again,' said Ian. 'They're behaving for now but we need to be careful.'

Will nodded, deciding it wouldn't do him any favours to point out that he had only left the group in the first place because while Ian was in his office, there had been nobody else to greet the actress. 'What about the final couple?' he asked.

'No sign of them. We can wait a little longer, but we might have to serve the starters without them if they don't arrive soon.'

'Have they got far to come?'

'They wanted rooms, so I suppose so. And it isn't a couple. It's a young woman and her father.' He fixed Will with a stern look. 'Is everything else ready?'

Will nodded again, forcing as much confidence into his voice as he could muster. 'The clues are in place, the letters are on the dinner table and the actors all seem happy. They'll wait in the lounge, just as you wanted.'

Ian let out a long breath and looked again at the guests. 'We just need to get through dinner. Once the game begins and we can split them all up, we should be in the clear.'

The sound of more clattering echoed from the kitchen.

'For Christ's sake.' Ian glared into the hallway. 'Stay here. Keep a close eye on them, and if it looks like someone might even *think* about that lighthouse, change the subject.'

'How should I do that?'

'Think of something! Ask if they want more drinks. Tell them a joke. Do whatever you need to; just make sure they're talking about something – *anything* – else.'

Before Will could reply, Ian hurried from the restaurant.

He understood why Ian was so nervous. With the *Herald* on hand to see any potential falling out between the guests, the pressure was most definitely on. But Ian wasn't the only one eager for the party to be a success. Nor was he the only one feeling uncomfortable about who had chosen to attend.

Will risked a glance towards the fireplace, where Hugh Holloway was hovering at Gwen's shoulder, sipping an Old-Fashioned while he made what looked like some painfully uncomfortable small talk with Nigel Cobb.

Will's greatest fear, *much* greater than a fight over the lighthouse, was that the guests might see through the mystery he'd prepared. That they'd spot the hidden purpose he'd buried among the clues, unbeknownst even to Ian.

If one of them saw through it . . . If *Hugh* happened to realise . . .

He tucked his hands into his pockets, to hide that they were trembling.

That day alone he'd relived the morning on the beach four times already. Four times he'd heard the shrieking of the gulls, seen the bulging eyes and felt the scream upon his lips.

It was a last resort. He knew that much. And if it didn't work, he had no clue where he'd turn next. But if the game went the way he hoped, then perhaps the party would be where he finally rid himself of it. Perhaps, when this evening was through, he would be free.

His chest tightening, he fetched the inhaler from his pocket again and took another pull. Then he straightened up, adopted the most confident expression he could manage and made for the guests.

2

'So, now I teach.'

In the lounge, Theo Bloom looked up from his script.

Upon discovering that the actress Will had recruited to play the maid looked to be somewhere in her forties, and was therefore much closer to his own age, Jack Marshall seemed to have completely forgotten his earlier suggestion that she might make good girlfriend material for nineteen-year-old Theo. This wasn't something that Theo would usually have been upset by. He might actually have been glad, if Claire, the actress, didn't look quite so uncomfortable about being the focus of Jack's attention.

A dozen armchairs of various sizes, patterns and states of decay were dotted around the lounge. And yet, Jack had insisted she sit beside him, on a padded green sofa. Clutching a champagne flute, he angled himself towards her, the leather squeaking as he wriggled his behind into a comfortable position.

Claire, meanwhile, sat with her hands planted firmly on her knees. With the plain dress she wore for her role as the maid, and her dark hair tied neatly behind her head, she looked as if she were posing for a Victorian photograph.

'Is that right?' she asked.

'Oh, yes. At Hamlet High School. The West End was wonderful, of course. A chapter in my life that I'll never forget. But you have to recognise when it's time to allow the next generation their chance. We can't be young for ever!'

She laughed obligingly, as Theo wondered how many times – and to how many women – Jack had recounted this particular anecdote.

'Young Theo was one of mine not so long ago,' he continued. 'So was Will, for that matter. But Theo's moving up in the world now. You're looking at a future star!'

'Oh?' Claire glanced at Theo, seemingly grateful for a reason to turn away.

'Yes, indeed.' The enthusiasm built in Jack's voice. 'One of my finest students, even before I recruited him to our little group, the Hamlet Players. But with the kind of auditions he's going for these days, one day soon you'll see his name in lights. Isn't that right, Theo?'

A yearning expression took form on Claire's face. Theo knew that look. He was pretty sure he'd even worn it a few times himself. After being cornered by Jack, sooner or later everyone searched for a lifeline.

'Have you actually looked at these?' He brandished the ring binder that Will had put together for them, his own notes scribbled across every inch of clear space. On the coffee table between them, a second, perfectly clean copy lay face down beside an old stethoscope.

'I've given them a cursory glance.'

'So, you haven't.'

'It's hardly Shakespeare.'

'All the same. There are some pretty specific lines that Will needs us to deliver. Instructions for the guests—'

'Theo.' Jack held up a hand to silence him. 'I went twenty-five years in London without once fluffing a line. I'm sure I can cope with a few glorified stage directions written by young Master Will.'

'What's your name, then?'

'My name?'

'Your character this evening.'

'I'm the village doctor.' Jack pointed towards the stethoscope.

'And what's his name?'

There was a long pause, during which Theo couldn't help but feel a flicker of satisfaction.

'Dr Wargrave,' said Jack, spitting out the words like a mouthful of spoilt wine. 'That's my character. You're Spade, the solicitor, and Claire is playing the maid. Now put down those notes, dear boy, and drink some champagne. It's not often you'll get stuff this good for free.'

Theo's vindication fizzled out just as quickly as it had surfaced. Admitting defeat, he took a flute from the coffee table and allowed himself a small sip. In fairness, Jack was right; it was good stuff. The problem was that they were on a job. No matter how far beneath him Jack seemed to think tonight's performance might be – or, for that matter, how small the fee Will was paying – some professionalism was required.

Jack turned back to Claire, determined to keep the conversation flowing. 'How did Will find you for this evening?'

She cleared her throat, trying hard, it seemed, to mask her

disappointment at Theo's failure to draw Jack's attention. 'I used to do a little am-dram in my twenties, back when I lived in the city. I've been thinking for a while about getting back into it, but I wasn't sure I'd be confident enough to join a group. When I saw the Facebook post, saying that Ian and Will were looking for an actress to take part tonight, I thought it might be a slightly less . . . *stressful* way of seeing if it's still for me.'

Jack scoffed. 'I'd hardly call this bizarre performance *drama*. When this evening's done with, you really ought to join the Hamlet Players.'

'I'm not sure . . .'

'Of course you should! There's some wonderful talent and we're very proud of our productions. You'll feel right at home among some like-minded thespians.'

'It isn't just the two of you, then?'

Jack laughed. 'No, there's a decent number of us. About fifteen or so. Theo and I were just the only ones available for this evening's performance. To tell the truth . . .' He leaned in a little closer. 'While I'm fond of our little group, there can be a certain amount of snobbery.'

'Is that right?'

'Oh, yes. I say that young Theo and I were the only ones available this evening. I suspect the truth is actually that we were the only ones willing to *make ourselves* available. The others saw it all as . . . shall we say, a little beneath them?'

Theo took a deep breath, keeping his eyes glued to his notes.

For a few seconds, nobody spoke. From the corner of the room, Theo heard the ticking of the grandfather clock, and from the direction of the restaurant, the muffled sound of distant music.

Jack tipped back the remnants of his champagne. 'Let me fetch you a drink.'

'Oh, no, that's all right.'

'No, no.' Already he was on his feet. 'I managed to convince Carl to pour a glass for Theo, but he doesn't seem to appreciate it. I'm sure he'll give me one for you instead.'

'I really don't want to be any trouble.' Claire was pleading now. 'Are we even supposed to be drinking?'

'It's no trouble!' Reaching the door, he turned back and gave what Theo took to be a cheeky wink. 'Let's have a small one and then we'll see if I can't sweet-talk you into joining the Players.'

He vanished before Claire could protest further, the door thudding shut behind him. The second he was gone, she whipped around to face Theo.

'Does he have a girlfriend?'

Theo recoiled into the back of his sofa. 'Are you *interested*?'

'Not remotely. But I didn't see a wedding ring, so I was hoping there might be a girlfriend I could threaten to introduce myself to. Otherwise I'm going to have to start thinking of excuses to shake him off.'

Theo smiled. There was something colder in Claire's voice now. Something more grounded. In an instant, the sweet facade with which she'd apparently been humouring Jack seemed to have disappeared.

'He does. But . . .'

'But what?'

He felt the smile slip from his face. 'But *she*'s married.'

Claire didn't reply, and in the silence, Theo found himself beginning to shuffle uncomfortably.

Jack's girlfriend was a subject he tried hard to avoid, having learned of her existence over the summer, during a meeting with the Hamlet Players. A few rehearsals later, after plucking up the courage to ask Jack if perhaps he should see someone who wasn't already married, all he'd been told in response was, 'I can't tell you how many married women I saw back in London. Never did a jot of harm.'

He wondered how the woman Jack was so proud of seducing would feel about the speed at which he'd taken a shine to Claire. Then again, as he thought of the round belly Jack had grown and the way middle age had caused his cheeks to sag, he couldn't help but wonder what it was she found so appealing at all.

He supposed Jack took care of himself in some regards. While he'd adopted a tweed suit and a gleaming pair of brogues for his performance as Dr Wargrave, he was always impeccably dressed and groomed, never going longer than a fortnight without having his grey hair closely cut and styled.

Or perhaps it was the stories of his time in London that had won her over. In a sleepy seaside village, the idea of a retired actor might seem a glamorous prospect.

'Is he serious?' asked Claire. 'Did he actually perform in the West End?'

'For nearly twenty-five years.'

'Why haven't I heard of him? He says he was in all the shows.'

Theo shrugged. 'They all need extras.'

'And is that what really brought him back here? He finally realised it just wasn't going to happen?'

'I suppose that depends on who you ask.'

'How so?'

'Well, if you ask him, he'll tell you that he'd had enough of the London lifestyle.'

'And if I asked you?'

Theo paused. 'His mum got ill a few years ago. Dementia. He didn't have any money for care, so he came home to look after her.'

He thought he saw Claire's features soften slightly, although only for a moment.

'What did he mean by what he said about you?'

'What about me?'

'He said you're up and coming. That you're going for some big auditions.'

'He exaggerates.'

'You're being pretty diligent with those.' She waved at the ring binder in his hand. 'You haven't put them down since I arrived. And he's right about the champagne, too. You've barely touched it.'

Theo forced a smile. 'If you're going to take on a job, you might as well get it right.'

'Very professional. I'll bet you even do that thing with your phone, don't you? Where you record yourself reading the other characters' lines so you have someone to rehearse with at home.'

He felt himself blush. He was too embarrassed to admit it, but she was absolutely right – he'd recorded dozens of one-sided scenes on his phone. Some were to help prepare for his role in the Hamlet Players' next show, others were from productions gone by and he hadn't yet had the heart to delete them. He even had a few for completely random roles that he simply hoped one day for the chance to play.

He glanced down at the folder, surveying the pages of notes that Will had prepared, and his own handwritten scrawling. As he did so, he thought again of Jack. This time, however, he pictured a twenty-five-year career as nothing more than an extra. He imagined pursuing fame and stardom, only to be brought straight back to Hamlet.

'What about you?' he asked, suddenly desperate to change the subject. 'Have you been in the industry?'

'I did some decent amateur productions when I lived in London. Never anything more than that, though.'

'And you really found tonight through Facebook?'

'That's right. Ian wrote something about needing an actress to take part in a murder mystery party. So I got in touch.'

Theo nodded. 'You really should join us at the Hamlet Players. I know Jack can be a bit . . . *much*. But I'm sure you'd love the others.'

She gave a little smile, then glanced towards the door. 'He's going to be back in a second, isn't he? How long can it take to pour two glasses of champagne?'

Theo watched her. He saw her shoulders slump, and a look of resignation spread across her face.

'You know, his name isn't really Jack.'

Claire frowned at him.

'It's a stage name. Jack Marshall. He took it on years ago. Thought it would help him get more roles when he was in London.'

Her eyes went wide. 'You're joking.'

'I wish I was.'

'What's his real name?'

Theo hesitated.

'Go on,' said Claire. She was smiling, though not in the polite way that she had for Jack. This time it was genuine. 'I won't tell.'

Theo relented. 'It's Jim. Jim McBride.'

A broad grin spread across her face. 'Jim McBride,' she repeated. 'So, these students at Hamlet High. Do they call him Mr McBride?'

Theo shook his head. 'He used to make us call him Mr Marshall. But we all knew it wasn't really his name. He has to put McBride on anything official. Test papers. Permission slips for theatre visits. That sort of thing.'

Claire's grin became even wider until she finally began to laugh. Theo felt a sudden twinge of guilt. Then, despite himself, he found that he was laughing, too.

At the sound of the door handle beginning to rattle, he quickly raised his notes again. Claire, too, managed to swiftly compose herself as Jack nudged the door open with his shoulder.

'Now,' he declared, pressing a champagne flute into her hand and settling himself back onto the sofa. 'What shall we drink to? I'd suggest new friends.'

Risking a glance away from his notes, Theo caught Claire's eye. As he did, he was sure that he could still make out the faint trace of a smile upon her lips.

'New friends,' she told him, before clinking glasses with Jack and taking a small sip.

3

'So, what's inspired tonight's event?'

Will looked down at the phone that was being waved under his nose, an angry red light blinking as he tried frantically to come up with an answer he'd be happy to read in the *Hamlet Herald*. All he could think of, though, was how Justin seemed not to have bothered with the 1920s dress code.

In fairness to Edward and Martha Finn, who had arrived in a tweed suit and a faded floral dress and cardigan, there was no way of being sure they hadn't actually come in their own clothes too. But the rest of the group had certainly made an effort.

Gwen had followed the code to the letter, with a bottle-green gown and a string of pearls hanging from her neck, while Sylvia Cobb appeared to have stepped straight from the pages of *The Great Gatsby*. She had swept into the restaurant in a glittering gold dress, a feather boa around her shoulders and silk gloves reaching for her elbows.

As for the men, Hugh had donned a pencil-grey suit with a polka-dot bow tie, a flat cap and a gleaming pair of black-and-white shoes. Nigel looked more like a cartoon gangster than a

Golden Age dinner party guest, hanging at Sylvia's shoulder in an oversized pinstripe suit. He carried a trilby in his hand, which, if his uncomfortable expression was anything to go by, she hadn't succeeded in convincing him to wear.

Justin, meanwhile, had come in a thin blazer and a crumpled pair of chinos, his *Hamlet Herald* badge hanging from a lanyard around his neck.

Will fought back a wave of resentment. They'd never moved in the same circles – in fairness, he hadn't moved in *any* particular circle – but he'd known during their time at Hamlet High that Justin hadn't been one for rules. There had always been an excuse; a cocky smile and a witty retort. As excited as Ian was by the prospect of some publicity, Will was sure he must have been disheartened that Justin was the reporter the paper was sending.

The little red light continued to blink as Will struggled for an answer. Gwen had spoken to Justin a moment earlier, his questions about the lighthouse having been promptly rejected by Nigel Cobb, and she'd made it sound so easy. So natural.

'Ah, now, Justin,' she'd said. 'While I'm sure we're in for a wonderful time, and I'm very happy to lend my support, you know just as well as I do that tonight's event has been organised solely by Hamlet Hall. I won't have any influence over whether it becomes a regular feature. What I will say is how pleased I am to see that such a local effort has brought this evening together. I know that the beautiful food we'll soon be enjoying has come from nearby farms, and that some props have been kindly sourced from Sue Bains on the high street—'

'At the bric-a-brac shop?'

'I'm sure she'd prefer you to write "antiques dealer".'

'Right.' Justin held the phone an inch closer. 'Any further comment on Damien White's project at the lighthouse? Or on Edward's petition? I've already tried speaking to Nigel, but—'

'No more than we've already given.' Suddenly, there was an edge to Gwen's voice. 'The development taking place at the lighthouse is a private project and not something for the tourism board to hold any kind of opinion on.'

'But surely—'

'Justin, I really think you should speak with Will, here. It's New Year's Eve, after all, and this *is* his party . . .'

And so, moments later, Will had found himself being questioned. A look of bored expectation was lathered across the young reporter's face, in stark contrast to the grinning head shot that hung from his lanyard. He gave the phone a little waggle. He was waiting.

'Well,' Will managed to force out. 'It's a murder mystery.'

Justin cocked an eyebrow.

'We're . . .'

Floundering, he tried to remember something he'd said a few days ago. Ian had decided it would be simpler to set up a Bluetooth speaker and find a decent Spotify playlist than to play music all evening on a gramophone. But Will had stood his ground. It wasn't about convenience. Nor, for that matter, was it about the fact that he must be the only nineteen-year-old in Devon without either a Bluetooth speaker or a Spotify account. It was about authenticity; taking their guests by the hand and leading them straight into the pages of a vintage detective novel.

It was a good little speech, Will had thought. Admittedly, one he'd rehearsed several times at home, having sensed Ian's growing reluctance to use the gramophone. But it had done the trick.

He looked Justin in the eye. 'We wanted it to feel like an old detective story.'

'But it's sort of a play, isn't it? Like a piece of interactive theatre. It's the guests who'll solve the murder.'

'In a sense. After dinner, when the game begins, there'll be actors around the hotel who lead them to clues—'

'And the guests are all playing characters.'

'That's right.'

'Is one of us going to *be* the murderer?'

'Yes,' said Will. 'But they don't know it yet. There are envelopes on the table – one for each of you – which contain details of all the characters.'

'And which story are we playing out? Is it an Agatha Christie? A Sherlock Holmes?'

'Actually, tonight's story is one I've come up with.'

For the first time, Justin looked genuinely interested. 'So, *you*'ve chosen which of us is the murderer.'

The phone inched closer to Will's face.

'I've chosen a character,' he said, a note of uncertainty creeping into his voice. 'In the story.'

'Aren't you worried what people might think about that? About your involvement in any of this, to be quite frank. Given your history with this sort of thing.'

Will said nothing. Justin had asked the question sweetly enough, but it landed like a punch to the gut. The little red light seemed to become all the more determined, blinking even more aggressively than it had before.

'I don't . . . I mean, I didn't . . .'

He could feel himself beginning to panic. He tried to laugh but it came out all wrong, the sound that tumbled from his mouth more akin to a whimper. He clenched his fists, palms beginning to sweat as he tried to resist; tried desperately not to drift to the morning on the beach.

In the far corner of the restaurant, the door creaked open and Ian stepped in from the hallway. 'Ladies and gentlemen,' he called. 'If you would please take your seats, we'll be serving the first course shortly.'

Justin drained his glass and tucked the phone into his pocket.

Will, however, remained where he was, fear gripping him as the guests searched for their seats. They chattered to each other, commenting on the gold confetti that had been sprinkled over the tablecloth and swapping theories on what Carl might have prepared. Martha Finn picked up the magnifying glass and began searching the table for an imaginary clue, announcing in a dreadful French accent that she was ''ot on the 'eels of ze murderer'.

But Will barely heard them. Instead, Justin's question was ringing in his ears.

Aren't you worried what people might think about that? Given your history with this sort of thing.

He'd hoped it wouldn't happen. Hoped that after so many years, he would no longer be associated with what happened on that beach. But he realised now how drastically he'd miscalculated. Justin had been a child when it happened, too. Barely old enough to remember it. And yet, the moment murder had been mentioned, his mind had gone straight to the place Will had prayed it wouldn't.

He thought of the speech he'd written, folded up inside his pocket. Was there time to change it? He had to do something. If he read it as it was, the other guests would surely make the same connection as Justin. They'd be appalled.

And as for Hugh . . . Jesus, what would Hugh do?

'Will!'

Ian was beckoning him to the doorway. Clutching his hands together, to hide how violently they were trembling, Will skirted the table and went to join him.

'I've spoken to the last two guests,' he said quietly. 'They're a few minutes away but I need to help Carl with the starters. Can you be ready to greet them when they arrive?'

'Of course.'

Ian looked at him. 'Are you all right?'

Will nodded, perhaps a little too enthusiastically. Ian seemed to weigh him up for a moment, before stepping back into the hallway. After he'd gone, Will fetched the inhaler from inside his dinner jacket and took a deep breath. Then another.

Changing the speech wouldn't be enough. What about the clues he'd planted? The actors' lines? He slowed his breathing, trying desperately not to hyperventilate. There was too much in motion. Too much that just couldn't be changed. And there was no chance of Ian agreeing to postpone.

'Where did you get these printed?'

Turning to face the table, Will saw that Sylvia had found the envelope bearing her name, and was running her fingers over the letters.

'I used my typewriter,' he said, voice trembling.

'You have a typewriter?'

45

He nodded and took a deep breath. He had to play the host. Keep the evening under control until he could come up with a plan.

'I have two, although it took a little work. A normal envelope wouldn't really fit, so I had to put each one through as a sheet of paper and then learn how to fold them.'

Sylvia hummed politely, setting the envelope down again before he'd finished.

'It's an excellent touch, Will.' Gwen flashed a smile across the table, and despite all that was happening – despite the raw fear that was now coursing through his veins – he couldn't help but feel soothed. He'd seen that smile photographed dozens of times in the *Hamlet Herald*, but it was different in person. Even in that moment, it was calming.

He gave her a small smile back. Perhaps it wouldn't be so bad. Gwen might even be his escape. If he took her to one side and explained what he'd done – told her that he'd made a mistake – she would help him with the others . . . Wouldn't she?

'Can we open them?' asked Martha.

'After dinner,' he said, his mouth going dry as the sense of dread returned. 'When we begin the game.'

As the guests sat down, Ian returned, popping open two bottles of champagne and pouring them each a glass. Then, he and Carl brought through the first course. Each summer, he hired a couple of waiters, but there was no point keeping them on for the winter months. Will had wondered if he might recruit one for the party, but Ian had grimaced at the idea. He and Carl could easily serve nine people between them. Why waste money – money he didn't have – on an extra pair of hands?

Will had never met Carl before that night. He was built like an old tree, with broad shoulders and branch-like forearms that were covered in tattoos. To tell the truth, with the chef's shaven head and thick beard, Will found himself a little intimidated. And yet, despite his enormous stature, there was a surprising delicacy to the way he placed down the steaming bowls of clam chowder – a 1920s treat, apparently.

Will seated himself at the far end of the table, closest to the Finns. Ian had insisted on keeping them apart from Nigel and Sylvia, using Gwen and Hugh as a buffer. Martha leaned forward and breathed in the aroma of the chowder, a satisfied smile on her face. Edward looked less sure, although he seemed to Will the sort of man who would describe any dish other than a roast dinner or fish and chips as exotic. Still, he picked up his spoon and dutifully tasted a small mouthful.

Watching them now, Will found it curious seeing just how different they were; Martha apparently still so youthful in spirit, while Edward appeared to be embracing old age a good deal sooner than he needed to. It wasn't a stretch to think which of them had decided they would attend the party.

'Do we have you to thank for the food, Hugh?' asked Sylvia.

'I don't know if I'd go that far. It's Carl who has to cook it. But yes, Ian's a customer.'

'And how's business?' It was Nigel who spoke this time.

There'd already been something cold in Hugh's tone when he'd replied to Sylvia, but when he turned to her husband, it was with a voice of pure ice. 'We're out of season,' he said. 'The hotels are empty and half the restaurants are closed. It'll pick up again in the spring when the tourists are back.'

'We're the same,' said Martha Finn. 'The shop might as well be shut until March.'

'Any more burglaries?' asked Justin.

A silence descended upon the table, as suddenly and as clumsily as a falling brick. Edward Finn, who had been blowing on a spoonful on chowder, glared so fiercely at the young reporter that he began to squirm in his seat.

'No,' said Martha, forcing some cheer into her voice. 'We haven't had any more trouble. Have we, Edward?' She looked expectantly across the table at her husband.

'We're doing just fine,' he said quietly.

For a short while, Sinatra's crooning was the only sound. Will tasted a small mouthful of chowder, but he'd lost whatever appetite his nerves had initially allowed. He was still trying desperately to think of how he could save himself once the game began, Justin's question echoing over and over in his mind.

Aren't you worried what people might think about that? Given your history with this sort of thing.

'Edward,' said Sylvia, so abruptly that Will's heart leapt into his throat. 'Nigel's boys aren't responsible for what happened to your shop. Whatever's going on with the lighthouse, you must know that he wouldn't allow—'

'Sylvia,' said Gwen gently. 'I think this might not be the time.'

'I need to say something, Gwen,' Sylvia snapped. '*We* need to say something.' She set down her spoon and looked across the table at Nigel. 'Let's do it now.'

Will began to panic, remembering Ian's warning to keep the conversation flowing. To keep it, at all costs, away from the lighthouse. Could things really be unravelling so quickly? They'd barely sat down.

He looked down the table towards Nigel, painfully aware that he had to do something; that whatever Sylvia was talking about, he had to put a stop to it. But the words wouldn't come. He was frozen, so completely overcome with terror that he was unable even to move.

'We have an announcement to make,' Sylvia continued. 'Regarding the lighthouse. And regarding Mr White.'

At the sound of Damien White's name, there was a sharp intake of breath.

'Darling.' Nigel tried desperately to catch his wife's eye. 'I'm really not sure now is—'

Before either of them could go any further, a pair of headlights swept past the window and came to a stop outside the hotel.

Will breathed a sigh of relief. Whoever the new arrivals were, it seemed they'd just thrown him a lifeline. 'That must be our final guests,' he said.

'Who is it, Will?' asked Gwen, apparently just as eager to change the subject.

He shook his head. 'I don't know.'

Hugh frowned at him. 'You don't know?'

'Ian booked them in.'

Ian had closed the restaurant door behind him when he and Carl went back to the kitchen, but Will could still hear the muffled sound of voices as he greeted the new arrivals in the hallway.

'There we are,' said Gwen. 'From here on out, let's agree to give our visitors a warm Hamlet welcome. Just for tonight, let's

49

have no talk of Nigel's workers. No more of the lighthouse and certainly none of Mr White.'

A murmur of unenthused agreement rippled around the table. Only Sylvia looked as though she might protest, seemingly furious that whatever announcement she had been about to make had been derailed. But for the time being, at least, she held herself back.

With a deep breath, Will got to his feet. Adopting the widest smile he could manage, he patted the creases from his dinner jacket and raised his glass, ready to welcome the new arrivals. All eyes watched as the handle turned and the door swung open.

The smile dropped from Will's face as if made of lead. Nigel and Sylvia's eyes went wide. Justin sat bolt upright in his seat and even Gwen, usually the epitome of composure, had to set down her glass.

Will had never met this man before. But like everyone else at that table, he knew exactly who he was. He was shorter than he looked in the *Hamlet Herald*, but Will recognised the tanned complexion, the steel-grey hair and the pale blue eyes, the same hue as his designer polo shirt.

A young woman followed. Her blonde hair tied back in a ponytail, she wore a Superdry hoody, Adidas leggings and a startling pair of orange trainers bearing the logo of a brand that Will didn't recognise. She looked from one disbelieving face to the next, taking them all in.

Will felt his lips move as he tried to say something. Anything. But the words wouldn't come. He thought he'd planned for every scenario. Predicted every problem they might have. But he hadn't planned for this.

'Sorry we're late, folks.' With a flash of gleaming teeth, Damien White gave a broad grin. 'Glad to see we haven't kept you waiting.'

Eight o'clock

4

It was quickly becoming clear to Lily White that suggesting they visit her dad's lighthouse had been the first of several mistakes.

She understood he wasn't popular. After he'd taken her up on her suggestion – one she'd only made for the sake of showing an interest in the property empire that would some day be hers – she'd frantically googled what, exactly, he was doing in Hamlet Wick. Skimming through half a dozen local news articles, she'd soon learned all about the outrage he'd sparked by buying the lighthouse. But she'd thought the people would at least be civil. After all, he'd once been one of them. He was born in Hamlet; spent the first eighteen years of his life there until, when he was only a year or two younger than Lily was now, he'd left for London to go to university. Whatever disagreement there might be over the lighthouse, it didn't seem too much to expect a little common courtesy.

But having arrived at Hamlet Hall, she realised this assumption had been her second mistake. And it was rapidly dawning on her that allowing her mum to sign them up for a murder mystery party at their hotel would prove to be her third.

After they'd parked the Range Rover and collected their room keys from the manager – a man called Ian, who'd looked like he might have a panic attack at the sight of the infamous Damien White – they went to join the other guests in the restaurant. From the entrance hall, Lily had heard conversation. The clinking of cutlery. Even some jazz music.

When they stepped inside, it was as if they'd flipped a switch, the expressions that greeted them ranging from blank to downright hostile.

'Nigel!' Undeterred, her dad strode to a man in a pinstriped suit and grasped him by the hand. 'I hadn't realised you'd be here. Wonderful to see you. And you must be Sylvia. How are you both?' He planted a kiss on the cheek of a scowling woman in a glittery dress and feathered headband. Then, without waiting for an answer, he motioned towards two empty chairs at the top of the table. 'I take it these are for us.'

A young man in a dinner suit looked as though he might speak, but before he could, White seated himself and motioned for Lily to take the chair opposite. She sat down cautiously beside the man he'd just identified as Nigel. He was staring at them, his eyes bulging and skin so pale that Lily wondered if he was about to be sick.

What the *hell* had her mum been thinking by suggesting this?

The logic might have been there, she supposed. While Lily and her mum went away on plenty of city breaks and spa weekends, this was the first time she'd ever been on a trip with just her dad.

'It's going to be awful,' she'd complained. 'We can barely fill twenty minutes on the phone these days. What am I meant to talk to him about for twenty-four hours?'

'Why did you suggest it, then?' her mum had replied.

'I didn't think he'd actually say *yes*! He's been talking for months about showing me some of the locations, getting me familiar with the sites before I finish uni. I couldn't just keep on smiling and nodding.'

'But why did you suggest the *lighthouse*?'

'I don't know! My mind went blank and it was the first thing I could think of. Besides, all I said was that it sounded like it might be cool. Suddenly he's talking about catching up, spending some quality time together – whatever that means. I had no idea I was signing myself up for some kind of cringey daddy–daughter weekend away.'

In the end, it had been her mum who came up with the idea of finding something to do while they were in Hamlet. At first it had seemed sensible. Even something as dull as the murder mystery party she'd found on Facebook sounded preferable to making an evening's worth of forced conversation in a pub somewhere.

'Think about it,' her mum had urged. 'Once you're there, this *mystery* thing will probably take up most of the evening, so you won't need to think about making conversation again until the journey home. There'll be other people, too. That'll make it easier. You can palm him off on them if you need a break.'

Now that they were here, the idea seemed laughable. Perhaps her mum really hadn't realised. They might have been married for twenty-one years, but Lily knew her parents had developed a distant relationship. It hadn't even come as a surprise that her mum wouldn't be joining them for New Year's Eve.

'Hi, Gwen.' Across the table, her dad gave a warm smile to the woman in the green dress.

Lily must have seen that smile hundreds of times. Whether it was inside his latest brochure or on the cover of an industry trade magazine, it was always flawless. The perfect white teeth matching the whites of his cool grey eyes. Her mum once said it could have made him a movie star. As it was, it had still paid for their six-bedroom house in Chelsea, each of their cars and even a yacht. It had charmed countless clients and investors, but as he turned it on Gwen, Lily saw a man in a grey suit and polka-dot bow tie scowl at him from across the table, nostrils flaring.

The starters were finished in total silence. Ian and someone who Lily assumed must be the chef came to clear the dishes, returning a moment later with plates of pink lamb and roasted winter vegetables. If she'd been in a London restaurant, it was the sort of meal she would have taken a dozen photos of, capturing it from several different angles to put on Instagram. But she felt hopelessly uncomfortable among these people. Every time she looked up, she caught someone quickly glancing away from her.

It didn't help that they couldn't have looked more out of place if they'd tried. Lily hadn't thought anyone would actually bother with the 1920s dress code. And yet, now, in her Superdry hoody and with her dad in his Ralph Lauren polo, she felt ridiculous.

'This lamb is beautiful,' said the woman in the glittery dress, who he'd identified as Sylvia.

'Which farm is it from, darling?' Gwen looked towards the man in the polka-dot bow tie.

'It's Jeremy's,' he muttered, his eyes still fixed upon White.

Sylvia forced a smile. 'Well, whoever's farm it's from, it's divine.'

A fresh silence fell upon the table. Even the record had reached its end, the only sounds now the crackling of the fire and the gentle clatter of cutlery.

Lily glanced up from her plate and caught two more sets of eyes flickering quickly away. This time, she felt a sudden flush of frustration.

'I have to say,' her dad announced. 'This isn't the homecoming I'd expected.'

'What exactly *did* you expect?' the man in the polka-dot bow tie answered straight away, as if the words had already been in his mouth, waiting to burst free.

'Hugh!' Gwen's eyes went wide.

'It's a fair question.'

She flashed him a dangerous look. 'I'm sorry, Mr White.'

'It's all right, Gwen.'

'Don't call her that,' Hugh growled.

'Her name?'

'It's Mrs Holloway.'

'It wasn't always.'

Lily flinched. She knew that tone of voice. To the untrained eye, her dad might seem perfectly amiable. Maybe even playful. But anyone who knew him well would recognise that he was drawing a line. Testing his opponent and seeing just how willing they might be to cross it.

'Can I fetch anyone another drink?' At the end of the table, the young guy in the dinner suit rose to his feet, but Hugh spoke again before anyone could reply.

'What did you expect, Mr White?'

'Hugh, stop it.' Gwen was speaking through gritted teeth now, a sudden intensity in her expression.

'No, I want to know,' he pressed. 'What, exactly, did you think you'd achieve by coming here tonight?'

Nobody spoke. Even Gwen, it seemed, was interested in the answer. Lily glanced at her dad and felt a growing sense of unease. He and Hugh were staring at one another. Sizing each other up across the table.

He gave a little laugh. 'Honestly, Hugh—'

'Mr Holloway.'

Lily saw him pause. That winning smile remained in place, but when he spoke again, his voice was lower than before. Colder.

'Mr Holloway,' he said. 'I only thought it would be a good idea for Lily and me to spend some time with the good people of Hamlet before my house is finished.'

'You don't seem to have noticed that "the good people of Hamlet" are less than thrilled by the idea of you coming here.'

'Hugh . . .' Gwen seemed now to be pleading with him, but it was no use.

'Someone has to say it, Gwen. You of all people know that it's appalling what he's doing to the lighthouse. And I'm sorry, Nigel . . .'

At the sound of his name, Nigel shrivelled into his seat.

'I know this contract means a lot to your company. But surely even you can see the damage this is doing to Hamlet. Just look at the Finns.'

The older man in the tweed suit glanced up from the end of the table.

'How long have the pair of you been here?' Hugh asked him. 'Forty years? Never once had a problem with crime. And now your shop has been broken into twice since work began on his house. Twice!'

'There's no proof that Nigel's boys are involved,' said Sylvia.

'But they aren't Nigel's boys, are they?' Hugh rounded on her. 'He's had to pull them in from out of town because none of his regulars will do the work. You don't actually *know* any of the men you've got working on that site.'

He was panting now, his cheeks flushed, and looking down, seemed to only just realise he was brandishing a fork.

'So, I'm responsible for the local crime now, too?' White addressed the older couple at the end of the table. 'Mr Finn, you've run the shop here since I was a boy. Do you really think I'd stand for my development to have this kind of impact on you?'

Lily joined the others in turning towards Mr Finn. His wife grasped his hand.

'We don't want any trouble,' she said.

'Really?' Hugh's voice rose again. 'You've been saying for months that Nigel's workers are involved in the thefts. And now the man responsible is sitting right in front of you, but you don't want to say anything?'

The Finns were silent, causing Hugh to stare at them, open-mouthed, as though personally affronted by their reluctance.

'Perhaps I could put another record on.' The guy in the dusty dinner suit rose once again to his feet, but Hugh had already launched into another impassioned tirade, turning this time towards a young man wearing a blazer and a lanyard.

'I'm sure that Justin, at least, will have something to say about it. After all, he's reported on both break-ins.'

'Damn-near ruined my business,' Nigel muttered.

'I just report the facts, Nigel.'

'What facts? You've no proof that my boys broke into their shop!'

'Either way.' Justin reached inside his blazer and fished out a mobile phone. 'I'd be interested in hearing how Mr White feels about it.'

He placed the phone on the table, a little red light blinking in one corner. Realising that he was recording, Lily looked towards her dad. But of course, he'd spotted it too. He'd been grilled by too many journalists in the city to be caught out that easily. She saw him glance down at the phone. Then, his eyes narrowed.

'Are you the one who's been calling my office?'

'Oh, Justin, you haven't . . .' An exasperated look passed over Gwen's face.

'You are, aren't you? From the *Herald*?' He raised his voice to address the table. 'Did any of you know about this? Night and day, he's been calling. For months. Trying to get an interview about my development.'

'And what if he has?' Hugh demanded. 'Don't we deserve to know what you're doing to our town? Justin's doing his job, I'd say.'

'I don't see why my affairs should be splashed across the front of your paper. And I'm certainly—'

With a loud creak, the door opened and the chef returned with a tray of newly filled champagne flutes. Starting at the head of the table, he placed one in front of White then set down a second for Gwen. Before he could go any further, though, the young man in the dinner suit leapt to his feet.

'I'll take those!' He scurried over to the chef and awkwardly took the tray, before making his way around the rest of the table. Lily noticed a slight tremor in his hand as he placed a glass in front of her.

She couldn't blame him. The famous Damien White could hold his own against the likes of Hugh. But then, that was exactly the problem. He wasn't fighting Hugh; he was tolerating him. And she wasn't sure just how long he'd be willing to keep it up.

'Dad,' she said. 'Maybe we should go.'

'We're not going anywhere.' He looked across the table, catching Hugh straight in the eye. 'We have just as much right to be here as anyone else.'

Hugh's nostrils flared, but a venomous scowl from Gwen seemed, for the moment, to stop him from saying anything.

White turned to Nigel. 'At least I have someone on my side. Here's to you, Nigel.' He raised his glass and then tipped back the champagne, drinking it all in one go.

Nigel said nothing, his eyes glued to the surface of the table.

'Tell him,' Sylvia hissed.

'This isn't the place,' Nigel murmured.

'Tell him now or I will.'

'Tell me what?' Lily watched as her dad set down the empty glass, the smile fading slightly. 'Nigel, what's going on?'

Suddenly, all eyes were on Nigel. He glanced around the table, apparently trying hard not to look at Sylvia. Then he breathed a heavy sigh.

'Mr White,' he said.

'Damien.'

'*Mr White*. I've thought about this a great deal and . . .' He took a deep breath. 'I've decided I have no choice but to terminate our contract.'

Lily saw her dad's eyes bulge.

'You won't build my house?'

'I'll honour all of the necessary—'

'Where's this coming from, Nigel? You told me this was the biggest contract your firm has ever had.'

'And it'll be the last if he sees it through,' snapped Sylvia.

Nigel breathed another sigh. 'She's right, Mr White. The truth is that I should never have accepted it.'

'What the hell are you talking about? I'm paying you a small fortune.'

'You might be,' said Sylvia. 'But the simple fact is that it's ruining our business. Nigel hasn't been offered any other jobs in months. His warehouse has been vandalised. He's had to bring in new men because none of his regulars will work for him.'

'And they're robbing the local shop,' Hugh muttered, earning a scowl from Sylvia.

'You're paying a handsome sum now,' she continued. 'But if Nigel sees your contract through, he won't have a company to come back to when the lighthouse is finished.'

A stunned silence fell upon the table. Lily looked at her dad. He was glaring at Nigel, cold fury in his eyes.

'Well, I, for one, think you're doing the right thing,' said Hugh.

'I don't accept.'

Nigel frowned. 'I'm sorry?'

'Your resignation,' he said, his voice completely level. 'I don't accept it. You're finishing my house.'

'Didn't you hear him?' Sylvia demanded.

'I heard him perfectly. And I'm telling him I don't accept.'

'But I've sent the paperwork,' said Nigel. 'I put it in the post yesterday.' He shook his head. 'I had no idea you would be here this evening.'

He looked around the table, searching for support. Again, Lily noticed that he seemed to avoid turning to Sylvia. Instead, his gaze settled on Justin. Then on the mobile phone.

'Are you recording this?'

'It's quite a story,' said Justin. 'Would you give me a comment for the *Herald*?'

'Yes, he will,' Sylvia jumped in.

'I don't want this to be in the paper!'

'Let him do it, Nigel,' said Hugh. 'It's the right thing. People should know.'

Nigel propped his elbows on the table and pressed his hands to his face. For a split second, Lily almost felt sorry for him.

'What about our shop?' said Mr Finn.

'What about it?' Justin replied.

'Are you writing about that too? And the petition?'

'I'm sure it'll feature somewhere. But right now, I'm more interested in a comment from Mr Cobb.'

Nigel glared at Sylvia. 'Look what you've done,' he hissed.

'Because you didn't have the spine to do it yourself! I'm trying to protect our business—'

'*Our* business? Your only worry is where your next holiday

will come from if there isn't another contract for me to slave over—'

'Enough!' Gwen stood, silencing the table in an instant. 'I know that tensions are high,' she said. 'But this is neither the time nor the place. Will and Ian have put so much work into this evening. Can we please be civil?'

As a begrudging murmur of agreement went around the table, Lily looked towards her dad, expecting to see his usual cool composure. Instead, she saw something else. He was suddenly pale, his eyes glazed over.

Gwen noticed it too, concern flashing in her eyes. 'Mr White, are you all right?'

'Yes,' he said, loudly clearing his throat. 'Yes, I'm just . . . Would you all excuse me for a moment?' He rose to his feet, smoothing the creases from his Ralph Lauren polo.

'Dad, what's going on?'

From the corner of Lily's eye, she saw Hugh break out into a smug grin.

'Trouble holding your drink?' he asked. 'Or are you finally starting to get the message?'

'D'you know what, Hugh?' White glared across the table, any trace of his composure now gone. 'Keep talking if it makes you feel better. It won't change how Rory ran himself into the ground. Just like it won't change the fact that I've shagged your wife.'

The grin fell from Hugh's face. Gwen's eyes flew wide open and Sylvia gasped, a gloved hand flying to cover her mouth.

But Damien White didn't wait to see the effect of his words. He was already striding towards the door and, in an instant, he had gone.

5

Will didn't like to swear. It had always struck him as something people did when they couldn't think of anything more intelligent to say. But this felt like an extreme case. Things had barely got under way and his evening was already a fucking disaster.

Ian arrived just as Damien White stormed from the restaurant. His eyes swept the room, taking in Hugh, who was now trembling with rage, and Gwen, still standing, white-faced. Then he looked at Will.

'Ladies and gentlemen,' he said through gritted teeth. 'Can I suggest we take a short break?'

'Fine by me.' Lily White sprang to her feet and barged past him into the hallway. She slammed the door shut behind her, causing Will to give a whimpering sound.

Ian grimaced, then took a deep breath. 'If anyone would like to get some air, maybe have another drink, let's all take a few minutes and then reconvene here. Will, perhaps you'd put on some more music for us.'

The guests began to rise to their feet. Hugh was first, striding from the room without a word. Will noticed that Gwen didn't try to follow him.

He moved to the gramophone and, with a trembling hand, lifted the needle. He thought about changing the record, but there hardly seemed any point. The moment Sinatra had struck up again, Ian gripped him by the shoulder, his knuckles white.

'We need to pull this back,' he hissed. 'Do you understand? We can't afford for it to go sideways. *I* can't afford it.'

Will nodded eagerly, Ian's fingers still digging into his shoulder.

'We're giving them half an hour to cool off,' he continued. 'Then you're going to start the game.'

'But the desserts—'

'Never mind the desserts! We can't have them sitting around talking again. Not with *him* here.' He looked around quickly, making sure nobody could hear. 'Pull yourself together. Explain to the actors what's going on. In thirty minutes, we're calling everyone back in.'

Will glanced around the restaurant. Most of the guests had filed out, the only ones who remained at the table being Gwen and the Finns. He almost wished he'd changed the record after all, Sinatra's cheerful rendition of 'Come Fly with Me' some-how making the whole scene even more depressing.

Then he saw it. The escape he'd been searching for since his conversation with Justin.

'You don't think . . .' He gulped. 'With Mr White here. You don't think we should call the whole thing off? Send the guests away?'

Ian glared at him. 'Do you have any idea how much I've spent on tonight? The food, the champagne . . . Money I don't have, on *your* idea. We aren't calling anything off. Not when we have a chance to split them up and distract them with the game, and *certainly* not with the *Herald* here to see it.'

Immediately, any hope that Will had allowed to flicker into life was snuffed out.

He thought of the speech, folded up in his pocket. In half an hour, he would be reading it. In half an hour, he would look into the guests' faces and know exactly whether they thought the same as Justin.

'Mr White . . .' he said, his voice now quivering. 'How did we not know that he was coming?'

Ian's expression softened slightly. 'The daughter booked them in,' he muttered. 'She only gave her first name. Just said that the other room was for her father.' His brow suddenly creased again, eyes like coal. 'Now, get this shitshow under control.' He jabbed a finger under Will's nose. 'Thirty minutes.'

6

Gwen had thought on more than one occasion about how it might feel to one day see Damien again. In the years since he'd left Hamlet Wick, she'd only seen his face in the pages of the *Herald* and on the covers of brochures. She'd even visited his website once or twice, just for a peep at how he'd changed over the years. To see him in person, though . . .

She'd often wondered if it might stir up old feelings; if she would be reminded of the headstrong teenager with whom she'd shared her first kiss. She'd known for years that he'd married someone in London. Some girl he'd met at university. Would she perhaps feel a glimmer of jealousy?

In reality, when Damien swaggered into Hamlet Hall, Gwen had been furious.

Why spend months dodging her calls, only to spring himself on them in person? Could he have come just to see how the lighthouse was progressing? And why bring his daughter – to show the place off to her?

No. Damien wouldn't want to show Hamlet off. When he'd left, all those years ago, he'd told her that he never wanted to come back. She remembered the look in his eyes. Remembered knowing with complete certainty that he was telling the truth. Deep down, she was all too aware that he had only bought the lighthouse because he was frightened. Because, with her plans to reopen it – to renovate it – Gwen had inadvertently forced his hand.

She watched the other guests file from the restaurant. If only he'd spoken to her. If he'd just picked up the phone and let her explain . . .

She thought of the article in the *Herald*, announcing her project at the lighthouse. Justin had written about how she planned to preserve it, to ensure that people never forgot the terrible tragedy that, for twenty-five years, had stained their town.

Hugh had wanted her to frame that article. After so many years of shaking hands and smiling for photos, this was the project that would finally make her Mayor of Hamlet. From there, who knew? She had the drive to go further. Much further. And it would all start with the lighthouse.

But six days after that story was published, Gwen had received an email from the council, explaining that her planning permission had been revoked. It had taken considerably longer to find out why. Four months, specifically. And even then, the truth only came out when a worker at Cobb Construction Ltd let it slip that Nigel had accepted a contract from Damien White to convert the lighthouse into a luxury home.

Gwen had no idea how much Damien had paid for it, although she suspected the brand-new Audi TT in the council building car park might be an indication. What she did know, however, was what must have set him on edge. She was fairly sure, in fact, that she knew which exact word in Justin's story had sealed the deal.

Preserve.

She'd called his office countless times to explain. Given her name and told his secretary that he would want to reply. But there'd been nothing. No matter how many times she tried, all Gwen ever received in return was silence.

She should have seen this coming, of course. Even as a teenager, once Damien had made up his mind, there was no changing it. He was a strategist, every decision a case of risk and reward. The lighthouse was no different. He must have read Justin's story in the *Hamlet Herald* and decided her plans were too great a risk. And so, in the space of just a few days and with a significant bribe to the council's planning department, the lighthouse – *her* lighthouse – had become his. His to protect; to cordon off and shield from the world.

No. Disappointed as she was, she couldn't allow herself the comfort of surprise. So, instead, she had been filled with rage.

She wasn't an idiot. Of course she would have taken precautions. She would have made sure that what needed to stay buried, *did* stay buried. It was just as much in her interest as his. She would hardly become Mayor if the truth of what had really happened, all those years ago, were to come out.

She looked towards the restaurant door. Hugh had gone to the kitchen for a drink with Carl. That was probably for the best. She thought of the look on his face when Damien swept into the restaurant, and then again when he fired his parting shot . . .

She was amazed Hugh hadn't punched him. Another

comment like that and she was sure he would. After all, he had reasons of his own to hate Damien. The loss he'd suffered was even greater than hers. It wouldn't take much to tip him over the edge.

Gwen stared at that door. And as she did, she knew what she was going to do. All those months spent trying to contact Damien and now he was right here.

She had to go after him. She wasn't going to let him stand in the way of her ambitions and she certainly wasn't going to allow whatever history might linger between them to hold her back. By the time the night was through, he was going to give her the lighthouse.

She smiled sweetly at the Finns, now the only others left in the restaurant. Then, with fire in her heart, she tipped back her champagne, rose to her feet and made for the door.

7

Edward sat in silence as Gwen followed the others into the hall-way. She gave him a smile as she went, but he couldn't return it. He was burning with rage. And not just for Damien White. He was furious with himself for having sat back and done nothing.

Confrontation wasn't something that came naturally to Edward, but over the past few months, there had been so many things he'd imagined he would say if they ever came face to face. He would demand to know who White thought he was, claiming the lighthouse as his own. He would insist on reimbursement for the damage caused by the men who had broken into the shop. He would even show him the petition and make him aware of just how widely hated he was; of how many people wanted him gone.

There was so much he wanted to say. But when the opportunity presented itself – when he and White had been sitting together at the same table – he had done nothing.

Martha took his hand. 'Are you all right?'

Edward didn't reply. Of all people, she should know. She should understand just how it felt to see this man again.

He hadn't changed, of course. Underneath, Edward could see that he was still the same cocky boy who used to sweet-talk Martha into giving him chocolate bars free of charge from the shop. And that final jab at Hugh . . . To have spoken about Gwen in that way had been unforgivable.

Martha squeezed his hand. 'Maybe it's good that he's here tonight. You heard Nigel. If there's nobody to do the work any more—'

Edward silenced her with a single look.

He knew what Nigel's news meant. What it *actually* meant. Nigel might delay the work on the lighthouse. If he was lucky, he might even claw back some of his standing with the community. But White would just find someone else, and that was if he even let Nigel go. Just a few moments earlier, he'd outright refused the resignation. Nigel might find himself finishing the work by force, if not out of choice.

Either way, Edward was sure that all was not said and done. When it came down to it, Nigel's display at the dinner table would mean nothing.

Bristling with rage, he rose to his feet, pulling his hand from Martha's.

'Where are you going?' she asked.

'I want a coffee.'

She gave a little nod, but he didn't see it. He was already striding from the restaurant, leaving her alone at the table.

73

8

In Theo's opinion, Will had never looked especially healthy. But in that particular moment, when he came to see the three actors in the lounge, he looked dreadful. His eyes were wide, his skin like a sheet of blank paper. Even the vintage dinner jacket seemed to hang from his shoulders as though he were an undersized mannequin.

'What's happening?' asked Theo.

Will looked at him blankly, Jack and Claire hovering at his shoulders. 'We're taking a break,' he said. 'Half an hour. Then we're calling everyone back and starting the game.'

'But Carl's only just served the mains,' said Jack.

'Ian wants to get started. The other guests haven't taken well to Mr White.'

Theo watched as Will fetched an inhaler from his pocket, shook it and took a deep breath. His hand was trembling, causing it to rattle gently in his palm.

'Sit down, Will,' said Claire. 'Give yourself a minute and we'll make a plan.'

Will looked unconvinced, but he allowed her to guide him

onto one of the sofas, murmuring quietly to himself as he went. He shook the inhaler again, more vigorously this time, and took another breath.

'You're running low,' Claire observed. 'Do you have a spare one of those?'

He nodded, holding his breath for a moment before replying. 'My rucksack's hanging up in Ian's office.'

'Can I fetch it for you?'

'It should be fine,' he said, his eyes glazing over. 'This one will last a little while longer.'

'What are the guests doing now?' asked Theo.

Will gave a half-hearted shrug. 'Nigel's smoking by the back door. Hugh's gone to see Carl in the kitchen and I think Sylvia's taken herself upstairs. Justin's—'

'Justin?' Theo glared at him. 'Justin's here?'

'The *Herald* wanted to send someone. Thought it would make a nice feature, or something like that.'

Theo's heart sank. It had been months since he and Justin last crossed paths – no small feat in a place the size of Hamlet – but still, he wasn't yet ready to see his old classmate again. Even the mention of Justin's name left him fighting to restrain a sudden swell of resentment.

'Who's Justin?' asked Claire.

'He's a reporter,' said Jack when it became apparent that Theo wasn't going to reply. 'Gave Theo something of a bad—'

Theo stopped him with a look that could cut glass. Claire looked for a moment like she might ask again, but held herself back.

Theo took a deep breath, trying to stay composed. 'What about White? Where's he?'

'He was the first one to go,' said Will. 'Ian mentioned that he was staying the night, so I suppose he's gone to his room.'

'Is there anything we can do?' asked Claire.

'I don't know. I honestly don't. I think . . . I think I'll just have to hope that when we call them all back, they'll have cooled off.' He blew a long sigh. 'Ian's going to kill me. He's going to—'

'Don't worry about Ian,' said Claire. 'Take a moment. Clear your head. He'll be all right.'

As she continued attempting to soothe Will, Theo felt Jack take him by the shoulder and steer him briskly towards the door.

'Listen, dear boy,' the older man said quietly. 'If Nigel's having a cigarette, I might pop out and join him. Just for a quick one, you understand. You can manage without me for a moment, can't you?'

He was almost whispering, as if they were schoolboys planning to smoke behind the bike sheds. Theo looked him in the eye, his face just inches away. He felt Jack's arm draped around his shoulder, smelled the alcohol on his breath and realised that he wanted nothing more in that moment than for him to just go away.

'Yes, Jack,' he said. 'I'm sure we can manage.'

With a cheerful grin and a clap on the back, Jack made for the door. The moment he'd gone, Theo scooped his own barely touched glass of champagne from the coffee table and held it out to Will.

'Drink this. It'll calm you down.'

Will looked suspiciously at the glass.

'It's all right,' said Theo. 'I've only had a sip.'

'That's not it.' Will gave a weak smile. 'I'd actually prefer something a little stronger. Maybe a whisky? There used to be some in the restaurant, but we had to empty the drinks globe to make room for one of the props.'

Theo swept a glance around the lounge, scanning the grandfather clock, the sideboard and the bookcase. There was no sign of any whisky.

Claire rose to her feet. 'I'll look around. See what I can find.'

'You're sure?'

She nodded and gave a warm smile. 'I'll be right back.'

Theo returned the smile, quietly hoping as she slipped into the hallway that Jack wouldn't put her off joining the Hamlet Players by the time the evening was over.

Will ran a hand through his hair. 'What am I going to do, Theo? Ian told me to get things under control. How am I supposed to do that? Hugh was going for blood out there, and I'm sure the Finns must want to, as well. Then there's Justin. He's going to write about this, isn't he? Every word. It'll be all over the front of the *Herald*.'

The pair of them were silent for a moment, listening to the ticking of the grandfather clock. Will had another go on the inhaler, his breathing now a fraction steadier.

'I'm sorry about Justin,' he said. 'I really am. Ian was so excited by the idea of some publicity that there was no chance of him turning the *Herald* down. But I should have told you he would be here.'

Theo said nothing.

'He shouldn't be difficult to avoid,' Will continued. 'He'll be clinging to Mr White all evening, hoping for a comment on the lighthouse. Nigel, too. He and Sylvia announced over dinner that they're—'

'How did this happen?' Theo leapt in, eager to steer the conversation away from Justin. 'Why would White even come here?'

'His daughter's here too.'

'His daughter?' A note of surprise crept into Theo's voice. Despite the *Herald's* coverage of the development at the lighthouse, he'd never heard anything about White having a daughter.

'And there's more,' said Will. 'I think . . .' He paused, collecting himself. 'I think he's having an affair with Gwen.'

'What makes you say that?'

'He more-or-less admitted it. He told Hugh that he'd slept with his wife. Said it right in front of all the others.'

Theo let out a long breath. 'Maybe that's how he managed to get his hands on the lighthouse.'

'You think so?'

'The guy's clearly a piece of work. Perhaps there's some arrangement between him and Gwen that we don't know about.' He sat down on the sofa and grasped Will by the shoulder. 'But there's no point worrying about that now. Sit up straight and I'll show you some breathing exercises; the kind we use in the Players before we go onstage. We need to get your head back in the game. And we don't have long to do it.'

9

With a trembling hand, Nigel Cobb lit his second cigarette.

The first seemed barely to have lasted a minute. He'd fished it from his jacket pocket while leaving the restaurant and lit it before he'd even reached the French doors at the far end of the entrance hall. Now, he stood there in the open doorway, the bitterly cold air brushing his face while the tip of his second glowed in the darkness.

In the daylight, a garden would have been visible, a gravel pathway stretching perhaps thirty paces before the ground banked sharply upwards towards the moor. A year or two earlier, when Ian had first taken over Hamlet Hall, Nigel had heard him speak about putting up some fairy lights or a couple of paraffin heaters. Instead, the only light was a sliver from a small window twelve feet to his right, which he knew was Ian's office.

That was fine by Nigel. He stood, puffing frantically on his cigarette as he stared into the night.

What the *hell* was White doing at Hamlet Hall? In the six months since they'd signed their agreement, he'd never once visited in person. The designs and the paperwork had all been drawn up and agreed over email or the phone. Why make an appearance now?

Could he somehow have got wind that Nigel was planning to pull the plug on the job? And what did he mean when he said that he wouldn't accept his resignation?

Nigel swore under his breath. He'd never known anyone with wealth like White's, but he could imagine the connections it came with. The power. More than that, he'd heard the stories about White himself; the rumours that had circulated all those years ago, when Will had found the body on the beach.

He should never have let Sylvia talk him into this. Never have let her pressure him into working with White, and then feed his instinct to back out. It had seemed like the best thing to do. The *only* thing. But now . . . It had gone wrong in a way he couldn't possibly have imagined.

Where had Sylvia disappeared to, anyway? She hadn't been far behind Hugh and White's daughter – Lily, was it? – when she'd left the restaurant.

He supposed he shouldn't be surprised. He knew all too well just how typical it was of her to wash her hands of a situation the moment it became tough. Why should this be any different?

From the end of the little corridor to his right, the sudden clattering of pans in the kitchen made him jump so violently that he almost dropped his cigarette. He checked his watch, taking a moment to compose himself.

Irritating as it was, he dismissed the question of where his wife had gone to sulk. There were more important things to worry about. He had approximately twenty minutes before Ian called this interval to an end and White returned to the restaurant. Twenty minutes to determine how he might save his career, his company and perhaps even his life.

He heard footsteps behind him, a pair of heels clicking on the tiled floor of the hallway, and then the creak of wood as someone began to climb the stairs.

Nigel didn't turn around. Whoever it was, he didn't want to engage. He needed quiet. Some time to think of how he could climb from this hole.

His eyes fixed upon the inky darkness, he tossed the butt of his second cigarette onto the ground, crushed it beneath his shoe and immediately lit a third.

10

If she was being kind, Lily would have said that her room looked comfortable enough, with a double bed, a small desk and a flatscreen TV mounted on the wall. But right now, the last thing she was interested in being was kind.

Flicking on a low light, she went to inspect the view from the window. She'd been given a room overlooking the front of the hotel, with a view of the shingle beach. The water was pitch black, the moon's reflection off its surface the only proof that it was there at all.

On the last trip she'd taken with her parents, during her Easter break, she had woken to an ocean view from a Caribbean villa. Admittedly, it was one she hadn't been able to fully enjoy, with an exam to study for and two assignments to write before her return to university at Durham. But in that moment, even the thought of a week spent reviewing lecture notes was more appealing than that of a grey English sea heralding the start of a new year.

She knew her lifestyle was a luxurious one, and she was all too aware it was her father who funded it. He paid for her car, her university fees, the various international trips she took during the summer . . . But over the last couple of years, he'd begun gradually introducing her to the inner workings of his empire, preparing her for the day it would eventually become hers. He had sites in nearly every major city in the UK – a few abroad, too – and she knew just how much pride he took in overseeing the entire operation single-handedly. He took his laptop everywhere, was forever on his phone. Even on Christmas Day, she'd come downstairs to find him hunched over a contract at the breakfast bar. He'd built all of this, he once told her. Some day she would need to look after it herself, just as he had. They couldn't trust anyone to manage it but themselves.

Most days, she tried not to dwell on the idea of taking the reins, simply because the thought of having to somehow maintain everything he'd built was, frankly, overwhelming. She knew her accounting degree would help. It was the reason she'd chosen it, just as it was the reason she pushed herself twice as hard as any of her course mates when there was an assignment due or an exam on the horizon. She wasn't interested in something as mundane as being top of her class – although she undoubtedly was. What she wanted was to not be stranded when the time eventually came to take over. Damien White's career was his life. And one day, it would be hers, too. With no siblings to share the work, it would be her shoulders alone that propped everything up.

The lighthouse, however, was different. Already, she could see that this place would be a particular weight on her mind. The people here *hated* him. When the time came, she imagined they would hate her, too. And it was so far away . . .

After four painstaking hours on the motorway, they'd spent another weaving through winding country lanes among sheep-filled fields. The daylight gone, she'd felt sure they must finally have arrived when they turned into Hamlet. But, to her dismay, they'd passed straight through the little town and dropped onto a narrow track, shrouded in darkness and flanked on both sides by tall hedges.

Her dad hadn't seemed phased. The track looked like it would barely have been wide enough for Lily's Mini Cooper, and yet he barrelled down it in the Range Rover.

'The Lane,' he said. 'We used to come joyriding down here when we were kids, pretending we were rally drivers. It's the only way in or out of Hamlet Wick, at least by road.'

She frowned at him. 'Hamlet *Wick*?'

'The harbour,' he explained. 'It's technically part of Hamlet, but just far enough out of town that it gets its own name.'

After what must have been a couple of miles, the hedges gave way and they burst from the track. To their right, a beach hugged the shoreline, leading a short distance to the harbour, and in the glow of an old-fashioned lamp post she could make out Hamlet Hall.

But Lily hadn't been interested in either. Instead, her eyes had settled on the lighthouse. The reason they were there. Her legacy.

Pressing her face now against the window of her room, she swept a glance left. There it was, up on the little hill, floodlights casting it in a harsh light.

She'd wondered if, when she saw it, she would understand why he'd bought it. For the life of her, though, she couldn't see what made it so special. And after his performance in the restaurant, she was now doubting whether it had even been the lighthouse that had brought him back to Hamlet in the first place.

Keep talking if it makes you feel better. It won't change the fact that I've shagged your wife.

Was that it, then – had all of this been for the sake of being closer to some mistress? And what about her mum? Was she waiting to have this dumped on her just as unceremoniously?

Lily understood that her parents no longer had the closest of relationships. They seemed to have become indifferent to each other, to the extent that it would hardly surprise her if they went their separate ways. Most days, they barely even acknowledged each other. But they were, ultimately, still together. And as long as that was the case, she couldn't imagine him doing something like this.

Sitting down on the bed, she wanted desperately to be back in London. Or in Durham, getting drunk on cheap spirits with her housemates before going out to mark the new year in some grimy, overpriced club. Either would do. She just wanted to get away from this crumbling hotel and these bitter, resentful people.

Taking out her phone, two notifications reminded her of messages that had arrived as they'd left London. One was from a boy in her seminar group, who she'd broken up with before Christmas and who seemed keen to chat things through when she was back in town. He was nice, she'd told him, but far too clingy. Clearly, he hadn't taken the hint. The second was from a guy on the rowing team, who, on the same day, she'd taken home from a bar and was asking now if she'd be out again for New Year's.

She swiped them away and instead saw her mum's face smiling up from the lock screen, all blonde hair and gleaming teeth. Lily wanted desperately to call her. To hear her voice and tell her what was happening. There was no chance, though. Glancing at the top corner of the screen, she could see she didn't have a single bar of signal.

Before she had the chance to be frustrated by this latest disappointment, she heard footsteps on the landing. She'd left the door open a crack, to make sure she heard if her dad left his room, and the footsteps sounded close. She tensed, bracing to rebut one of the other guests. But there was no need. The footsteps passed and, instead, came to a stop at the neighbouring door.

'Mr White.' Immediately, she recognised Justin's voice. 'Mr White,' he said again, his voice drifting through the crack in Lily's door. 'I was hoping I could have a word.'

The door opened and Lily heard another creak on the landing, as if Justin had suddenly recoiled.

'What do you *want*?' she heard her dad hiss.

'Just to ask some questions. About the lighthouse. I think we should speak—'

'Get inside.'

Seconds later, the door slammed shut.

At the sound of his voice, Lily began to seethe. In that moment, she hated him. Hated him for bringing her to this place. For the future he'd inflicted on her. For whatever was happening between him and Gwen.

Desperate for a distraction, she reached for her rucksack, which Ian had brought upstairs while she'd been in the restaurant, and fished out a pair of wireless earbuds. She unlocked her phone, swiping away her mum's face, and put on a recording she'd made of some lecture notes, nudging up the volume until her ears began to ring. Lying back on the bed, she stared at the ceiling and tried to focus on the sound of her own voice, reciting back to her on tax and compliance.

Try as she might, though, she couldn't keep her mind on the recording. Just as she couldn't keep her rage from slipping through her fingers. Something, just now, in her dad's voice worried her. It had sounded wrong, somehow. Strained.

She thought of the way he'd gone pale before he stormed from the table. The way his eyes had been wide and unfocused.

Could Hugh have bothered him more than he'd let on? Or perhaps it had been Nigel. If he did, truly, care about the lighthouse, she could appreciate that for Nigel to have given up on their contract – and so publicly, at that – must have been a serious blow.

And yet, even as she pondered this theory, another was occurring to her. When she'd booked the rooms, she'd been clear over the phone about his nut allergy. He took his EpiPen everywhere, and if the quality of the food had been anything to go by, Hamlet Hall's chef seemed to know what was he doing. Even so, could something have gone wrong? Could the message not have been delivered?

It was a few minutes before she noticed the other sound coming through. At first, she ignored it. It was probably just some background noise on the recording; one of the other girls moving around the house as she'd read her notes into her phone. But the sound persisted, coming through more sharply than before. Taking out one of her earbuds, she sat up on the bed.

Immediately, she realised what she had heard.

It was a knocking sound. Specifically, someone knocking on the door to her room.

She turned to face it. But even as she did, it occurred to her that she was only half-interested in who her visitor was. Instead, she found herself considering an altogether different detail.

She had deliberately left the door open. Admittedly just a crack. But it was now closed.

Someone had pulled it shut.

11

Lily rose cautiously from the bed as another knock came at the door.

'Who's there?' she called.

'It's Gwen.'

She froze. Then, with a glimmer of resentment, she wondered if Gwen had come to the wrong door; if she'd meant to knock on her dad's instead.

She would soon send her on her way.

Throwing open the door, she found that Gwen was alone, fiddling with a string of pearls and wearing a gentle smile.

'Did you close this?' she demanded.

'I'm sorry?'

'The door. I left it open. Did you close it?'

Gwen frowned. 'No, it was shut already.'

Lily looked at her. Could Justin have shut it? There was no noise coming from the neighbouring room, despite how thin the walls appeared. Perhaps her dad had sent the young reporter packing while she listened to her notes. But why would he close her door?

'It's Lily, isn't it?' asked Gwen.

'That's right.'

She heard the steel in her own voice. But if Gwen was phased, she didn't show it.

'I thought I'd just check on you. I actually came to see Damien, but he isn't answering his door.'

'That journalist must have really riled him.'

'Justin was up here?'

'A few minutes ago. He came to try and get his interview.'

Gwen sighed. It hadn't escaped Lily that her dad was now 'Damien', as opposed to 'Mr White'. She wondered if that would still be the case when Hugh was next there to hear it.

'I passed him on the stairs,' said Gwen. 'I hoped he hadn't been to bother Damien, but I suppose that was wishful thinking.'

So Justin *has* gone, Lily thought. Not much of an interview, then. He couldn't have been there more than a few minutes.

Gwen shook her head, before adopting that warm smile again. 'Listen, I wanted to make sure Hugh hadn't upset you. I'm so embarrassed by the way he behaved down there.'

'He seems to really hate my dad.'

'I'm afraid Damien hasn't made himself popular around here.'

'You don't seem to mind.'

Gwen winced, prompting Lily to feel a flash of guilt. She quickly quelled it, thinking of her mum. There was no need to worry about upsetting this woman.

'Damien and I . . . We go back a long way.' Gwen paused, and when she spoke again, there was a sudden edge to her voice. 'I'm not having an affair with your dad. He was my high-school boyfriend.'

Lily felt her cheeks flush. 'So, you aren't still . . .'

'No.'

'Then why did he say that? Down in the restaurant?'

'He must have known it would upset Hugh.'

Lily felt a sudden flicker of fury. She'd known already that his final jab at Hugh had been vicious. But she realised now it had been something more. To use this woman as a weapon had been nothing short of cruel.

'Well . . .' Gwen started to turn away. 'If you're sure you're OK . . .'

Lily hovered in the doorway, watching her leave. She stood there for several seconds, rooted to the spot. As Gwen reached the staircase, though, she stepped onto the landing.

'Why do they all hate him so much? Why's it so terrible that he's bought the lighthouse?'

Gwen didn't reply at first. Fixing Lily with a quizzical look, she retraced her steps, until they were only a few feet apart. 'How much do you know about the lighthouse?' she asked quietly.

'Nothing. I didn't even know it existed until a few months ago, when he told us he'd bought it.'

Gwen swept a nervous glance back down the landing. 'Can I come in? If you'd really like to talk about this, it's something that would be better discussed in private.'

Lily didn't move. Gwen might not be the homewrecker she'd first assumed, but that didn't mean she could be trusted. If nothing else, the question still remained as to why she had come at all to her dad's room. Lily doubted it was to check that *he* was all right too.

But as she weighed her options, she knew she had no choice.

At the very least, Gwen was speaking to her, something she suspected none of the others would do in a hurry. If she wanted to know about the lighthouse, it seemed this was how she'd do it.

Reluctantly, she stepped aside, pushing the door closed as Gwen slipped into the room.

'Were you listening to something?'

Lily followed her line of sight to the earbuds. 'Just some lecture notes. I have exams in January.'

'Are you going into property too?'

'Accounting.'

'Damien will like that. He'll have you managing his books before you've even qualified.'

Lily forced a smile. 'I was actually hoping to check in on my mum,' she said, eager to change the subject. 'But I can't get any signal.'

'You won't in Hamlet Wick. You might just get a bar by the lighthouse, up on the hill. But your best bet would be going back up the Lane to Hamlet.' Gwen paused. 'It was Wendy, wasn't it? Your mum?'

'Do you know her?'

'I've heard about her. They met in London?'

'That's right. In the student drama society.' Seeing the surprise on Gwen's face, Lily rolled her eyes. 'Hard to imagine, isn't it? The way Mum tells it, he only joined to get her number. He dropped out as soon as they were an item.'

Gwen sat down on the bed. 'That sounds more like the Damien I know.' Catching sight of Lily's expression, she gave a little laugh. 'Don't get me wrong, he could be sweet when he wanted. But most of the time he was a nightmare. So ambitious.

And the smoothest talker you'd ever meet. Give him an inch and he'd have anyone he wanted in the palm of his hand.'

'Is that why Hugh hates him? Because the two of you were an item?'

The smile slipped from Gwen's face. 'Hugh has his reasons.'

'The lighthouse?'

For a moment, Gwen just looked at her. Then she asked, 'Is Damien happy? We lost touch after he went to London. We haven't spoken in such a long time.'

Lily didn't reply. She looked down at the bed and then out of the window. Finally, she sighed. 'I don't know,' she admitted. 'He and Mum . . . They're still together, but I don't really know why. They've slept in different rooms nearly as long as I can remember. They say it's because they have such different work schedules, but I'm not so sure. Mum said once that she only married him for the name. She was joking, of course. But I do wonder sometimes.'

The corners of Gwen's mouth twitched. 'Wendy White. Like a cartoon character.'

'She prefers to say like a movie star.'

'Ah, of course. The budding actress.'

Lily nodded. 'She works in the industry. She's a West End make-up artist.'

'That must be exciting.'

Lily was silent, her gaze still fixed on the window. The lighthouse was out of view from where she was standing, although she could just make out the glow from the floodlights.

'Did Damien really not tell you *why* he'd bought the lighthouse?' asked Gwen.

'He said it'd be nice to have a place in the village where he grew up. Somewhere we could visit as a family.'

'But you don't believe him?'

Lily shook her head. 'He'd never spoken about wanting to come back here before he bought that place. Never brought me here when I was little or spoke about any family.'

'So you think he's lying?'

Lily paused. 'He did mention one other thing. He told me he'd beaten the local tourist board to it. That there were plans to turn it into an attraction, but he'd convinced the council to give him the planning permission instead.' She looked Gwen in the eye. 'That was you, wasn't it? I've read some of Justin's articles in the *Herald*. He beat *you* to it.'

Gwen nodded. 'Yes. That was me.'

'Is that what you wanted to talk to him about?'

Gwen hesitated. 'I've been trying to speak to Damien for months, but he's been dodging my calls. Ignoring my emails. It isn't too late to reverse what he's doing to the lighthouse. While he's here, I had to at least try speaking to him.'

Lily looked again towards the window. 'I just can't understand it. I get that you'd all rather it was some kind of tourist attraction. Honestly, I do. But is it really enough of a reason to hate him so much?'

Gwen fixed her with a frown. 'I'm sure you're going to hear about this at some point tonight. After the way the others behaved in the restaurant, I suppose I'd rather it came from me than from one of them.' She took a deep breath. 'That lighthouse means a great deal to the people here. It has a history.'

'What kind of history?'

'The kind that people feel very sensitive about.' She paused, choosing every word with care. 'Something happened up there. It was years ago now, but there was an accident, with a boy from the village.' She broke off for a moment. 'His name was Teddy. One evening, he climbed to the top. It would have been windy up there. It was dark . . .'

She didn't finish. But Lily didn't need her to. She could see clearly enough from the look in Gwen's eyes how this story ended.

'You have to understand,' she continued. 'It broke the town apart. After he fell, half of Hamlet wanted to tear the lighthouse down and the rest wanted to turn it into a memorial.'

'And you came down on the memorial side?'

Gwen nodded. 'That's why Damien's upset so many people by buying it. It was going to become a viewing tower, dedicated to Teddy. Yes, tourists would have been able to go up it. Frankly, we need the income. But it was just as much about reclaiming it after what happened. For Teddy's family. For all of Hamlet.'

For several seconds, neither of them spoke.

'Did my dad know about this?' Lily asked.

'He knew. Although I don't think he ever truly understood what it did to the town. He moved to London just a couple of months after it happened. And as you've said yourself, he met your mum and never looked back.'

Lily didn't know what to say. Gwen must be right: he *couldn't* have understood. She knew how bullish he could be when it came to a development. But to buy the lighthouse, with the knowledge of what it meant to these people, would be something else entirely.

'What was Teddy even doing up there?'

'Nobody knows. There are theories, of course. Accusations were thrown around at the time. But we never knew for certain.'

Lily looked down at the ground. Then she glanced up, a sudden realisation taking hold. 'Did *you* know Teddy?'

Gwen hesitated. 'I didn't know him, as such. I was a few years older than him. But I remember him.'

'Did my dad?'

Before Gwen could answer, Lily heard the neighbouring door open and then quickly shut again. She frowned to herself. With Justin having been sent away and the silence that had apparently greeted Gwen, she'd assumed her dad must have left. That he'd taken himself downstairs while she listened to her notes.

'Dad?' she called.

There was no answer. He hurried along the landing, the floorboards creaking as he made for the staircase.

Lily thought about calling out again. Why wasn't he taking her with him?

'We'd better follow him,' said Gwen, rising from the bed. 'They'll be wondering where we are.'

Lily nodded. 'Listen,' she said. 'Gwen, I . . .'

She tailed off. She had been about to thank her. To say how grateful she was for coming to check on her. For making her feel less alone.

But she stopped herself. Whatever kindness Gwen had shown her, she was still one of them. When all was said and done, she still wanted the lighthouse back.

Gwen gave that warm smile again. 'Come on,' she said. 'They'll be waiting.'

Nine o'clock

12

Will nudged half-heartedly at the fireplace with an iron poker. The embers crackled, casting a soft glow while the theme tune from David Suchet's *Poirot* pranced from the gramophone. The restaurant looked exactly as he'd imagined. In just three hours' time, they should – in theory – be celebrating both the beginning of a new year and the end of a successful night. Everything was where it needed to be. And yet, Will's evening was on the brink of falling apart.

Carl arrived with two fresh bottles of champagne and a furious expression on his face. After he'd slaved all afternoon over a beautiful batch of soufflés, the decision to skip dessert and minimise the opportunity for Damien White to further antagonise the other guests had put the chef in a foul mood. But Ian wouldn't budge. The clues were in place. Theo, Jack and Claire had their lines. When the guests had all returned, they would get the murder mystery portion of the evening under way.

Will, meanwhile, was still trying frantically to think of whether he could change the story before they began.

When he'd first learned that Hugh would be joining them,

he'd considered a different murder weapon. Perhaps a drop of poison in the cognac or a shot from a Boer War revolver. He'd even briefly toyed with the idea of finding the victim in the garden with a pair of shears in his back. Nobody would have thought twice about any of those.

But it was too late now. He might be able to rewrite his opening speech but there was no time to change the clues or for the actors to learn new lines. And even if there had been, the question remained: would he actually want to?

Ian might have been hoping simply for a successful event that he could replicate. But an altogether deeper purpose lay at the heart of what Will had planned. To change the story – to be dishonest about what he'd found on that beach – would defeat the entire purpose of what they were truly doing at Hamlet Hall.

His mind began to wander. He felt shale under his feet and a stiff breeze on his face. Heard the cawing of seagulls and the flapping of wings. Gripping the poker, he began to jab at the logs, hauling himself from the memory before it could carry him any further.

He wished Claire had found the whisky. That might have steadied his nerves a little, but it was no good. She'd looked in the kitchen, the library and even in Ian's office, but had ultimately come back to the lounge empty-handed.

He couldn't change the story. He'd waited years for this opportunity. Wanted for so long to finally put that morning on the beach behind him. He would just have to carry on, and hope that what he'd planned would slide past Hugh.

Justin had been the first to make his way back to the restaurant. Will heard from Martha Finn, who it seemed hadn't even left her seat during the interval, that he'd only been gone a few minutes. When he'd reappeared, he'd apparently poured himself a large glass of champagne, draining what had been left in the bottles from dinner, and sat scowling at the table.

Nigel was next, having chain-smoked three cigarettes at the back door. Sylvia followed, sitting beside him and offering a smile. He seemed unable to return it, his arms folded on the table and his shoulders slumped. She quickly turned away, any hint of affection vanishing in an instant.

Hugh, who Will understood had spent the entire half-hour in the kitchen with Carl, arrived shortly after, wearing a ferocious expression which did nothing to bolster Will's confidence. Damien White's final jab seemed to have done lasting damage. He didn't even mellow when Gwen joined them. If anything, when she paused to hold the door open for Lily, his eyes gleamed with even greater contempt.

Ian came last. With all the guests seated, he eased the door shut and hovered in the corner, his hands behind his back like a soldier standing to attention. Or rather, *almost* all of the guests. It hadn't escaped Will that Damien White was yet to reappear. He supposed he couldn't blame him. After the barrage of abuse that he'd taken over dinner, Will would be hesitant to come back, too.

He glanced at Ian, who gave a single nod. It was time to begin.

Setting down the poker and taking his place at the foot of the table, Will turned to Lily. 'Is Mr White joining us?'

She frowned at him. 'I thought he was down here.'

'We haven't seen him.' Will looked to the other guests, searching for support. Nobody stepped in.

'But he came downstairs,' Lily insisted.

'She's right, Will,' said Gwen. 'We heard him leave his room, just a few minutes ago. He was making for the stairs.'

'And what were you doing up there?' Hugh muttered.

Gwen glared at her husband, causing Will to wrestle with a sudden glimmer of panic.

'Let's make a start,' said Ian, his voicing rising before she could respond. 'Mr White can catch up when he joins us.'

Hugh scowled and turned towards the bay window, prompting Gwen to sigh.

From across the room, Ian gave Will another nod. Eyes blazing, it was less of a self-assured nudge and more of a frantic plea to get under way.

With trembling hands, Will took two pages of notes from inside his dinner jacket.

He'd pored over this speech for weeks, writing several iterations by hand before typing up the final version on the better of his typewriters. At the time, there'd been something oddly comforting about how the letters had been punched into the paper, the bulky, angular font so cleanly imprinted. But now that the time had come to finally read the words aloud, there wasn't a jot of comfort to be found.

Aside from Hugh, who was still glaring at the window, all eyes were upon him. Justin's phone was on the table, although Will was relieved to see that the little red light wasn't blinking. He didn't want this recorded. Across the room, Ian lifted the needle from the record, the only sound now the crackling of the fire.

Will cleared his throat, took a deep breath and in as confident a voice as he could manage, began to read. 'Good evening, ladies and gentlemen. My name is Bartley and I'm the butler here at Hamlet Hall, home of the noble Lord Ashcombe.'

Following a handwritten note he'd left himself on the speech, he waved towards the fireplace, where a portrait hung of the first Earl of Hamlet.

'Lord Ashcombe,' he continued, 'has invited you here – his closest family and dearest friends – to share a tremendous piece of news. What this news is, I cannot say, but I do know he has anticipated this evening keenly. In ordinary circumstances, it would be my most sincere pleasure to welcome you all to this house. But these are not ordinary circumstances, for an unspeakable crime has taken place. Lord Ashcombe, ladies and gentlemen, has been murdered!'

Will paused for effect. As he did, he caught Justin smirking quietly to himself. Gwen gave him an encouraging smile.

'Inspector Monroe has since inspected the body but, alas, is clueless.' Will motioned towards Ian, who cocked a disapproving eyebrow. 'I, however, saw the crime take place from an upstairs window. No more, I'd say, than thirty paces from the house. Having served Lord Ashcombe for many years, I know that most evenings it is his way to take an after-dinner walk on the beach. Indeed, I have often seen him doing so from the window. This evening, however, was different. For tonight, I saw a second figure join him.'

Will paused again, wrestling with a sudden urge to look up at Hugh.

'I watched them speak for several minutes before Lord Ashcombe turned away and began to walk back towards the house.

It was then that his companion took a rock from the beach, struck him across the head and ran back towards the manor!'

Will continued, not daring this time to look up from the page.

'I went to him at once, hoping I might be able to assist him. But it is my solemn duty to inform you, ladies and gentlemen, that Lord Ashcombe was killed on that beach. A great man, taken too soon. A philanthropist. A gentleman. We can, at least, take some comfort in knowing that he is now reunited with his dear departed wife, Lady Agatha.

'But who was the murderer? I hear you cry! I cannot say. Darkness had already fallen, such that I couldn't make out the shadowy figure. Even as they ran back to the house, I couldn't see if the culprit was a man or a woman.

'One thing we can be sure of, however, is that nobody has entered or left Hamlet Hall since this dreadful crime took place. This leads me to one terrible conclusion. The murderer must be among us; seated here at this very table. And with Inspector Monroe so helpless, it falls to you, Lord Ashcombe's friends and family, to identify them.

'On the table, you will each find an envelope, which you may now open. Inside is a letter containing details about the characters you will be portraying. One of you will find that your letter identifies you as the murderer. Whichever one of you this may be, it is imperative that you keep your identity secret until the end of the evening.

'Around the house, you will also find two associates of Lord Ashcombe: Mr Spade, who was his trusted solicitor, and Dr Wargrave, the local physician. Both of these gentlemen were called here tonight, though for what purpose, I cannot say. You will also find Miss Chambers, who has been a maid here at Hamlet Hall for twenty years. They will help lead you to the truth, but they won't do so willingly. You will need to present each with a clue, hidden somewhere in the house. Present the correct clue to each associate, and only then will they reveal what they know.

'Tread carefully, ladies and gentlemen. Remember, at all times, that the murderer is among you!'

Will waited several seconds before looking up. It was done now. There was no way back.

For a fleeting, fevered moment, he imagined looking up at his audience and seeing eager, amused faces. In his mind, he saw them snatching up their envelopes, separating into groups and asking him where they should start in their search for clues.

But when, finally, he tore his eyes from the page, that fantasy faded in a heartbeat.

Gwen, Nigel and Sylvia all gawped at him, wide-eyed. Justin had sat bolt upright in his seat, his hand hovering over the phone. Ian glared from his spot in the corner and even Martha Finn had abandoned her expectant smile.

And then there was Hugh. He stared with such contempt that Will couldn't look him in the eye.

The only one, of course, who remained oblivious was Lily White.

'Hold on,' she said, breaking the terrible silence. 'Are we really starting this without my dad?' She rounded on Will. 'I know that none of you care, but I, at the very least, want to know where he is.'

'Perhaps Will and I can check on him,' said Ian. He might

have been speaking to Lily, but his eyes were still fixed on Will. 'We'll go now,' he growled, teeth gritted, 'and knock on his door.'

'But he came downstairs,' Lily protested.

Nobody replied. Not even Gwen spoke up this time.

'Will,' said Ian quietly. 'Come with me.'

Will had no idea which way to turn, the thought of what Ian would say when they were alone in the hallway frightening him as much as anything had ever frightened him in his life. But he knew that he couldn't stay in the restaurant. He couldn't take another moment under Hugh's piercing, hate-filled gaze.

Resigning himself, he tucked the notes back inside his jacket and walked the length of the table. He could feel the weight of every pair of eyes upon him as he went, the sound of his shoes on the wooden floor deafening in the silence.

The moment they slipped into the hallway, Ian seized him by the shoulder and shoved him roughly towards the staircase. Will realised immediately what was happening. The torrent of fury was coming. Ian just wanted to make sure they were out of the guests' earshot when it did.

He went slowly, one foot trudging after the other. With each step, he thought of the conversation that must be taking place in the restaurant. He wondered what they'd be saying about him, which of them would be calling him crazy. And he thought again of his conversation with Justin.

Aren't you worried what people might think about that? About your involvement in any of this, to be quite frank. Given your history with this sort of thing.

When, finally, they reached the top of the stairs, Ian turned on him.

'What the *fuck* were you thinking?' he hissed, his eyes blazing. 'A body on the beach? A rock to the head? *Jesus*, Will! You knew that Hugh was going to be there. And even if he hadn't been, what made you think you could *possibly* get away with that?'

Before Will could even speak, Ian raised a hand to silence him.

'No. I don't want to hear it. I shouldn't have agreed to this. Any of it. When we go back downstairs, we're going to . . .' He tailed off. 'I don't know *what* we're going to do. We can't play this *game* of yours now. Christ, the looks on their faces. On *Hugh*'s face . . .'

Will tried to speak but the words refused to come. He felt as though he was drowning. Being tossed about in the water outside, icy hands dragging him down while all of the guests stood and stared.

Ian watched him for a few seconds. When he realised no solution was coming, he scowled and turned away, marching towards Damien White's room.

'Mr White,' he called, with a sharp knock upon the door. 'Is everything all right?'

There was no answer.

'Mr White,' he called again. 'Are you in there?'

Still, there was silence.

Despite everything, Will found himself momentarily distracted from the panic attack that he was wrestling into constraint. Perhaps Lily was right. Perhaps Damien White really had left his room. But where would he have gone? And how could nobody have seen him leave?

He stepped closer, closing the distance until he was standing shoulder to shoulder with Ian. Muttering something under his breath, Ian stood up straight and forced what Will imagined must have been the most amiable expression he could manage. Then he turned the handle and opened the door.

The first thing Will saw was the blood.

Ian eased the door open gradually, presumably to avoid startling Damien White if he had still been in the room. The effect it seemed to have, though, was to reveal the scene in slow motion. Inch by gory inch.

White lay face down on the floor, his body angled towards the window and arms spread like a discarded doll. A savage wound at the back of his head was wet with blood, matting his hair and staining his polo shirt.

Will's stomach turned. Ian might have said something, but he didn't hear it. He simply watched as the older man sprang into the room and crouched down low, inspecting the body. There was no questioning the sight before them. Damien White was dead.

Ian recoiled, breathing hard as he staggered back into the corridor and collapsed against the wall. Will hadn't moved. He'd barely drawn breath. He was fixed in place, staring at the gruesome spectacle.

And then, of course, came the inevitable. Because this wasn't the first time Will had seen death. Instantly he heard the seagulls, shrieking as loudly as if they were right there in the corridor. He felt an ocean breeze, brushing so vividly against his skin that he could practically taste the salt on his lips. He closed his eyes, trying desperately to block out the image of Damien White's lifeless body. But in his mind, all he could see instead was the mound of sodden clothes, heaped upon the shale, twelve years ago. He saw pale skin, damp hair and wide, bulging eyes.

He felt Ian grasp him by the shoulder.

'Tell me this wasn't you,' he snarled.

Will gawped at him.

'Is this fake?' Ian jabbed a finger towards the body, but Will couldn't follow it. He couldn't bear to look back. 'I swear to God, Will,' said Ian. 'Tell me right now that this isn't part of your game. That you haven't—'

'This isn't me!'

Ian stopped, what little colour had been left draining from his face. 'So he is actually . . .'

He didn't wait for Will to reply. Gently, he closed the door. Then he buried his face in his hands, pressed his back to the wall and slumped to the floor.

He sat there for several minutes, swearing viciously between deep, shuddering breaths. Will stood, watching. He should say something. *Do* something. But he was completely paralysed. He could feel a sense of nausea building. If he tried to speak – if he so much as *moved* – he was certain that he'd either break down or be sick. Maybe both.

When Ian finally lifted his face from his hands, he'd gone completely pale, his eyes bloodshot. 'We can't let the others know,' he said slowly, forcing each word. 'Not yet. I'll call the police. You need to go back to the restaurant and make sure they stay put until someone comes.'

Will's eyes flew wide, the thought of returning to the restaurant proving enough to snap him from his daze. 'How am I supposed to do that? What do I tell them?'

'Don't tell them anything,' Ian hissed. 'Not a bloody word. Nobody can know what's happened. Act normal. If they ask where he is, say that White is in his room and is fine. Whatever you do, until I can get the police here, we need to keep them all in that restaurant.'

13

Lily was seething.

It must have been her dad who she'd heard leaving his room. It had to be.

The Range Rover was still parked outside, so he hadn't driven off. Maybe he'd sneaked out for a walk. He clearly hadn't been safe upstairs, with both Justin and Gwen calling on him during the interval. But why hadn't he taken her with him? He wouldn't leave her with these people. Would he?

Perhaps it was a test. Leave her with this group and see if she could stand her ground. It would be a horrendous thing to do, but she wouldn't put it past him. Anything to make sure she was worthy to one day fill his shoes. Or maybe he was resentful at her making the suggestion that they visit the lighthouse in the first place. That would hardly be fair. Shouldn't it be her mum he was furious with? After all, she'd been the one who insisted they come to this party.

Wherever he'd gone, Lily was furious that he'd have the gall to leave her. She'd had no idea about Teddy or the full extent of the local hostility. If anything, *he* should have warned *her*. He might have left Hamlet shortly after Teddy died, but he must have had an idea of the anger he'd provoked by buying the lighthouse. Had he not heard about the petition? Seen the stories in the *Herald*? Was he oblivious or did he just not care?

The longer she sat there, though, the more difficult it became to give his whereabouts her full attention. It was painfully clear that something in Will's speech had changed the tone of the evening. The fire had dwindled to a pile of faintly glowing embers, while the absence of a new record on the player had allowed an uncomfortable hush to descend on the room. The Finns muttered to each other and shook their heads. Even Sylvia, without any desire to natter at Nigel, looked unsure of herself. She sipped cordially at a newly filled glass of champagne, but she couldn't hide the troubled glances that she kept sweeping towards the top of the table. Towards Hugh.

Without a doubt, he was the most severely affected by Will's opening speech. His eyes had glazed over and his jaw was set as Gwen whispered to him. She was holding his hand, a strained expression on her face as if she was trying to gently deliver a terrible piece of news. It was quite a change from how embarrassed she'd been about his outburst over dinner.

Lily wondered if it might all have something to do with Teddy, but she struggled to think how. The victim in Will's story had been hit around the head with a stone on the beach. He hadn't mentioned the lighthouse, and even if he had, she couldn't imagine why it would have such an effect on Hugh.

She thought about what Gwen had told her upstairs, when

she'd asked if it was their teenage relationship that had caused Hugh to be so angry at her dad's arrival. She remembered the way Gwen had suddenly seemed so uncomfortable. What was it she'd said?

Hugh has his reasons.

Perhaps he did. But whatever those reasons were, Lily was still none the wiser.

In her mind, she replayed the moment her dad stormed from the restaurant. *Keep talking if it makes you feel better*, he'd said. *It won't change the fact that I've shagged your wife.*

It had been brutal. But the more she thought on it, the more Lily began to realise it wasn't all he'd said. She'd been so furious about the possibility of an affair with Gwen that she'd missed the other part of his final blow:

It won't change how Rory ran himself into the ground.

Her entire life, she'd only ever known one Rory. A friend of her parents from their student days, by all accounts he'd been a big part of their lives when they were younger. He'd been best man at their wedding and gone into business with her dad, helping get his first few developments off the ground. When she was small, she'd even called him 'Uncle Rory'.

She could barely remember him now. Hardly surprising, she supposed, considering that she was fairly sure it must have been around fifteen years since she'd last seen him. But if she tried hard, she thought that perhaps she could hear his laugh. She pictured broad shoulders. Dark, scruffy hair.

She did remember once asking her parents why they hadn't seen him for so long, but all they'd say was that he'd fallen out of love with London. He'd had something of a midlife crisis,

113

sold his stake in their company to her dad and disappeared into the sunset.

Could it be the same Rory? It didn't *sound* as if he'd run himself into the ground. He'd just needed a change of scenery. And why would her dad mention him to Hugh? He'd met *their* Rory in London. Why hurl his name, like a dagger, at a stranger in Hamlet Wick?

Across the table, Justin caught Lily's eye. He was the only one who appeared not to have been troubled by Will's speech. If anything, he seemed energised.

When they'd returned from the interval, Justin had been slumped in his seat; bruised, Lily assumed, from his 'interview' with her dad. But after Will had finished speaking, he'd sat bolt upright, phone in his hand. Whatever had sailed so cleanly over Lily's head – whatever had upset Hugh and the others – seemed to have struck Justin like a jolt of electricity.

She looked away, refusing to make eye contact. Whatever gossip-fuelled story he was composing behind those dark eyes, she wanted nothing to do with it.

As an excuse to keep her attention elsewhere, she took the envelope from the table in front of her. She'd noticed it when they arrived, but with all that had been said over dinner, she'd barely thought of it. Now, half curious and half determined to avoid a conversation with Justin, she cracked the seal and drew out a folded sheet of thick, cream-coloured paper.

In fairness to Will, he deserved some credit for attention to detail. There was a coat of arms at the top of the page, with *Hamlet Hall* inscribed beneath. Further down, a few short paragraphs had been typed up, the letters punched onto the paper in dark ink. Glancing over the first, Lily read:

Tonight, you will take on the role of Jane Ashcombe, nineteen-year-old daughter of Lord Ashcombe's reckless younger brother, Lester. Though Jane's birth is something of a scandalous affair – Lester has a long-standing reputation as the black sheep of the family, and a great many rumours surround the identity of Jane's mother – she is loved by all and has been warmly welcomed into the family. Lord Ashcombe was especially fond of his niece before his untimely demise.

So she wasn't the murderer. Will had mentioned that one of the guests would be told in their letter they'd killed Lord Ashcombe. Skim-reading the remaining paragraphs, she saw there was nothing to suggest that her fictional counterpart was guilty.

Before she could think about Jane Ashcombe any further, Martha Finn pulled out the neighbouring chair.

'Do you mind?' she asked. Without waiting for an answer, she tucked herself smoothly under the table, a champagne glass in one hand, and held up her own letter. 'I'm married to the butler. Fifty years in Hamlet Wick and that's what I've been relegated to. I don't know who you've got, but I'd much rather be a lady or a duchess. Something a little more glamorous. I'm not sure I'd have bothered coming if I'd known Will was going to make me a glorified housekeeper.'

Lily couldn't help but give a short laugh. Lowering her guard a fraction, she looked closer at Martha Finn. She and Edward were easily the oldest of the guests, and yet, as Lily weighed her up properly, there was something vibrant about her. A warmth which, by the look of his combed grey hair and sedate expression, her husband didn't share.

'Fifty years,' Lily repeated. 'I thought everyone in Hamlet must have been born here.'

'Not me.' Martha nodded towards Edward. 'Nineteen years old, I was. He was twenty-four. The navy stationed him in Plymouth for a couple of years while I was clearing tables at one of the bars by the harbour. When he reached the end of his time, he asked me to marry him and convinced me to come back with him to Hamlet.'

'And you've been here ever since?'

'That's right.'

'What's it like?'

Martha thought for a moment, tilting her head as if considering it for the first time. 'It's beautiful,' she said.

Lily waited for her to expand, but the way she raised the champagne glass to her lips seemed to suggest she was going no further.

'Did you know my dad?' she asked. 'When he was younger?'

Martha snorted gently. 'Everyone knew your father.' She set the glass down on the table, before saying, 'I shouldn't worry about him. I'm sure he'll be along soon.'

'I just want to know where he is.'

'Is he really the sort to be frightened off by a crowd like us? Because I'll tell you something – he wouldn't have been when he was your age.'

Lily paused. 'I guess not.'

For a split second, she was desperately grateful. There was

no chance of making peace with the likes of Hugh or Sylvia; their resentment ran far too deep. But with some kindness from Gwen and now Martha Finn, the evening might not be quite so unbearable.

'I'm sorry about what's happened,' she said. 'To your shop.'

'It's not your fault, dear.'

'Do you really think my dad's to blame?'

'There are plenty who'd say so.'

Lily was silent for a moment. She was sure Hugh had said that the Finns believed it was men from the lighthouse who had broken into their shop. Perhaps Edward clung more tightly to that theory than his wife.

'I'm surprised you'd even want to speak to me.'

Martha looked her in the eye. 'How much sway do you have over what your father's doing to that lighthouse?'

'I didn't know it existed until a few months ago.'

'And if you could convince him to call it off, would you?'

'I think so. Seeing tonight how much it means to all of you, I'd at least consider it.'

'There you have it. You and your father aren't the same, dear. Some might say he deserves a lot of what was said to him over dinner. But I don't see why you should be treated in the same way.'

Unsure how to respond, Lily glanced across the table towards Gwen and Hugh. 'What have I missed?' she asked.

Martha frowned at her.

'Will's speech,' she explained. 'It seems to have really killed the mood. I can't help feeling like everyone knows something I don't.'

117

Martha paused, deciding carefully what to say.

'Is it about Teddy?' asked Lily.

At the sound of his name, something changed in the older woman's expression. 'Your father told you about Teddy?'

'No, I heard about him from Gwen.' Lily frowned. 'I didn't think my dad really knew him.'

Martha's expression darkened even further, the warmth that had radiated from her seeming to all but vanish. 'Make no mistake. Your father knew Teddy.'

'Were they friends?'

'I don't think friendship is quite the right word.'

She paused, a cold silence hanging between them. Lily sat completely still, watching as this curious change overcame her.

'There were two of them,' Martha said quietly. 'Your father and another boy from the village. Teddy idolised the pair of them. Followed them everywhere they went. They never paid him the slightest jot of notice, of course. But that didn't stop him trailing after them like a lost lamb.'

'So my dad knew him?'

'He did.'

'Who was the other boy?'

Martha's eyes softened slightly. 'He isn't here any more.'

Again, Lily waited. But it seemed clear, this time, that Martha wasn't going any further.

'All right,' she pressed. 'But what does this have to do with Will's story? I'd understand why mentioning Teddy would put you all on edge, but I don't see a connection. He didn't even mention the lighthouse—'

'It isn't about Teddy.'

'What, then?'

Before Martha could reply, the door opened and Lily turned to see Will stepping into the restaurant.

The sudden change in Martha's tone had already set her on edge. But with one glance at Will, she knew for certain that something was wrong. He had the look of a hare, startled from having narrowly escaped the tyres of a speeding car. His face had run pale, and his eyes were wide and distant. Even his hands trembled slightly.

For several seconds, everyone watched him. Then, tired of waiting, Lily broke the silence.

'Well?'

He gave a little jump.

'Is he up there?' she asked.

'Yes, he's up there.'

'And is he coming back?'

Will shook his head.

'Why not?'

'I can't say.'

'What do you mean, *you can't say*?'

She was acutely aware of the other guests watching her, but she didn't care. She liked to think that she wasn't one for fretting – it was never something her dad would do – but the truth was that Will was beginning to frighten her.

'Is Ian up there too?' asked Gwen.

'He's in his office.'

'Why?' asked Lily.

Will turned to her again. 'I'm sorry?'

119

'If my dad's still up in his room, and you're down here, why is Ian in his office?'

Will took a deep breath and twisted his features into what Lily could only imagine was meant to be a smile. 'Can I pour anyone another drink?' he asked.

'What are you talking about?' Lily's voice rose, the concern she was trying to pretend wasn't there beginning to show. 'I don't want more champagne. I want to speak to my dad.'

'Will,' said Justin. 'Has something happened to Mr White?'

'Wouldn't you like to know?' Lily spat.

'What's that supposed to mean?'

'I heard you up there, trying to get an interview out of him. You'd be thrilled if something had happened, wouldn't you? That'd be just what you need for a juicy story.'

Gwen stood up, her hands raised. 'Lily, please . . .'

'Just tell us what's going on, Will.' It was Sylvia who chimed in this time, though in a tone that sounded more irritated than concerned.

'I am,' Will protested, the pitiful smile vanishing as quickly as it had been forced into place.

'No, you're not!' Lily rounded on him.

'Everyone, please . . .' Gwen tried again to calm the group, but they were too far gone. Sylvia was jabbering like a canary, demanding that Will just be frank, while Justin had launched into a monologue about journalistic integrity. Lily, meanwhile, was finding her own frustration reaching breaking point.

'Tell me what's going on,' she blazed. 'Tell me right now or I'll—'

With an almighty crash, Hugh brought a fist down upon the

120

table. The blow echoed from the wood-panelled walls, landing with such force that half of the crockery leapt an inch into the air and the glassware began to sing. Beside her, Lily saw Martha Finn jump.

Gwen placed a hand on her husband's shoulder. 'Will,' she said delicately. 'Are you saying that Mr White won't be joining us?'

He nodded.

'Will you please tell us why?'

A moment passed. Then another, the silence now crippling. Lily rose to her feet.

'What are you doing?' Will asked.

'I'm going to see my dad.'

'No!'

He sprang towards the door but she shoved him easily out of the way.

'Wait,' he cried as she barged into the hallway. 'Please, you can't go up there!'

But Lily wasn't listening. She reached the stairs within seconds and began taking them two at a time.

'What's happening?' She heard Ian's voice behind her, emerging, she assumed, from his office. Immediately he took up Will's protests. 'Miss White!' he called after her. 'Miss White, you can't go up there!'

But he was too late. Lily had already reached the landing, and at the end of the corridor, she saw her dad's door.

The stairs creaked behind her, but she didn't turn back to see whether it was Ian or Will in pursuit. Something was being hidden from her, and she had to know what.

The footsteps continuing to follow her, she ran the last few paces. Her fingers brushed the handle, and she turned just in time to see Ian reach the top of the stairs, his eyes wide with sheer terror.

With a single swift movement, she turned the handle and threw the door open.

14

The scream filled Hamlet Hall, ringing out so clearly that, even in the lounge, Theo heard it as if the woman it came from had been right there with them.

Across the coffee table, Claire flashed him a panicked glance, while Jack jumped so violently that he spilled half of his champagne.

Springing from the leather sofa, Theo threw the door open just in time to see a young woman tearing through the hallway. Ian and Will looked like they'd tried to pursue her but were both now standing at the foot of the staircase, Ian's face in his hands. Across the hall, the guests were gathering outside the restaurant, the young woman barging past them as she made frantically for the front door.

'Lily!'

Gwen jostled her way to the front of the group, shoving the others roughly out of the way. But it was no use. Lily had made it to the door and was now sprinting from the hotel.

Theo couldn't say what, exactly, possessed him to follow her. Perhaps it was the sound of that scream, still echoing in his ears.

It might just as easily have been the sight of the others simply standing and gawping as she fled into the night. Either way, he was aware only of the slightest hesitation before he found himself lurching after her.

He heard Jack call his name, but he didn't stop. She had a good lead. By the time he was even outside, she'd already crossed the road, covering the short distance to the beach.

'Wait,' he called after her. 'Please!'

He had no idea if she'd heard him. If she had, she wasn't listening.

He pushed himself onwards, slipping and stumbling as he struggled in his shoes to find his footing on the shale. Ahead of him, she carried on running right up to the water's edge, where eventually she stopped, her shoulders heaving. The waves crashed at her feet, the surf lapping at the toes of her running shoes.

'Please,' said Theo again, panting slightly. 'Come back to the hotel.'

Still she ignored him.

'It was Lily, wasn't it?' he tried. 'Lily White?'

Finally, she turned back. Even in the darkness, he could see that there was venom in her expression. Pure, undeniable resentment. Her eyes glittered in the moonlight and Theo realised that there were tears on her cheeks.

'It's OK.' He lowered his voice as much as he could without being drowned out by the waves. The wind caused his tie to flutter in front of his eyes, but he didn't dare move it out of the way. He stood completely still, as if she might bolt at the slightest movement. 'It's all right,' he said gently. 'I'm Theo. I'm one of the actors.'

'I'm not going back in there,' she said breathlessly.

'Why not?'

She said nothing.

'Why won't you come back with me, Lily?'

'Because one of them killed my fucking dad!' she screamed at him, so suddenly – so fiercely – that Theo took a sudden step back, almost losing his footing on the shale. 'And for what?' she demanded. 'For *that*?'

She swept her head right, Theo following her gaze past the harbour to the lighthouse. It stood proudly on the hill, the wire-topped fences jagged in the glare of the floodlights.

His mind raced, the sound of the waves filling his ears. Could she be right? Could Damien White really be dead?

She turned away from the lighthouse, but when the moon-light caught her eyes again, Theo realised that she wasn't look-ing at him. Rather, she was looking past him, towards Hamlet Hall. He turned as well and saw the guests beginning to gather outside. Light poured from the door, silhouetting them as if they were lining up for a team photo.

'It was him,' said Lily, her voice laced with malice. 'It was that boy, Will.'

'Will . . .' Theo thought that he could just make his shadow out from the others, hovering at the back. 'Please,' he said, facing Lily again. 'Just come back inside. You must be in—'

'Don't try to tell me I'm in shock!'

Theo took another step back, wishing desperately that the others would go inside again. He was already hopelessly out of his depth. This would surely be easier without a crowd of spectators.

125

'Listen to me,' he said, raising his voice over a sudden gust of wind. 'Will couldn't ever—'

'How do you know? You're part of his story, aren't you? Did he tell you how his murder happens?'

Theo hesitated. 'He was worried about the game being ruined if the actors knew too much. We only got the details we needed.'

'And that doesn't seem odd to you?'

Theo couldn't answer straight away. Will had been so sure of himself that he hadn't even questioned it. In the end, it had just been part of the job.

'What don't I know, Lily?' he asked. 'Why does it matter what happens in Will's story?'

But she wasn't listening any more. She was looking again towards Hamlet Hall. She was trembling, but Theo couldn't tell if she was shivering or – despite her protests – if she might genuinely be in shock. The wind was piercing, making him wish for the tweed jacket he'd brought as part of his solicitor's costume. They must only have been standing there for a few minutes, but already he could feel his cheeks beginning to sting, his hands going numb.

'He's a psycho,' Lily said quietly.

Theo took a deep breath, choosing every word with pristine care. 'I don't know what's happened to Mr White. Or why you'd think that Will has something to do with it. But he can't have. He was with me in the lounge for the whole interval and then in the restaurant with you and the others. When would he have had the chance to hurt your dad?'

She said nothing.

'Lily.' Theo took a single tentative step forward. 'Whatever's happened, I promise you, Will can't have been involved. He's not a psycho.'

'What is he then?' She rounded on him, her voice rising again. 'Tell me. Explain to me how my dad ends up dead just minutes after Will tells a fucking story about it!'

Theo stopped dead, as if suddenly treading on a sheet of ice.

'Will's story,' Lily continued. 'His *mystery*. The victim was hit on the head with a rock, right here on this beach. Well, I saw my dad, dead on the floor in his room. And it sure as hell looked to me like he'd been hit around the head.'

Theo's stomach turned. 'It isn't your dad that Will was talking about.'

This time, she stopped. Her shoulders still heaved, breath steaming in front of her face. But her expression softened a little, her eyes narrowing into a frown.

'Who, then?'

Theo looked away, cursing himself for not insisting on more information. For letting Will tell him that it was better they didn't know. A rock on the beach . . . What was he thinking?

When he turned back, he saw that Lily was still watching him. Waiting.

'It really isn't my place,' he said.

'I don't care.'

He looked down at the shale, feeling himself being dragged further down. A shiver ran through him, and he shoved his trembling hands into his pockets to stave off the cold.

'Please,' he said. 'Just come back inside and we'll—'

'No!' she shrieked. 'What is it that nobody's telling me? If it isn't Teddy and it isn't my dad, who was Will talking about?'

Her voice was rising again, her eyes wild. Theo felt his lips move, but there were no words any more. Mind racing, he was now searching frantically for an escape.

Over his shoulder, he heard the low rumble of an engine. Grateful for a reason to break Lily's gaze, he turned and saw a police car emerging from the Lane, blue lights flashing as it pulled up outside Hamlet Hall.

A woman stopped the engine and stepped briskly from the car, silhouetted by the light from the Hall as she patted down her uniform. Wasting no time, she marched promptly up to the group and gave a series of instructions, although Theo had no chance of hearing them from where he stood. By the time the words reached him, they had long been engulfed by the wind and the waves.

For a few seconds, nothing happened. Then, to Theo's relief, the guests began to file back inside. All except one, who stepped onto the beach, clutching her arms to protect herself from the cold. As she approached, the wind causing her ball gown to flutter, Theo saw that it was Gwen Holloway.

'Lily,' she said gently. 'We need to go inside now.'

'I'm not going back in there.'

'Please, Lily . . .'

'No!' Finally, her voice broke, her eyes glittering with fresh tears.

At first nobody moved. Then Gwen put a tentative arm around Lily's shoulders. For a moment, she stood firm. But within seconds, her whole body seemed to slump and she allowed herself to be guided back towards the house.

Theo took a moment to collect himself before he followed.

He stared into the dark water, tasting the salt on the air as he tried to grasp just what was happening inside Hamlet Hall.

What was Will thinking? Was he really trying to recreate what he'd seen all those years ago? For some unfathomable reason to relive it? If Lily was right – if his story really hinged on someone being struck on the beach – then it seemed he just might. But what would it achieve? And what had happened to Damien White?

He turned his head, swearing aloud as he settled again on the lighthouse.

Could White really have been murdered? Whatever Will was doing – whatever madness seemed to have possessed him – Theo couldn't believe he would be capable of that. If White had been killed; if Lily had really seen what she claimed to have seen . . . wasn't it more likely it would be connected to the lighthouse? Everyone knew its terrible history, and everyone resented Damien White for buying it.

Even so . . . Theo had spent his entire life in Hamlet; grown up with the people now gathered inside the Hall. He'd spent his pocket money in Edward and Martha Finn's shop. Gwen had given him a trophy on Sports Day. Whatever their feelings towards Damien White, and towards the lighthouse, the thought of any of them committing murder was too terrible to even consider.

Finally, unable to bear the cold a moment longer, he began to walk towards the house. All of the guests had disappeared inside, but in the light from the hallway, he saw that the police officer remained. She stood in the doorway, looming like a statue, and Theo realised she was watching him approach.

He walked slowly, treading carefully on the shale, and with every step a sense of dread set in deeper. Because as much as he wanted to deny that anyone inside Hamlet Hall could be responsible for murder, one of them must be.

Someone, it seemed, had killed Damien White. And unless they'd managed to slip away unnoticed, they were still there. Hiding among the guests.

Ten o'clock

15

Despite twelve years having passed, Will remembered his first meeting with Constable Natalie Fay as clearly as if it had happened that very day.

From the beach, he and his dad had been sent to Hamlet police station, where two officers took their statements. The first had fetched a plate of biscuits and a plastic cup of orange squash. He'd smiled kindly at Will and said he could call him Toby, if he liked. The second had sat bolt upright in her seat, hands clasped on the table, and told Will to call her Constable Fay.

In the weeks and months that followed, they'd met a handful more times. Toby would come to the house and ask Will gently if there was anything else he remembered. He could say whatever he needed to; he wouldn't be in trouble.

PC Fay, meanwhile, would ask them into the police station. She would show them pictures of the beach and demand to know if Will was *sure* he was being honest; if he wasn't leaving things out on purpose.

Eventually, when Fay had clearly decided there were more

productive lines of inquiry for her to follow than a frightened seven-year-old, those meetings came to an end. It was now more than a decade since they were last face to face, but she still looked exactly as Will remembered. She wore the same stern expression, her eyes sweeping the room as she collected every possible detail. Even her uniform was just as pristine, hair tied tightly beneath her chequered hat.

After ushering the guests back into Hamlet Hall, her first action was sending them to wait in the restaurant, and the actors back into the lounge. Then she instructed Ian and Will to take her to Damien White.

Ian led the way, guiding her upstairs, while Will hung a few steps behind. It didn't matter that he was an adult now. It didn't even matter that he was a few inches taller than her. He seemed to naturally place himself out of PC Fay's line of sight.

When they reached the room, she didn't pause to ask what they made of the scene. Instead, she held out a hand, signalling for them to wait on the landing, and went straight inside. Will couldn't have been more relieved. The thought of being made to look again at Damien White's lifeless body was too much to bear.

While she was away, he thought for a moment about how she was still a PC. He was certain that wouldn't be by choice. There were officers in Hamlet who had kept the same beat for decades, but Fay wouldn't be one of them. The woman he remembered was the most single-minded person he'd ever met. He didn't know much about working for the police, but he had no doubt that she would have the drive to seek out a promotion, if there was one to be sought.

After a few minutes, she re-emerged, pulling the door gently

134

closed as she joined them on the landing. If she'd been fazed by the sight of the body, she didn't show it. 'The two of you discovered him?' she asked.

Ian nodded.

'And you were together?'

'That's right.'

'What were you doing?'

Ian spoke slowly. 'His daughter was worried about him. We offered to check that he was all right and when we came upstairs, we found . . .' He trailed off, unable to finish.

'The body hasn't been disturbed in any way?'

'No.'

'Did Miss White have any particular reason to be concerned about her father?'

'She thought he'd left his room. Claims to have heard him. But nobody else had seen him come back downstairs.'

'Did anyone else hear him leaving?'

'Gwen. She was in Miss White's room with her.'

Fay pointed towards the neighbouring door. 'Is this Miss White's room?'

'That's right.'

'And who was the last person to actually *see* Mr White?'

Ian turned to Will. Fay followed, and for the first time since she'd arrived, they locked eyes. She didn't even flinch, but he knew she recognised him. It wasn't a case that he imagined she would forget in a hurry.

He felt his heart begin to pound in his throat. Of all the police officers working in Hamlet, why had it been her? Why couldn't someone else have taken Ian's call?

'Justin,' he said, his voice quivering. 'At least, I think it must have been Justin. He'd been up here to ask Mr White for an interview.'

'And we're sure it wasn't actually Mr Fletcher who they heard leaving?'

'He was only up here for a few minutes. As far as I'm aware, he was already back in the restaurant.'

Fay thought for a moment. 'Assuming Miss White and Mrs Holloway did hear someone leaving this room,' she said. 'How much time then passed before the two of you discovered the body?'

'Can't have been more than half an hour,' said Ian. 'We gathered the guests in the restaurant, Will gave his speech . . .' He flashed Will a glare. 'And then when Mr White still hadn't joined us, we came upstairs to make sure everything was all right.'

'Do you know if anyone visited the room in that time?'

'No.'

'No, you don't know? Or nobody else visited?'

Ian floundered. 'I don't know.'

Fay paused again. Will knew the look that was playing on her face. To someone who didn't, there might appear to have been no change, but he saw the way her eyes had narrowed a fraction. She was mentally dissecting and cross-referencing every piece of information she'd just heard.

'How many ways out of the building are there?'

'Three,' said Ian. 'The main entrance at the front, a pair of French doors at the back to access the garden and a service door from the kitchen.'

'Do you have CCTV?'

'Over the French and kitchen doors, yes.'

'Not the front door?'

Ian shuffled on the spot, looking down at his feet. 'The camera over the front door is broken. I haven't had the money to replace it, and even if I did there's hardly seemed much point while we're out of season.'

Fay took a short, sharp breath.

'This has been done deliberately, hasn't it?' There was suddenly a note of distress in Ian's voice. 'The injury at the back of his head . . . That can't have been an accident. Someone's attacked him.'

Fay looked hard at him. 'Is there a key for this door?'

'Yes.'

'But you didn't lock it after you'd found the body?'

'I didn't think to. The key was in the office when we found him . . . I was focused on getting through to the police . . . Honestly, I just wasn't thinking clearly.'

With a trembling hand, Ian drew a bulky, old-fashioned key from his jacket, and handed it over to Fay, who locked the door and then tucked the key into a pocket.

'I'd like to see the footage from the cameras,' she said.

Ian looked into space. As he did, Will thought about what must be running through his head. The collapse of his business – of the reputation of Hamlet Hall altogether. He remembered hearing somewhere that Ian had bought the place with money left to him after his parents had died. It must have been difficult to imagine that whatever dreams he'd had of running a luxury hotel might end like this.

The pause only lasted a moment. Composing himself, Ian

gave a stiff nod and set off towards the stairs. He descended quickly, as if keen to put some distance between himself and the terrible scene in Damien White's room. At the bottom, he turned left, guiding Fay down the corridor that led to the kitchen.

The office was little more than a glorified cupboard, with barely enough room for all three of them to stand comfortably inside. An old desktop computer sat on a cheap plywood desk. Behind the monitor, a cork noticeboard filled the wall, bearing a handwritten cleaning rota and a leaflet from the council containing a rubbish collection calendar. It was so tight that even Will's rucksack, which hung from a peg on the back of the door, seemed to be hoarding valuable space. Its one saving grace was a broad window which, in the daylight, would look onto the garden at the rear of Hamlet Hall.

Right now, though, that window was open a crack, causing Will to shiver as they all crammed inside. Ian went straight to it, yanked it shut and flipped a catch on the frame to lock it. Then he sat down at the desk, tucked a green plastic box into a drawer and waved the mouse, bringing the computer screen to life.

With a few taps on the keyboard, he brought up the feed from the cameras. Three screens filled the monitor, although one – the front door, Will supposed – was completely dark.

'This is live,' Fay observed.

'Yes.'

'Could you rewind, please?'

'How far back would you like me to go?'

'When did the last guests arrive?'

Ian thought for a moment. 'Must have been around half-past seven,' he said. 'It was Mr White and his daughter.'

'Then I'd like to see all footage recorded since half-past seven.'

Ian waved the mouse again and tapped obediently at the keyboard. But as he did, Will noticed something curious. Something that must have been in front of him for a while, but until now, he hadn't seen.

There was a bandage wrapped around Ian's hand.

He peered at it, certain that Ian hadn't been wearing it when he first arrived at Hamlet Hall that evening. Did that mean it was fresh? It certainly looked it. It was wrapped cleanly around his palm, the linen still tight and without a single scuff or fray.

He tried to think whether he'd seen it when they went to check on Damien White, although with the discovery of the body, it was fair to say he'd been somewhat preoccupied. He cast his mind back further, to the moment when he gave his speech. Again, he had been more than a little distracted, but he distinctly remembered Ian standing with his hands behind his back, as he watched from the door.

To hide the bandage?

With a start, Will thought of the green box that Ian had just tucked into the top drawer of his desk. A first-aid box. The bandage must have been applied during the interval, before the guests were called back to the restaurant.

He was sure there'd be a perfectly innocent explanation. Ian had probably been helping Carl in the kitchen; perhaps he'd broken a glass. Though, with a strangely unpleasant realisation, it occurred to Will that he knew nothing about what Ian had done after they parted ways at the beginning of the interval.

He looked back up at the computer screen. If it hadn't been for the timestamp reading 19:30:00, he wouldn't have known anything had changed. Ian tapped the enter key and the footage whirred into action.

The digits on the timestamp began to roll at speed. For a few seconds, nothing happened. Then, Will saw Carl emerge from the kitchen door, dressed in his chef's whites. He lugged a black bin liner into a bulky waste collection bin, his movements almost comical as the footage continued to scroll through at a rapid pace, before disappearing again from view. A few seconds later, there was movement on the second screen, as Nigel Cobb appeared at the back door and lit a cigarette. Smoking it down to the butt, he immediately lit another. Will watched the timestamp continue to roll over, as Nigel stood there for the full half-hour.

Finally, the interval over, Nigel went back inside and the screens were once again motionless.

PC Fay, who had been leaning over Ian's shoulder to peer closely at the monitor, straightened up. 'So we have no way of telling whether anyone has come or gone via the front door since Mr White arrived?'

Ian shook his head. 'As I said, the camera's broken.'

'There isn't an indoor camera? Looking over the entrance hall, perhaps?'

'No.'

A glimmer of irritation flickered over her face. Then, before Will could stop himself, he said, 'They would have been seen.'

They turned in unison to face him, a baffled expression on Ian's face.

'They would need to pass by the restaurant,' he continued. 'As far as I'm aware, there's been someone in there all evening. If anyone left by the front door, they'd have been noticed, wouldn't they?'

'You're saying there were people in the restaurant when Miss White and Mrs Holloway heard someone leaving Mr White's room?'

'I think the Finns were in there. Martha, certainly.'

Fay stared at him, and for a split second Will wished he hadn't spoken. Then she took a deep breath and returned her attention to the monitor. 'I'll need to interview each of your guests in turn. The actors, too.'

Panic danced across Ian's face. 'What for?'

'Because your assessment upstairs seems to have been correct. Mr White's injury suggests he's been the victim of an assault.'

'Will there be more police?'

'There will, but it'll take time to mobilise. Forensics will need to take charge of the body, but our pathologist and divisional surgeon have already been called to attend a car accident on the other side of Lynmouth. We'll need to wait until either they've finished or a different team can be sent from elsewhere. For now, our priority is to contain the scene. Mr White's room will remain locked, and nobody is to leave the building.'

'You don't think we should send people home?' said Ian. 'Surely, the Finns at least—'

Fay silenced him with a single look. 'The footage you've just

141

shown me is clear. And if Mr Hooper is correct, nobody could have left via the front door without being seen. I don't mean to alarm you, but given what we know, we can only assume one thing.'

'And what's that?'

'That whoever's responsible is still here, in Hamlet Hall.'

16

Lily had completely ignored both the flute of champagne and the glass of water that had been placed for her on the mantelpiece. The champagne had come from Martha Finn, who said it would help with the shock. The water had then been provided by Gwen, who had sent Nigel scurrying to the kitchen to fetch something more sensible.

Lily didn't see how either would help. Her hands were so numb from standing on the beach that she doubted she could even have held the needle-like stem of the champagne flute. Seeing how badly she was shivering, Gwen seemed to make it a personal mission to warm her up, telling Hugh to put more logs on the fire and forcing her into the nearest seat.

If she was honest, Lily barely noticed the fuss being made of her. As she was ushered back into Hamlet Hall, she felt as though she was entering some kind of trance. A numbness overcame her, and her thoughts swam with the image of her dad, splayed on the floor with that wound gaping on the back of his head. She took out her phone, wishing desperately that she could speak with her mum, hear her voice. But it was no use. She still didn't have even a single bar of signal.

It was Sylvia who finally asked. Standing by the sideboard, she looked Lily square in the eyes and with a bluntness that snapped her abruptly back to reality, said, 'How did he look?'

The others froze. Hugh peered over his shoulder, the poker in his hand hovering in the fireplace. Justin looked up from the table. Even Gwen was silent.

They all watched, mortified. But nobody challenged Sylvia. It seemed they all wanted to know.

The silence was shattered by the creaking of the door as Ian and Will returned to the restaurant.

'Ian.' Gwen took a step towards him, grateful for the distraction. 'What's happening? Where's Constable Fay?'

Ian didn't answer straight away. He just looked at them all, twitching from face to face. Lily noticed Will hovering at his shoulder. He was looking down at the floor, trying desperately, it seemed, to avoid making eye contact.

'She's speaking to the actors,' said Ian. 'Telling them to stay put in the lounge. Then she'll be coming to . . .' He cleared his throat. 'To explain the situation.'

Before Gwen could reply, Lily asked, 'Can I use a phone?'

Ian frowned at her, and for a brief moment she thought he was going to turn her down.

'There's one in my office,' he said, once he seemed to have collected himself. 'Down the corridor at the bottom of the stairs. First door on the left.'

Gwen said that she would come too, but Lily waved her away.

She wanted to be alone for this. With a vicious glance at Sylvia, she got to her feet and slipped from the restaurant.

Closing the door behind her, she crossed the hall, pausing at the foot of the stairs. She managed to avoid looking up towards the landing. But even so, she couldn't hold back the horrifying image of her father's corpse.

Perhaps this police officer would work out which of them it had been. She seemed able to keep them in check, which with a group like this was no bad thing. Lily thought of how Hugh and Sylvia had tried to protest being made to wait in the restaurant, and how PC Fay had scolded the pair of them like bickering children.

But at the same time, she forced herself to remember that everyone in Hamlet seemed to know each other far too well. This officer would be just as well informed – and presumably just as disapproving – of her dad's work at the lighthouse.

She hurried on past the stairs, frightened of losing the composure she was fighting so desperately to maintain.

As Ian had instructed, she stopped at the first door on her left and let herself into the office. Closing it behind her, she caught sight of her reflection in the window. In the daylight, she supposed she'd have looked out onto a garden. Not now. It was pitch black outside, and with the harsh electric light that seemed to fill the little room like cold water, all she saw was her own dishevelled self. Her eyes were bloodshot, her hair wild and skin sheet-white from the bracing wind on the beach.

She felt tears forming again in the corners of her eyes. She almost let them come. Without the others watching her, she wanted to let them fall; to simply despair.

A few bottles of whisky sat on the desk, tucked away behind the computer screen, and she considered taking a swig from one. She knew it wouldn't help, though. She remembered her dad telling her about business functions where he'd paid the bar staff a generous tip to ensure that, unbeknownst to whoever he was trying to schmooze, every other drink he was served was non-alcoholic. It was a dirty tactic, but a good one. Always ensure yours is the clearest head in the room.

Eyeing the telephone on the desk, she took a deep breath. How would her mum take the news? Would she burst into tears? Give a heavy sigh? Lily had often wondered just how much love was left in her parents' marriage. Even mused about it to Gwen. It seemed she might finally have that curiosity satisfied.

She picked up the receiver in one hand and scrolled through her mobile in the other until she found the number. Before she could dial, though, she hesitated.

Was she being selfish? What would she even say? Whatever the state of their marriage, how do you tell someone their husband has been murdered? More than that, at an event *she* had insisted they attend? It had been her mum who found the murder mystery party; who had been so sure it would be a good idea. What would it do to her, knowing that *this* was where her husband had met his end?

Lily almost changed her mind. The one thing that stopped her was the thought of the others waiting for her in the restaurant. She couldn't face them again on her own. Her mum might not be there with her, but she would still know all the right things to say. And the second they were off the phone, she would leap into her Mercedes and speed all the way to Hamlet.

Lily held up the receiver and dialled. It was a bulky handset, each of the buttons sinking with a thud. Bringing it to her ear, she heard a moment's silence, before the call went straight to voicemail.

Burning with frustration, she thrust the receiver back down so violently that the entire phone rattled on the desk.

Why wouldn't she answer? She never let her battery run low, and she'd be hard-pressed to find somewhere in London without any signal. Could she have switched it off for some reason? Picked up last-minute tickets for a show?

Lily began to rummage around on the desk, looking for a Wi-Fi router, but found no sign of one. There was only the whisky, a stack of invoices and bank statements and a tangle of wires connecting the computer to an antique-looking printer. She scanned the cork noticeboard on the wall instead, hoping a code might be written somewhere. Again, she had no luck. Reaching for the computer, she nudged the mouse. If it happened to be unlocked, she could send an email or a Facebook message. The screen lit up, but as she'd feared, a password was needed there too.

Propping her elbows on the desk, Lily felt the tears returning. She pressed her face into her hands, took a deep breath and held it as long as she could. Then she took another. Finally, when she felt as composed as she could manage, she reached for the phone and dialled.

Just as before, she was directed straight to voicemail. This time, however, she waited for the message to play out. As she heard her mum's voice, cheerfully telling her to please leave a message, she almost broke down again. She braced herself, holding her breath until the tone finally came.

'Mum, it's me. I need you to call me back when you hear this. As soon as you can. I'm OK, but . . . but something's happened to Dad. There isn't any signal here, so don't call my mobile. Try this number and someone will hopefully pick it up.'

With a trembling hand, she put the phone down. Then she sank into the chair.

The thought of going back to the restaurant – of being in there with his killer – was almost unbearable. But she couldn't stay in Ian's office all night. Even if none of the others came looking for her, the police officer would round her back up. Soon enough, she would have to face them all.

Looking again at her reflection in the window, she pulled her hair into a tight ponytail, dabbed at her eyes with the cuff of her sleeve and took another deep breath. She refused to succumb to shock. When she went back, she would look unfazed, just as her dad would have done. She was going to show them she wasn't afraid.

She stepped into the corridor, closed the office door, and from the darkness behind her, heard a voice murmur her name.

With a start, she spun round to see Justin. He was just a few steps away, watching her. 'What are you *doing*?' she hissed.

'Nothing.' He held up his hands. 'Really, nothing. I just wanted a word.'

'Were you listening to me?'

'No!'

'So you were just lingering in the corridor.'

He gave an awkward little laugh. 'I'm sorry. I wasn't trying to be a creep. I just wanted to talk. Away from the others.'

Lily glared at him. 'I'm not speaking to you.'

'Please,' he said hurriedly. 'Please, just hear me out. When what's happened here gets out, you'll have reporters trying to get to you. Dozens of them. And they'll all have their own agendas; want to spin things in a certain way. I thought I could help get your story across. You know, properly. Honestly.'

It took Lily a moment to fully register exactly what he was asking for. 'Are you joking? My dad's dead on the floor upstairs and you want an *interview*?'

There was such venom in her voice that she saw him physically recoil, the smug smile slipping from his face.

'I only thought—'

'I heard you come to his room earlier. What happened? He sent you packing when you came sniffing around, so now you're trying me instead?'

'Lily, please. You've got it all wrong—'

She rounded on him so abruptly that she saw him flinch. 'You're disgusting. Sneak up on me again and I'll report you to that police officer for harassment.'

'Lily . . .'

But it was too late. She'd turned her back on him and was already halfway to the restaurant.

17

The champagne fizzed on Theo's tongue. Almost two hours had passed since Jack first fetched it from the kitchen and it was now room temperature. He didn't care, though. He wasn't drinking it for pleasure.

'It isn't your fault, Theo,' said Claire.

Swallowing the champagne, he set the flute down on the coffee table. 'I just . . .' He hesitated, the words refusing to come. 'I should have done something to help her.'

'Like what?'

'I don't know. Just something more. *Anything* more.'

'It sounds like you did all you could.'

'But—'

'That's enough.' An edge crept into Claire's voice. 'There's nothing any of us could have done for her. Not after what she'd just seen.' She sank into the sofa, the leather squeaking. 'That poor young woman. To see her father like that . . .'

Theo said nothing. Honestly, he didn't know what more there was to say.

He glanced across the lounge, to see if Jack might have any

wisdom to share, but if anything, the older man seemed oblivious to the fact that Theo and Claire were even there. Once P C Fay had ushered them all inside, he'd taken himself off to a tartan armchair in the far corner and begun typing away on his phone. But after a few minutes he'd sworn loudly and tossed it onto a table. He'd looked up when Fay came to explain that they were to stay put until she called for them. Otherwise, he'd been completely disengaged.

Theo could guess what was bothering him: presumably, he'd wanted to message his anonymous married girlfriend. But like everyone else in Hamlet Wick, he'd found himself without any signal.

He felt a sudden swell of resentment. With all that was happening – a murdered man above their heads and an ensuing police investigation in which they were about to be questioned – could Jack not turn his mind to other things? Could he really not find something more useful to do than sulk?

Doing his best to suppress his frustration, he looked back at Claire. 'How about you?' he asked. 'Are you O K? I couldn't help noticing you were the first back inside.'

She nodded. 'I will be. It was just that scream . . . Such a terrible sound. When we were all watching the pair of you on the beach, I couldn't stop hearing it. Over and over in my mind. And then when the police arrived, I suppose I just . . .' She looked down at her maid's costume. 'I've never known anyone be murdered before. It seems I don't have much of a stomach for it in real life.'

Theo didn't reply. He wanted to say something soothing, but the words wouldn't come.

'You said that Lily thinks Will had something to do with it,' Claire continued. 'With what's happened to Mr White?'

He nodded. 'She seemed convinced of it out on the beach.'

'Do you think she might be right? He doesn't seem the type to do anyone any harm. But then . . .' She paused. 'Well, I have only just met him tonight.'

Theo looked down at the coffee table. 'No. Will couldn't do something like this.'

'You know him quite well, then?'

'I don't think anyone does, really.'

He looked up again and their eyes met. He tried to remember a time when Jack had listened to him so closely. None came to mind.

'We were at school together,' he explained. 'In Hamlet. But he was quiet. He'd always hover at the back, keeping out of everyone's way. Whatever's happened to Mr White . . . I don't think anyone would have Will down as the sort to be involved. But this story of his . . . A rock to the head, Lily said. That's apparently how the murder he's come up with for tonight's game is committed. And she's convinced something similar has happened to her dad.'

'It doesn't look good,' said Claire.

'There's more. Even without whatever's happened to Mr White, there's . . .' Theo hesitated. 'How long have you lived here?'

'A few years.'

'And you've never heard about what happened on the beach?'

She frowned at him. 'I know about the boy who fell from the lighthouse.'

'No.' Theo shook his head. 'No, this is something else. The murder in Will's story . . .'

For a few seconds, he wrestled with just how much to say – and how much he ought to hold back. But there was something so welcoming in Claire's expression. A sense that she wanted, genuinely, to hear him.

'Will found a body,' he said. 'Out on that beach.'

Claire's eyes went wide. 'Recently?'

'No! No, it was years ago. Back when we were just kids. I always knew it had stayed with him, but I'd never have thought . . .'

Claire watched him for a moment. 'Stayed with him how?' she asked.

Theo sighed. 'There was a birthday party, for one of the boys in our class. We'd have been about seven, I suppose. We'd been swimming, and on the way back, this kid's mum took us to Hamlet Wick to buy ice creams from the Finns. As you'd expect, we all got pretty excited. All of us except Will. He just went so quiet and pale that he looked like he might be sick.

'When we got to Hamlet Wick, we jumped out of the car, chattering about which flavours we were all going to have. I can remember getting to the shop and turning back. That's when I saw that Will wasn't with us.'

'Where was he?'

'On the beach. He stood still as a statue, staring at this one spot in particular. The kid whose birthday it was . . . his mum

153

went over and asked Will if he was all right. And that's when he started screaming.'

'Screaming?'

'It was like she'd snapped him from a trance or something. He just stood there, screaming and crying until she had to round us all up and put us back in the car.'

Claire said nothing. She sat attentively, hanging on Theo's every word.

'It really freaked us out,' he continued. 'Of course, *now* I know that the spot Will had been staring at was where the body had been. But none of us realised that at the time, he was just this weirdo who'd had some kind of meltdown. And after a little while . . . Well, even at that age, children can be cruel. When word got around of what had happened, it became a bit of a joke. Kids at school screamed at him in the playground, pretending to cry and seeing if they could get him to do it again. The teachers weren't impressed, of course. Parents tried to stop them, too. But for some of the nastier ones, it was too good a game.'

Theo shook his head. 'It went on for months. I remember the teachers would find him in the toilets or in the corner of the playground. Sometimes he was crying, other times he was just standing there in shock. The more the others reminded him of it, the more he seemed to close himself off. Even when we moved on to high school, he was still jittery all the time. Never really had any friends. In class, he always had this vacant look, like he was somewhere else. Then, the moment we'd be let outside for a break he'd immediately be on high alert, as if the whole world was out to get him.'

'You can imagine how that would stay with someone,' said Claire.

'Of course. To be honest, I think it did some pretty lasting damage. In Hamlet, everyone knows everyone. But not Will. I can't think of anyone who you'd say was his friend. He's never had a girlfriend or a boyfriend that I know of. He just works in that antiques shop on the high street, must only have about one customer a day. What happened to him on that beach, and the way the other kids tormented him after . . . I don't think he's ever been able to move past it.'

'That poor boy . . .' Claire stared at the coffee table, taking it all in. 'And you really don't think all of this could lead him to . . .'

Theo shook his head, more vigorously this time. 'I just can't see it. What he's organised tonight is bizarre. But can I imagine him actually murdering someone? Never in a million years. If nothing else, I don't think he'd have the nerve. The guy's scared of just about everything.'

Claire nodded. 'So who do you suppose it was?' She gave a little shrug, apparently seeing the confusion in his expression. 'I'm sure it's occurred to you, too. This police officer wants us all to stay put; she must think someone here's involved. If you don't believe it was Will, who else would want to kill Mr White?'

Theo gave a short laugh. 'I don't think you'll find anyone in Hamlet who'd be opposed to getting rid of Damien White.' He looked down and considered draining what remained of the champagne. 'I should have made Will tell us more,' he said, more to himself than to Claire. 'If I'd known how he was

155

planning for this murder to take place, I'd have tried to talk him out of it. Make him see how much trouble it would land him in.'

'Why didn't you?'

He shrugged. 'It was part of the job. We had our lines, our directions. When I asked about the parts of the story he hadn't shared, he said he wanted to keep that to himself. He thought that the more we knew, the more likely it was to be spoilt for the guests. It sounds ridiculous now, but he seemed so adamant. I just wanted to be professional about it.'

He tailed off, his eyes glued to the coffee table.

'You're far too hard on yourself,' said Claire. 'What do you really think you were supposed to have done for that young woman on the beach? And this obsession you have with being professional . . .' She paused. 'When Will told us earlier that Justin was here . . . You stopped him before he could finish, but I'm guessing Jack was about to tell us he'd written you a bad review. Is that where all of this is coming from?'

For a long while, Theo just looked at her. Even if he'd wanted to, he wasn't sure he could bring himself to talk about it. It was still too raw. And yet Claire waited, meeting his gaze with quiet determination.

He glanced across the lounge, making sure Jack was far enough away to be just out of earshot. He quickly realised he had nothing to worry about. Jack was still staring so intently towards the window that Theo reckoned they could call his name and he'd be oblivious.

'It was more than just a review,' he said. 'At the start of the year, the Hamlet Players put on *An Inspector Calls*. Justin came to see it, and the next day he wrote something in the *Herald*. Something that cost me an opportunity.'

He looked at Claire, hoping she'd be satisfied. Instead, she let the silence hang between them.

Theo sighed. 'Believe it or not, I'd been cast as the inspector. It was a big deal; my first major role. But on the morning of our opening night, one of the core cast members called in sick.

'It was a disaster. All morning, we spoke about how we'd have to cancel the production. But then . . .' He nodded towards Jack, dropping his voice. 'Jack told our director that he knew the lines. Said he'd learned them for the auditions and could step into the role.'

Claire grimaced, and Theo imagined she must already know where his story was leading.

'We were all sceptical. But what choice did we have, other than to call the whole thing off? The director asked if he'd like to read from a script – they were all friendly faces in the audience, they'd understand – but he said he didn't need it. To be fair to him, he made it almost to the end before it went wrong.'

A sudden anger began to stir, deep within Theo's gut. 'It was the last scene. The grand finale. And he forgot his line. Even now, I don't know if he realises that what he came out with was wrong or if he just managed to style it out. Either way, he threw me off. Made it look like it was *my* mistake.

'I recovered. It took me a minute but I managed to get back on track, and when we came offstage everyone told me not to worry. Said it hadn't ruined the performance. By the time we were on again the following night, I'd all but forgotten it. I didn't think about it again until a week later, when I went to Bristol for an audition.'

He put his head in his hands, taking a moment to compose himself. 'It was the biggest audition I've ever done. A touring production of *West Side Story*.'

'What were you up for?'

'Tony. The lead role. Gillian, who set up the Hamlet Players, knows the casting director. She put in a good word for me, convinced them to give me a shot.'

'And how did it go?'

Theo paused, struggling to go on. 'I nailed the lines. The songs. The dancing. You could see in the director's face that she was pleased. But the next day, she called to say I hadn't got the part.

'At first, she wouldn't tell me why. But I needed to know. I had to understand what I'd done wrong. Eventually, she said she'd seen a review in the *Herald* of *An Inspector Calls*.' He clenched his fists. 'It was Justin. He'd written about that scene. Made it out to be ten times worse than it had actually been and said that, for him, such a terrible blunder in such a crucial part of the play had almost ruined the entire performance.'

He shook his head. 'The *West Side Story* director said she couldn't take a risk like that. She understood these things happen, but there was too much money being poured into the show. She had to go with someone else.'

Claire reached across the coffee table and put a hand on his arm. 'I'm sorry. Truly I am. But Theo, you're an actor. Opportunities come and go. You can't beat yourself up every time an audition doesn't go your way.'

He grimaced and looked towards the far end of the room. Towards Jack. 'I just don't want to end up like . . .'

Claire gave him a warm smile. 'I don't think you need to worry about that. I'm sure of it, in fact.' She dropped her voice low. 'Do you think Jack sees how he's turned out? Do you think he's even considered the possibility that his career hasn't been one tremendous success?'

'I'd never really thought about it like that.'

'Well, try to. He might be a crappy mentor, but there's one thing, at least, that he's doing for you. He's inspiring you to be better.'

Theo had no idea what to say. For a long moment, they sat in silence, listening to the ticking of the grandfather clock. Then the smile slipped from Claire's face. Her eyes twitched towards Jack, her voice dropping so low that even Theo struggled to hear her.

'I want you to be careful around him,' she whispered. 'There's something he isn't telling us.'

Theo said nothing, prompting her to give a small sigh.

'When Will came in here to tell us about the interval, Jack mentioned that he was going to have a cigarette with someone.'

Theo nodded. 'Nigel Cobb.'

'Well, I saw him. Nigel, I mean. When I went to find Will some whisky, he was at the back door, having his cigarette.'

'And?'

She looked once more at Jack, making sure that he was still out of earshot. All of a sudden, there was something cold in her eyes. Something fearful.

'Jack wasn't with him.'

'You're sure?'

She nodded vigorously. 'Certain. I saw Nigel, clear as I'm seeing you now. But I'm telling you – Jack wasn't there.'

Theo looked at Jack, still slouched in his tartan armchair, staring towards the window. When he turned back to Claire, he could already feel the frown on his face.

'Then where the hell was he?'

18

Constable Natalie Fay looked down at her radio.

It would take seconds to make the call. Suspicious death at Hamlet Hall; assistance required.

And yet she was hesitating. *Why* was she hesitating?

Deep down, she knew the answer. Even if she wasn't ready to admit it. Because this wasn't the first time murder had come to Hamlet Wick. Nor was it the first time Natalie had been the officer to respond. Twelve years ago, when a body had been found on the beach, she'd been the one who'd secured the scene. Sent for an ambulance. Even escorted young Will Hooper and his father to the station for a statement.

But aside from speaking a few more times to the Hoopers, that had been the end of her involvement. CID snapped up the investigation in a heartbeat, and there'd suddenly been no assistance required from a young constable, barely a year into her first policing role.

She stared at the radio, remembering exactly how she'd felt when she arrived on the beach. It wasn't just horror at the sight of the body. There'd been a quiet rush of excitement, too. *This* was why she'd joined the police, and the thought of proving herself so soon in her career had given her an undeniable thrill. She remembered that feeling just as well as the sting of being so quickly shrugged off by the detectives – and the frustration that had consumed her when the murderer was never found.

She could have done so much more. She was clever. Observant. There were officers who spent most of their careers as constables and who were perfectly happy, but that wasn't Natalie. If those detectives had only let her help, she would have been relentless. And perhaps, if she'd just had chance to show what she could do, she imagined she would have spent the last twelve years working in CID herself, rather than wasting her potential as a response officer.

In her mind, she pictured the scene she'd just inspected inside Hamlet Hall. She'd recognised the victim, of course. Everyone in Hamlet knew Damien White. But she knew the others, too. Because while she might not have played a role in that first investigation, she'd followed it. Studied it. And when she'd arrived that evening at Hamlet Hall to find the guests lined up outside, she'd quickly realised she was looking at almost exactly the same cast of suspects as before.

Carl Gifford. Hugh Holloway. Both had been questioned last time around. Even White himself. He might be playing the role of victim tonight, but twelve years ago he'd briefly been suspect number one.

And then, of course, there was Will Hooper. Far too young to have been considered a suspect before, but linked to the case and very much an adult now. For him to be present yet again was undeniably strange.

Admittedly, there was another element at play. Natalie hadn't failed to also notice Nigel and Sylvia Cobb, Edward and Martha Finn, even Gwen Holloway . . . None had been suspects twelve years ago, but with White's project at the lighthouse, she had to consider that one of them might have struck tonight's killing blow.

Whatever the motive – whether it be the lighthouse or what happened all those years ago on the beach – there was one thing she could be certain of: the culprit was inside Hamlet Hall. She'd seen the CCTV. Since White had arrived, there'd been nobody in and nobody out. If she could grill them on their alibis, find out who had been where at the time of death . . . All she needed was to ask the right question and she'd solve it. Not only the murder of Damien White, but perhaps also the other case. The murder that had lingered over Hamlet for twelve long years.

This was the opportunity of her career. And the moment she called it in, she would need to hand it over, just as she had before. Protect the evidence, sit tight and surrender the scene once CID had arrived. Those would be her instructions.

She *had* to make the call. If nothing else, someone would notice if she didn't check in. But if she was careful – if she was very, *very* careful – perhaps she could give herself a head start. Some time alone with the scene. Even police comms were notoriously unreliable in the more rural parts of the county. In somewhere as remote as Hamlet Wick, nobody would doubt her if she claimed a temporary radio blackout. More than that, it was New Year's Eve. The radios would be swamped, resources stretched to breaking point. When she did eventually make the call, it would be a while before support arrived. And until then,

163

the extra noise on the airwaves would give her a little more time before her own silence was noticed.

She stared at the beach, feeling the weight of the radio in her hand.

The lighthouse might be involved, but it couldn't be as simple as that. This was connected to the old murder. She was sure of it. The same suspects, the same place . . . Point to point, there couldn't have been more than fifty metres between one body and the other.

The answer was inside Hamlet Hall. Waiting for her.

If it went wrong – if anyone realised that she'd deliberately waited to call it in – it would likely mean the end of her career. But then what did she have to show for that career anyway? She imagined another twelve years going by. She pictured herself, still patrolling as a response officer, wishing she'd had the nerve to show just what she was capable of.

She clipped the radio back onto her uniform. One hour. She'd give herself that. Just one hour's head start. She would speak to the witnesses, gather enough initial evidence that CID would have no choice but to let her play a role.

After that, she would call it in.

19

'Ladies and gentlemen, I'm sorry to confirm that Damien White is dead.'

Will flinched as PC Fay delivered the news.

Her voice was cold, chiming from the wood-panelled walls like a fork rapping against a glass. But it wasn't her bluntness that unnerved him. He remembered all too well that she wasn't one for pleasantries. It was the way that, at first, nobody moved. Not even Lily White, whose line of sight he had been particularly keen to make sure he avoided.

If anything, it was the Finns who seemed most badly affected. When Fay had come back from the lounge, she'd taken the old couple into the hall before addressing the rest of the group. They'd only been gone a few minutes, but when they returned, they looked utterly distraught. Edward sank into his seat, put his elbows on the table and dropped his head into his hands. Gwen had looked as though she might say something, her face pinched in concern, but Fay took control of the room before she had the chance.

'How?' Hugh spat out the question. He was leaning against the mantelpiece, too agitated, apparently, to join the others at the table.

Will held his breath, his heart pounding in his ears.

'I won't be disclosing exact details just yet.'

'Will there be more police coming?' asked Gwen.

'I've called for CID, but it'll take time for them to arrive. Forensics likely won't make it here until the morning. Until they can come, I'll be asking some questions.'

'And what does that mean, exactly?' Sylvia Cobb glared at her, as if the very idea of an investigation was some sort of personal insult. If Fay noticed, though – and Will was sure she would – she didn't seem fazed.

'I'll need to interview each of you in turn,' she said firmly. 'The actors as well. I understand a short interval took place after dinner. I'll be asking each of you for your whereabouts during this time—'

'But why?' Sylvia protested. 'Why do we need to be interviewed? What is it we're being accused of?'

'Sylvia!' Hugh snapped. 'Will you stop your squawking and just let her speak?'

She gawped at him, lips parted in a perfect circle, before turning to Nigel. 'Are you going to let him speak to me that way?'

Nigel locked eyes with Hugh. For a second, he looked as if he might retort. But he seemed to think better of it and receded into his seat.

'Mrs Cobb,' said Fay. 'While I shan't divulge any unnecessary details, I can tell you that Mr White has not dropped dead of his own accord. The questions I'll be asking will be to determine your whereabouts around the time he was killed. If you'd prefer not to answer then, of course, I can't force you. But I'm sure you can imagine how that might look to those who *will* speak with me.'

Sylvia opened her mouth to protest, but before the words could pass her lips, she seemed to catch sight of the cold looks from the other guests. She scowled, apparently reconsidering.

'For the time being,' Fay continued, 'I need you all to remain in this room. I've also instructed the actors not to leave the lounge.'

'Would it not be safer if we stayed together?' asked Gwen.

'It's more a question of reliability. As I understand it, you and the actors remained almost entirely separate during the hours leading up to Mr White's death. I'd like to keep it that way until I've taken statements from you all, to avoid any contamination of your accounts.'

'You're worried we'll corroborate our stories when you aren't listening,' said Hugh.

'I'm trying to take the most concise and efficient statements that I can; something which is very much in your interests. Right now, I have the opportunity to interview two groups that have not only witnessed this evening's events from separate vantage points but have also had virtually no opportunity to confuse what might prove crucial details. I'm therefore insisting you don't communicate with the group in the lounge, and also that nobody communicates with anyone outside the hotel. That includes press.' She flashed a glare at Justin. 'Mr Davies,' she then said, 'I'd like to start with you.'

Ian had positioned himself in the opposite corner of the

restaurant, by the bay window. Will noticed his arms were behind his back, like a soldier at ease, and couldn't help wondering if he was hiding the bandage wrapped around his hand.

'And also Mr Hooper.'

Will glanced up. 'Me?'

'You and Mr Davies have arranged this evening's event together?'

He nodded.

'Then I'll speak with the pair of you first.'

He took a deep breath, feeling the eyes of each of the guests following him as he skirted the table.

'Hold on.' They turned back to see Sylvia calling after them, her usual defiance returning.

'What have you told *them*?' She pointed to the bottom of the table, where Martha Finn still sat with her arm around Edward's shoulder. 'You said something to them out in the hall. Whatever it was, it's left quite the mark. Don't you think the rest of us should hear it too?'

Ever so slightly, Fay's expression softened. 'It isn't my place to say.'

'What does that mean? If it's to do with what's happened to Mr White, how can you not explain it to us?'

'Because it *isn't* to do with Mr White.'

With an embarrassed 'ah' sound, Sylvia settled back into her seat.

Martha Finn looked up at the constable. 'Should we tell them?' she asked.

'That's entirely up to you. I'm sure it'll be public knowledge soon enough. Although, given the present company' – she treated Justin to another glare – 'you might want to keep it to yourselves for now.'

Before Martha could reply, Edward spoke up. 'It's the shop,' he said quietly, seemingly speaking to nobody in particular. 'It's . . . It's happened again.'

Gwen's eyes went wide. 'Another break-in?'

Martha gave a mournful nod. 'All the money from the till is gone, and from the safe in the back.' She sighed. 'And of course, they've wrecked the shop as well.'

Gwen turned to Fay. 'When did this happen?'

'We're not yet sure exactly, although the call came in an hour ago.' Will saw the sympathetic expression vanish just as quickly as it had appeared. Her voice was completely level again, as if she was discussing the most mundane subject imaginable. 'It was reported shortly before we received Mr Davies's call about Mr White.'

Will looked at the Finns. For a split second, everything else was forgotten. All that mattered was this wounded old couple.

'We'll support you.' Gwen reached down the table and took Martha's hand. 'All of us. We'll make sure you're all right.'

Martha gave a weak smile. Edward didn't respond.

'You know what this means, though.' Nigel leaned forward in his seat, a desperate gleam in his eye. 'You see it, don't you? This means it can't have been my lads. You said it yourself, Hugh. I've had to hire in a team from out of town to work on the lighthouse. They've all been home for Christmas; they aren't due back for another three days.' His voice rose. 'You said a safe had been broken into this time. How would one of my boys manage that? Surely, there's a key or a combination required—'

169

'Nigel!' barked Hugh. 'For God's sake, will you *get a hold* of yourself?'

Nigel stopped and looked at the Finns, as though just seeing them for the first time. His enthusiasm ebbed away. 'Of course,' he said, suddenly embarrassed. 'You're right. I'm sorry.'

Sylvia took his hand and gave it a squeeze, the first sign of affection that she had showed him all evening. Lily White pulled a face, making no effort whatsoever to hide her distaste.

Nigel's outburst apparently over, Fay once again addressed Ian and Will. 'Mr Davies, Mr Hooper. If you'll come with me, we can begin.'

20

As Ian and Will followed PC Fay from the restaurant, the door clicking shut behind them, all Lily could think of was how tedious her dad would have found this.

She remembered, a year or so earlier, reading a profile article that had been written about him in *Property Week*. The reporter had been made to wait three months for an hour-long appointment, and even then, had needed to accompany him on a first-class flight to France, where he was inspecting a potential site for a new development. When the plane touched down in Nice, the interview completed en route, he'd shaken the reporter's hand and pointed him straight towards the arrivals desk, to catch the first flight home.

'Ridiculous,' Sylvia muttered. 'Just ridiculous.'

'She only wants to know where we were, Sylvia,' said Gwen.

'But why? Why should we need to answer that?'

'A man has died,' Nigel said quietly.

Sylvia threw away his hand, as if it had turned red hot. 'And one of us is responsible,' she demanded. 'Is that it?'

'Yes.'

At the sound of Lily's voice, the room seemed to stop. Sylvia swept her a glance, a hint of uncertainty dancing across her face.

'Unless you've seen someone leaving,' Lily continued, 'who the rest of us have missed, then yes. Someone here is responsible. Someone in this hotel has murdered my dad.' She looked around the table, settling on each of them in turn. 'How does it feel? Knowing that somewhere in this quiet, quaint little community of yours, there's a killer? And what do you suppose they'll do to make sure they aren't caught? It's only been my dad so far. I'd imagine most of you are perfectly happy to see him dead. But who's going to be next? Who around this table are you going to allow yourself to be alone with before the police let us leave?'

Nobody replied. Even Sylvia's defiance seemed to have slipped, her eyes twitching nervously between the other guests.

'Where were you, Sylvia?' asked Hugh.

She turned slowly towards the fireplace. 'I beg your pardon?'

'You're making an awful lot of fuss at the prospect of simply telling the police where you were during the interval. Now I come to think of it, you're the only one of us who's unaccounted for.'

'That's absurd.'

'Nigel was at the back door,' Hugh pressed. 'Martha was in here with Justin. Gwen was upstairs with . . .' He paused and briefly bit down on his bottom lip, as if Lily's name tasted sour in his mouth. 'With Miss White,' he finally finished. 'And Edward joined me in the kitchen with Carl.' He straightened up, stepping away from his perch by the mantelpiece. 'Where were you?'

Lily tilted her head curiously. At the far end of the table, Justin sat a little straighter in his seat, like a terrier catching the whiff of a scent.

'I was upstairs,' said Sylvia irately. 'In one of the rooms.'

'Why?'

'Why shouldn't I have been?'

'Hugh,' said Nigel. 'I think that's enough.'

Hugh rounded on him. 'Are you really saying that you wouldn't like to know why your wife was next door to Damien White while he was killed?'

All eyes turned to Nigel. Even Edward Finn, who still looked completely bereft at the latest looting of his shop, glanced up. Nigel shrivelled under the weight of their gaze, his lips trying to form words that simply weren't there.

'If you must know,' said Sylvia, 'I was fixing my make-up. And I wasn't *next door* to Mr White. His room's in the far-left corner, isn't it? I was in the far-right.'

'Fixing your make-up?' Hugh scoffed. 'Are we supposed to believe that?'

'Why should I need you to? Why should any of us need to explain ourselves when it's painfully obvious that Will's the one who's involved?'

'Sylvia,' Gwen hissed. 'Making assumptions won't help anyone. Let's just answer the questions, and I'm sure we'll—'

'But how can you not be suspicious? He tells that story about a murder on the beach just minutes before someone turns up dead. It should be you and Hugh thinking these things, not me.'

'Sylvia,' Gwen urged, but it was no use. She was now in full flow, the bile pouring from her mouth like water from a broken tap.

'He isn't right. He's never been right, ever since he—'

'Sylvia!'

It was the first time Gwen had raised her voice all evening. Looking at the reactions around the table, Lily suspected it was the first time many of them had *ever* heard it. Even Hugh looked taken aback.

'What was in Will's story?' she asked.

Gwen looked at her, her face paling.

'I know there's something I've missed.' She peered around the room, lingering on each face before moving on to the next. 'My dad's lying dead on the floor above our heads, and you all seem to think it has something to do with Will's story. Is anyone going to tell me why?'

Nobody spoke. She looked to Gwen last. The closest she had to a friend in this group of strangers. But she received nothing in return.

'Unbelievable,' she muttered, rising to her feet.

'Lily . . .' Gwen stood too, as if to follow her. 'Please, you heard Constable Fay. We need to stay put—'

'I don't care.'

'Then at least let someone go with you. You can't go out by yourself.'

'Why?' Lily snapped. 'Is someone going to kill *me*, too?'

This shot seemed to find its mark. There was genuine hurt on Gwen's face.

'Don't,' said Lily. 'You might be playing the mediator, but I'm sure it hasn't escaped you that you'll probably get your lighthouse back now he's gone.'

'That's enough.' It was Martha who spoke up this time,

raising her voice from the far end of the table. 'You're upset, Lily. We all understand that. But no one in this room is capable of murdering your father. Least of all Gwen.'

Lily met Gwen's eye. When she spoke again, there was something dangerous in her voice. 'Is that right, Gwen? Are you on my side?' She took a step closer, narrowing the gap between them. 'If you really want to show it, tell me what it is that I've missed in Will's story.'

For a split second, Lily thought she might have her answers. But before Gwen could speak, she locked eyes with Hugh. A cold look passed between them, his face creasing into a grimace, and at once Gwen seemed to reconsider. Whatever it was that Lily didn't know, it seemed she was to be kept in the dark.

This time, she said nothing. Sweeping one final glare around the room, she threw open the restaurant door.

Her running shoes padded softly on the tiled floor as she barged into the entrance hall. Once she was sure that nobody was following her, she paused at the reception desk, looking longingly at the heavy oak doors.

She could leave, if she wanted. Even now, she could feel her own key to the Range Rover, sitting in the pocket of her hoody. The police officer was occupied with Will and Ian, and it seemed none of the others had the nerve to follow her from the restaurant. It would be the easiest thing in the world to just get in the car and drive back to London.

She thought of the fireworks that would soon be lighting up the South Bank, and the tolling of Big Ben that would see in the new year. She pictured her housemates in Durham, drinking spirits in the kitchen before they went out to a club. She wanted to be far away from these people, from Hamlet Hall and, perhaps most of all, from her dad's lighthouse.

Except it wasn't her dad's. Not any more. The lighthouse was hers now. Just like everything else. There would be lawyers. Accountants. Business plans and inheritance tax.

She suddenly felt sick. She wasn't ready. There was so much else she wanted to do; things she needed to learn. How was she supposed to take it all on? Maintain everything he'd worked so hard to build? The pressure, the paperwork . . . The sheer relentlessness of running his empire.

Hearing footsteps, she tensed, turning back to see the chef emerging from the restaurant. He paid her no attention, though, stalking across the hallway in the direction of the kitchen.

She swallowed back her panic.

Later. There'd be plenty of time to worry about business. Right now, she needed to get out.

She looked at the doors, thinking of how she could climb into the Range Rover, drive back up that narrow track and make her way home. To somewhere with phone signal, at the very least.

But deep down, she knew that she couldn't. She couldn't leave her dad with these people. Not with his killer still under the same roof. She would have to wait, and just hope it wouldn't be long before her mum picked up her message.

Although perhaps there was still a reason to visit the Range Rover. As she stood there in the hallway, she thought about the glovebox, and about the gun that was concealed inside.

She could still remember the day, a little over a year ago, when she'd learned it was there. Sitting in the back seat, she'd seen her mum searching for a breath mint, her dad noticing just a second too late to stop her opening the glovebox.

Lily would have expected to feel shock – perhaps even disappointment – at learning that he owned such a thing. But the truth was that she understood. He'd explained that a few weeks earlier, while surveying a site in Naples, he'd been jumped by a mugger on the way back to his hotel. At the point of a knife, he'd lost his wallet, his Rolex and his phone. When he returned to London, he'd immediately sought a way of preventing such a situation from arising again. The gun had been the result of that search.

She knew it was still there. As they'd parked up outside Hamlet Hall and he'd leaned over to fetch a phone charger from the glovebox, she'd caught a glimpse of it. A small black handgun, barely larger than a closed fist.

Perhaps she should take it. It would take seconds to run out to the car, stuff it into her hoody and then make her way back inside. Wouldn't it be sensible for her to have a way of defending herself?

'Lily.'

At the sound of her name, she turned to see that Justin had followed her into the hallway, an expression of total innocence on his face.

'I've been thinking,' he said quickly. 'If you really want to know what it is they're talking about – in Will's story – perhaps there's an agreement we can reach.'

Lily didn't answer. She watched him for a moment, seeing if she could crack that porcelain facade. When she eventually spoke, the words were like grit in her mouth.

177

'You want your interview?'

He nodded enthusiastically. 'You answer a few of my questions, and I'll answer yours.'

Lily turned away, unable to look at those wide, innocent eyes.

Could she really stoop so low? Her dad would have done it. More than that, he'd have seen it as an opportunity. Grasped it with both hands and wrestled it into something that would work to his benefit.

She thought of him, laid out on the floor of his room. Perhaps she could be ruthless too.

'What did you discuss with my dad? At the beginning of the interval, when you came upstairs?'

Justin's smile faded slightly. 'I asked him for a comment on the lighthouse.'

'And?'

'And he told me that if I ever bothered him again, he would personally see to it that I spent the rest of my life writing for the *Hamlet Herald*.'

Lily allowed herself a single dark laugh. That sounded very much like the way he would play it. Steeling herself, she looked Justin in the eye. 'I want to know exactly what I've missed. Whatever it was in Will's speech that's set everyone else on edge.'

'Of course.'

'But we do my questions first. You tell me what I want to know and then you can have your interview.'

Justin's eyes narrowed. In a funny sort of way, if they'd met under different circumstances Lily thought her dad might actually quite like him.

Finally he nodded. 'Where do you want to start?'

'The character in Will's story. The one who was murdered on the beach. I thought at first that he was talking about my dad, but Theo said it was a reference to someone else. I want to know who that was.'

Justin looked at her. 'You really don't know?'

'Are you going to tell me or not?'

He took a deep breath, bracing himself. 'Theo's right,' he said. 'I don't know what Will was thinking by telling that story. But it seems to me – and by the looks on their faces, to everyone else – that it was certainly a reference to *someone*. Not your dad, though. A man was murdered on that beach.'

'How?'

An unpleasant smile passed over Justin's face. 'Can't you guess?'

'He was hit around the head.'

Justin nodded. 'Just like in Will's story. It was with a rock from the beach, they think. Mind you, they never found it. Whoever did it probably chucked it into the sea.'

Lily paused. 'What do you mean, "whoever did it"?'

'They never caught anyone.'

He tossed this detail into the air as if it was the most mundane piece of information imaginable, but it hit Lily like a blow to the stomach.

'When did this happen?'

'Years ago. I was just a kid.'

'How many years?'

'I don't know. Ten. Maybe twelve?'

'And what about Will? He must have been just a kid when this happened, too.'

'That's right. Me, him and Theo were all in the same school year.'

Lily shook her head, struggling to comprehend what she was hearing. 'So you're saying Will's using tonight to recreate this murder. To have us all *act it out*. Who does something like that?'

'I have a theory. But first . . .' He reached inside his blazer and slipped out his phone. 'It's time you answered a couple of *my* questions.'

'That's not what we agreed.'

'Well, I didn't know yours would be quite so demanding. Let's say you do a few for me and then we can swap back.'

Lily drew a deep breath. He was wearing a painfully smug expression now, the little red light blinking in the corner of his phone. She suddenly felt like a fish in a bowl, a cat peering at her through the glass.

'What do you want to know?'

'You've seen your dad's body.'

'Yes.'

'Can you tell me how he's been killed?'

She glared at him, repulsed. 'Do you really think I'm going to answer something like that?'

He shrugged. 'It's a perfectly valid question. I assume he's been hit around the head – or at least something similar – for you to think that it was him who Will was talking about in his story.'

Lily said nothing, her jaw clamped firmly shut.

'All right. How about this?' The grin remained in place, as if to assure Lily that she would be just as appalled by his next question as she was by the first. 'Your dad grew up in Hamlet.

He knew what happened all those years ago to Teddy. I'm sure a lot of people will be wondering – do you think he meant to upset them when he bought the lighthouse or that he just didn't care?'

She looked down at the phone, the little red light still blinking away. She wanted desperately to hear more about this murder on the beach; to understand why Will would recreate it as a bizarre piece of theatre. But was it worth *this*? Justin would probably write up the story during the night. Maybe even here, on his phone, if the police still refused to let them leave. His exclusive interview with the local villain's heartbroken daughter.

'You can't honestly expect me to answer these.'

'I'm only trying to report the facts, Lily.' He took a step closer, the smell of cheap aftershave filling her nostrils. 'More than anything,' he said sweetly, 'I want to understand if you're genuinely worried for your own safety.'

That was enough. Lily's lips curled into a snarl, but before she could snap, the door across the hallway opened.

'Lily,' said Theo. 'Is everything all right?'

21

Theo's question might have been directed at Lily, but his gaze was fixed firmly on Justin.

He seemed to be holding out a hand, and for a second Theo wondered if he was expecting Lily to reach out and take it. Then he saw the phone. Even that seemed to stoke his resentment. Had the words that ruined his audition been dictated into that phone? Had he perhaps even written the article on it?

At first, nobody moved. Justin tilted his head, apparently confused by the interruption, before flashing him a friendly smile.

'Theo,' he said cheerfully.

He didn't get any further. Whether it was the glare that Theo could feel on his own face or the disdain that he could see plastered across Lily's, Justin seemed to recognise that he was outnumbered. The smile slipped like grease from his lips and he tucked the phone into his pocket. Without a word, he turned back towards the restaurant.

'You didn't need to do that,' Lily muttered after he'd gone.

'I'm sorry.' Theo stuffed his hands into his pockets. 'I heard raised voices and . . .' He stopped, the vicious look she'd given

Justin now turning upon him. She clearly wasn't interested in chivalry.

'You should keep away from him,' he said plainly.

'I'm getting that impression.'

'I'm serious. He's bad news.'

Lily frowned at him. 'Do the two of you have some kind of history?'

Theo didn't answer. The Lily he was speaking to now seemed completely different to the woman he'd followed onto the beach. Her face was pale and her eyes were still slightly bloodshot, but they were no longer wide and wild, as they had been before.

'Justin cost me something,' he said. 'A part in a play.'

She rolled her eyes. 'Of course. You're an actor.'

'It was important,' he said, a little more defensively than he would have liked.

'I'm sure.'

He felt a glimmer of resentment, and for the briefest of moments, he didn't care about Lily's misfortune. Somewhere inside, there was a raging, primal part of him that wanted to let it all go. To tell her that he didn't need her condescension.

She nudged her head towards the door to the lounge. 'There are three of you in there, right?'

Theo took a breath, quelling his frustration. 'That's right.'

'And you trust the others?'

'I trust that Jack wouldn't have the patience to plan a murder. And Claire . . .' He paused. 'She's new here. But she isn't the sort that would hurt anyone.'

The muffled sound of raised voices drifted from the restaurant.

'What's happening in there?' he asked.

'Sylvia's causing more trouble, I'd expect.'

'Sylvia?'

'She's refusing to tell anyone what she was doing during the interval. She says she was upstairs, in one of the rooms. Fixing her make-up, apparently, but no one believes her.'

Theo snorted. 'I'm sure the police will get her to open up. That is, if Justin doesn't pester it out of her first.'

'You think he might?'

'If not, I reckon he could make up something suitably entertaining.'

The sound of footsteps came echoing from the back of the hotel. A moment later, Carl appeared, emerging from the little corridor at the foot of the stairs. He seemed to fill the archway, the sleeves of his chef's whites rolled back over a pair of broad forearms.

He looked at the closed door to the restaurant, then towards the top of the stairs. 'The police still up there?' he called to them.

Lily shrugged. 'I haven't seen anyone come back down.'

Carl grimaced and looked at an object in his hand. Peering at it, Theo was fairly certain it was a miniature bottle of champagne. It looked comically small, clutched delicately in Carl's enormous hand. It seemed to be empty, the screw-cap missing.

'Will you tell her to do me next?' he asked. 'It's important.'

Lily said nothing, her eyes narrowing.

'We'll tell her,' said Theo.

Carl mumbled something unintelligible in reply, before tucking the little bottle into his apron and disappearing again into the corridor. After the footsteps had faded and they'd heard the kitchen door shut, Theo returned his attention to Lily.

'What was Justin talking to you about?'

'Why?'

'I just . . .' He paused, searching for the right words. 'You really should be careful around him. You can't trust anything he says.'

Something cold took form in Lily's eyes. When she spoke again, there was an edge to her voice that could have cut through iron. 'He was telling me about the murder on the beach.'

Theo's heart sank. The undertone was immediately clear; Justin had told her what he'd refused to. She had pleaded with Theo to explain the meaning behind Will's speech. But it was Justin who'd obliged.

'Do you really think Will has nothing to do with it?' she asked.

Theo's cheeks flushed. 'He was just a kid—'

'Not with that,' she snapped. 'With my dad.'

He paused, choosing his words with the utmost care. 'Look,' he said gently. 'I don't know why he's done this. Any of it. But he's—'

'Answer the question, Theo.'

When he spoke again, it was in a firmer tone. It seemed that niceties were going to get him nowhere. 'He was with me in the lounge for virtually the entire interval. If that's when your dad . . . If that's when he was killed, it can't have been Will.'

Her nostrils flared. 'So he's just using us to recreate a decade-old murder as a twisted piece of theatre. That's all, is it?'

Theo didn't know what to say. It sounded ridiculous, and yet it appeared that was exactly what Will had done.

He took a deep breath. 'Will isn't involved with what's happened to your dad.'

'Fine,' Lily said quietly. 'But even if it wasn't Will, someone in this hotel has killed him.'

'We don't know that—'

'Everyone in that room hates him.' She jabbed a finger towards the restaurant. 'Every one of them. The Finns with their shop, Nigel and Sylvia with their firm, Hugh and his pathetic teenage rivalry. Even Gwen and the lighthouse. So yes, Theo, someone in this hotel has killed my dad. And it's pretty clear it's been done in the same way as both the murder in Will's story and the one on the beach.'

Her voice was rising, but not in the way it had done by the water. She was in control, each word landing with the precision of a marksman.

'Please,' said Theo. 'I don't know why Will's set this up tonight. But what happened to Rory on that beach . . . It was years ago. We were just kids—'

Lily stopped, her brow creasing. 'Rory?'

Theo frowned at her, not sure what she was asking.

'Did you say Rory?'

He nodded. 'The man who was murdered on the beach twelve years ago. His name was Rory.'

Eleven o'clock

22

Will couldn't stop his hands from trembling. He tried clutching them together like a vicar at prayer. He took slow, deep breaths. Nothing seemed to help. Whatever he did, there was no restraining the tremor that had completely overcome him.

He suspected the waiting made it worse. P C Fay had wanted to conduct the interviews somewhere with no risk of being overheard by the others, so Ian had suggested one of the vacant guestrooms. On paper, the room she'd chosen, in the back corner of the building, overlooked the garden. In reality, Will imagined it would offer a view of the same bins into which he'd seen Carl lug a bag of kitchen waste on the security camera footage. Two chairs had been fetched from the neighbouring rooms, one of which was taken inside for Ian, while the other was positioned in the corridor for Will to wait on until it was his own turn.

Voices drifted through the door, Fay's sharp bursts interchanging with Ian's nervous vibrato, but they were far too faint for Will to make anything out. He looked up at a framed oil painting of a galleon, tossing upon a writhing, furious ocean.

The ship was being battered by the rain, the clouds pitch black behind her bulging sails.

He shivered, tearing his eyes from the painting. The front door had stood open for several minutes after Lily dashed out onto the beach, and while the crackling fire meant that it had been less noticeable in the restaurant, the December chill had made itself very much at home in the hallway and on the landing. He pulled the material of his vintage dinner jacket a little closer, but it was no use, in part because it wasn't just the cold that was causing him to tremble. From his position on the landing, he could hear voices in the hallway. Specifically, he heard Lily White, speaking first with Justin and then with Theo.

He couldn't make out each word – he was too far away for that – but he caught snatches, their voices ricocheting up the stairs. At the sound of his own name, he'd considered creeping a little closer, but he knew he'd never manage it. The floorboards on the landing creaked so loudly that not even a dancer on tiptoe would make it to the top of the stairs without alerting them.

Instead, he made do with what little he could hear. Even that was frightening enough.

Between them, it seemed Lily and Justin had managed to find out everything he had hoped to keep buried. Lily now knew about Rory, and with that information, she must surely have drawn a connection between his murder, Will's Lord Ashcombe and the death of her dad. Three men – one, admittedly, fictional – all murdered in Hamlet Wick with a blow to the head.

Will propped his elbows on his knees and dropped his head into his hands. How could it have all gone so wrong? This evening was meant to be about healing. About moving on. And yet, he seemed only to have made things worse.

He fought with the instinct to look to his left, towards the far end of the hotel. The narrow landing that ran from one side of Hamlet Hall to the other was perfectly straight, offering a clear line of sight towards Damien White's room. Of course, Fay had locked the door. And even if she hadn't, from this angle there was nothing to be seen. But it didn't stop Will, whenever he failed to restrain his wandering gaze, from being taken straight back to the moment he and Ian had discovered the body, splayed upon the floor.

He thought of the wound on the back of White's head, the scorn on Lily's face as Gwen guided her in from the beach and the guests' horror as he'd read his opening speech.

He felt as if he was standing on a cliff, his toes hovering over the edge. All it would take was for Lily to reveal the apparent means of her dad's death to the others, and they would surely nudge him over.

As for the guests themselves . . . Could one of them really have delivered the killing blow?

Will thought of the footage they'd watched in Ian's office. Unless someone had managed to creep past unseen and make it out through the front door, nobody had entered or left Hamlet Hall. And it was true that there seemed plenty of motive in the restaurant. But could he really see one of them going through with it?

That is, if Lily didn't convince the police that he, himself, was responsible.

Thank God for Theo. From what Will had heard of his

conversation with Lily, he, at least, seemed to be defending him. If White's murder really had taken place during the interval, Will could rely on him to tell Fay that they'd been together in the lounge. He might have backed himself into a corner with the invention of Lord Ashcombe, but she couldn't argue with an alibi.

And then there had been Carl. Again, Will couldn't make out all of what he'd said, but there was no mistaking the deep timbre of his voice. He'd wanted to speak to Fay, it sounded like. He'd said it was important.

Could he have seen something? Something that would further prove Will's innocence?

He hoped so. When Fay was through with Ian, he would have to tell her. Make sure she spoke with Carl next.

He looked up again at the painting of the galleon, peering at the ant-like figures as they swung from the rigging. He knew how they felt. Tossed upon the waves, the elements themselves conspiring against them. It was a feeling of utter helplessness.

He sat bolt upright, hearing the sound of chairs scraping against the floor. A moment later, the guestroom door opened and Ian stepped into the corridor. He fixed Will with a nervous look.

'She's ready for you.'

23

Like every other room that Lily had visited in Hamlet Hall, the library had seen better days. An electric chandelier, half its bulbs missing, cast the place in a murky light. Wooden floorboards creaked beneath her feet and dusty shelves lined the walls. A few tattered armchairs were scattered lazily about, piles of leather-bound books heaped on a broad oak table.

There was a tired, mournful quality to it all, as if the room itself knew its own glory days were behind it. But that was all right. Lily hadn't insisted on it for its atmosphere. It was privacy she wanted.

'What is it, Lily?' asked Gwen. 'What's happening? Have you got through to your mum?'

Lily closed the door gently behind them, her hand trembling slightly as she turned the handle.

'When I was little,' she said, 'my parents had a friend called Rory. He was Dad's mate from university. Best man at their wedding. His business partner when he set up the firm. We haven't seen him in years. I haven't even thought about him until tonight, when Dad stormed out of the restaurant.

'But if I had to guess *exactly* when I last saw Rory, I'd say it's been at least a decade. Probably a little longer. So, you can imagine my surprise when Theo and Justin tell me about a murder that happened here, twelve years ago, on the beach. A local man struck around the head with a rock, very much like in Will's story. A man whose name was Rory.'

Lily saw the fear in Gwen's eyes. If she was trying to warn her away, though – to convince her that she shouldn't ask – it was no use. Lily was on the offensive, just as she knew her dad would have been.

'Who was he?' She let the question hang in the air, filling the tired old library.

'Lily,' said Gwen quietly. 'Please. These aren't things that—'
'*Who was he?*'

Gwen flinched, her whole body tensing. Then, with a sigh, her shoulders slumped. Lily watched as she approached the oak table and traced her fingers over a hardback book. They left trickles of colour, the dust coming away with her fingertips.

'I wish they hadn't told you,' she said. 'But the boys are right. The Rory your parents knew is the same man who was murdered here in Hamlet Wick. And yes, the same man who, it would seem, Will has based this evening's mystery on. Damien didn't meet him as a student, though. They go back way further than that.'

'They met here,' said Lily.

Gwen nodded. 'They were best friends, inseparable as teenagers. And when the time came for university, they went to London together. Dead set on taking over the world.'

'But you must have known him too,' said Lily. 'My dad's

girlfriend and his best friend. If they were really so close, the two of you must have spent your fair share of time together.'

Gwen gave a small, pained smile. 'Yes, I knew him.'

'What was he like?'

She thought for a moment, the smile becoming a grimace before slipping away completely. 'He was sweet,' she said at last. 'Although I suppose they were an odd pair, looking back on it. Rory had all of Damien's ambition but none of his charisma. He was never as witty. Never as clever. Never as . . .'

She faltered, struggling for the words. 'If you want the truth, he was never as ruthless. He couldn't charm himself out of trouble in quite the same way. But he was kind. And he never left Damien's side.'

She stared into the window, a faraway look in her eyes. 'People used to joke that Rory was Damien's shadow. Depending on who you ask, Damien was either propping him up or leading him astray.'

Lily followed her gaze to the window. There was nothing to be seen, of course. Only their own reflections gazing back at them. But as she listened to Gwen, she was struck by a sudden image of two teenage boys on the beach.

'Martha told me something,' she said. 'She told me that, before he died, Teddy used to follow two older boys around. Like a lost lamb. One of those boys was my dad. And the other . . .'

Gwen tilted her head slightly. She seemed to catch herself, though, the quizzical look quickly vanishing. 'I'm surprised Martha told you that. But yes, that was Rory. Teddy was enamoured with the pair of them; desperate to be the third member of their group.'

Lily took a deep breath, trying hard to stifle the frustration that was building inside her. They'd all kept her in the dark. Her dad. Gwen. Every other guest in that fucking restaurant.

'In my room,' she said, 'you told me accusations were thrown around after Teddy fell.'

Gwen nodded. 'Plenty of people knew how much Teddy had idolised Damien and Rory. When we all learned what had happened, there were suggestions that they'd dared him to climb the lighthouse.'

'And . . .' Lily hesitated, almost too afraid to ask. 'Did they?'

'No, Lily. Of course not. Rory's parents were away for the weekend and Damien had managed to get hold of some cider, so we were having a party at their house. Just Damien, Rory, Hugh and I.'

'Hugh?'

Gwen gave a little shrug. 'Even in those days, he and Damien didn't get on. But he used to spend a little time with the three of us. Mostly to keep an eye on Rory and make sure they didn't do anything too reckless. But he's since told me . . .' She looked away, embarrassed. 'He's said that even back then, he was carrying something of a torch for me. I suppose that might have had something to do with it too.'

'So my dad and Rory had nothing to do with Teddy's death?'

'Nothing,' Gwen said firmly. 'We were at Rory's house and hadn't invited Teddy. He was only thirteen – we couldn't risk him being caught drinking with us. Nobody knows what Teddy was doing at the top of the lighthouse, but the police ruled out any chance of Damien and Rory being involved. Not long after, they went to London.'

Lily felt a sudden surge of resentment for her dad, dead on the floor above their heads. More than ever, she wished she'd never come to Hamlet Wick. Wished he'd never bought the lighthouse. Never involved her in his dirty secrets.

Tears began to sting the corners of her eyes. 'Why didn't you tell me any of this? When we spoke in my room . . . Why did you let me go back into the restaurant not knowing?'

'I didn't know what Will was planning, Lily. And even if I had, what would I have said?' Gwen took a step closer, looking as if she might burst into tears herself. 'When you asked why Hugh hated Damien, it was so clear you didn't know what had happened on that beach. And if you didn't know Rory had been killed, you wouldn't have known—'

She stopped mid-sentence, her lips parted but no sound emerging.

'Known what?' asked Lily.

Gwen said nothing.

'*Known what?*' Lily gritted her teeth, clawing back the tears.

Gwen looked down at the ground. 'When Rory was murdered, Damien's name came up.'

'He was a suspect?'

Gwen nodded. 'You say you haven't seen Rory since you were young. That was when he came back to Hamlet, and when he arrived, he hated Damien.'

'Why?'

'He . . .' Gwen hesitated, clearly straying into uncomfortable territory, but Lily wasn't letting her slip away.

'Damien did something terrible,' she explained. 'Unforgivable, depending on who you ask. Rory had run into some trouble in London. Gambling. He'd been doing it for years and it had finally got the better of him. The debt he'd run up . . . There was no chance of anyone here giving him that kind of money. So he turned to Damien.'

'And Dad refused to help?'

'No, he helped. But there was a catch. Instead of just giving him the money or even loaning it, Damien wanted Rory's share of their firm.'

Lily gawped at her.

'It's true,' Gwen insisted. 'It was all Rory would talk about when he first came back. How Damien had cheated him; how everything was his fault. You have to understand, Lily. The debt he'd racked up was significant, but it wasn't worth his stake in their firm. Damien . . . He'd always been cunning. Ruthless, even. But to take advantage of Rory like that was something else entirely.'

She shook her head. 'You can imagine how Rory was after that. When he came back to Hamlet, he was just so angry. He stayed with Hugh and me for a little while and he was always drunk, raving endlessly about what a back-stabbing liar Damien was.

'Then, almost two years later, he was killed. Don't get me wrong, he'd managed to clean himself up a little in that time. Hugh even took him on as a driver. But all that talk about how much he hated your dad had left an impression on the people here. So when they found his body, naturally Damien's name came up.'

'Was Dad ever accused of anything?'

Gwen shook her head again. 'Your mum confirmed that he

was at home in London on the night Rory was killed. I'm surprised the police didn't want to speak to you as well.'

Lily thought for a moment. 'They sent me to a boarding school. If all of this happened during term-time, I wouldn't have been there.'

'That would explain it, I suppose. Either way, once your mum confirmed his alibi, the police had to let him go.'

'And nobody else was arrested?'

'There was one other who was accused of being involved. Someone who'd had a . . .' Gwen paused. 'A *disagreement* with Rory, the day he died. But in the end, their alibi was too strong as well.'

Lily's mind raced, the tears that had lurked in the corners of her eyes just moments earlier now gone. She thought of her dad, picturing the wound on the back of his head. Surely his murder was connected to Rory's. They were too similar, the link between them too obvious. And if the killer had never been caught . . .

'Where does Will come into this?' she asked. 'The murder he talked about in his speech . . . What's Rory to him?'

'Will . . .' Gwen hesitated. 'Will has a connection to Rory's murder. One that, until tonight, I think we all believed was long behind him. It seems that isn't the case.'

'Was he a relative?'

'No, not a relative.' Gwen sighed. 'It was Will who found Rory's body.'

Lily paused. She imagined a boy – what would he have been? Six? Maybe seven? – seeing what she had seen that evening. What would that do to someone? How would it haunt them?

199

'And Hugh,' she said. 'What about him?'

Gwen said nothing.

'I know there's something there,' she pressed. 'When dad stormed out of the restaurant, and said about Rory running himself into the ground, it was Hugh he was speaking to. Now you're talking about him wanting to keep an eye on Rory as a teenager, and about him staying with the pair of you when he came back to Hamlet.'

Gwen turned away again and pressed a hand to her face. Lily let the silence hang in the air between them. She was done with being the only one in Hamlet Hall scrambling in the dark.

Finally, Gwen turned back to face her. It was difficult to be sure in the dim light, but she seemed to have gone deathly pale. 'Rory . . .' she said quietly. 'He wasn't just Damien's best friend. He was Hugh's brother.'

24

Jack still wasn't speaking. While Theo had been with Lily in the hallway, Claire explained he'd barely moved, picking up his phone once only to scowl at the screen and drop it again onto his table.

'Got a message he didn't like, perhaps,' she suggested.

It was a possibility, Theo supposed. He thought of the woman Jack was seeing and wondered how a message from her might have put him in such a foul mood. But he shook his head. 'Not likely,' he whispered. 'The phone signal's dire. You'll get a couple of bars in Hamlet. Maybe one up by the lighthouse, if you're lucky. But there's virtually nothing down here.'

Still, looking at Jack it was clear something had bothered him. And if Theo was right about the phone signal, it must have been something happening there, in Hamlet Hall.

But for the time being, it would have to wait.

Claire had guided him onto the sofa, seating herself across from him and asking what he'd discussed with Lily. She listened closely, a grave expression on her face as he explained exactly what had happened with Rory Holloway, twelve years ago.

'You really don't know about any of this?' he asked her.

'I've told you, Theo, it was a good few years before I moved here. I know about the boy who fell from the lighthouse. But nobody's ever spoken to me about murder.' She shook her head. 'I know you don't think he would be capable of hurting Mr White, but what Will's doing tonight . . . You must see how it looks.'

'I do,' he admitted. 'But even if I thought Will *did* have it in him, he can't have been involved. He was in here, with me, for virtually the entire interval.'

'So you think it must have been one of them?' She tilted her head in the direction of the door.

'I'd like to think none of them would do it. But Damien White's an unpopular man. Gwen has the lighthouse, the Finns their shop. Hugh has Rory and if we're to take Will at his word, it sounds like White didn't take at all well to Nigel phoning in their contract.'

'What about the chef?'

'Carl?'

Claire shrugged. 'He was here, just like everyone else. Would he have had any reason to do it?'

Theo thought for a moment. 'I think he and Rory might have worked together at one point. Hugh's company delivers produce to hotels and restaurants. I'm sure I remember hearing that Carl and Rory were both drivers for a little while.'

'He doesn't have any connection to the lighthouse, though? Or the boy who died?'

'Not that I'm aware of.' Theo paused. 'Although there was something else. Something strange that happened out in the hallway.'

202

Claire's eyes narrowed slightly.

'He wanted to show something to the police,' Theo explained. 'A little bottle.'

'A bottle?'

'It looked like one of those single servings of champagne. The kind you'd get in a bar at the theatre.'

'What was he doing with it?'

'I've no idea. He didn't say any more; just that he needed to speak to Constable Fay. Lily told him she was upstairs and he went back to the kitchen.'

Before Claire could question Theo further, there was a knock on the door. Without waiting for a reply, it eased open and Justin poked his head through the crack.

'Theo,' he said sweetly. 'Could I have a word?'

Claire's expression suddenly became grave. Across the room, even Jack raised an eyebrow.

'It'll only take a second.' Justin flashed a cheerful smile.

Slowly, Claire rose to her feet. 'Jack,' she called. 'What do you say we give Theo and Justin a minute alone?'

For a split second, Theo thought Jack might refuse. But he eventually got to his feet, muttering to himself as he followed Claire into the hallway.

Closing the door behind them, Justin sauntered into the lounge. He strolled through the room as if on a country walk, hands in his pockets as he weaved between the furniture. 'I don't think I've been in this one before. Doesn't hold a candle to the restaurant. But still. Not quite as crappy as the library.'

'What do you want, Justin?'

The young reporter looked at Theo like he was seeing him

for the first time. There was an eagerness in his eyes now, the innocent smile with which he'd charmed his way into the room no longer needed. 'You've been talking to Lily White,' he said. 'Out on the beach. Then again in the hallway.'

'And?'

'And I need your help.' Justin settled himself on the sofa which Claire had just vacated. 'I'm trying to get her to do an interview. But she won't agree to it.'

'An interview?'

'That's right. When what's happened here gets out, every paper in the country will be reporting on the murder of Damien White. But think of the story *I'd* get. An inside look at the investigation and an at-the-scene interview with his daughter. It'd be incredible.'

Theo glared at him. He hadn't thought it possible to feel any more repulsed by Justin than he already did. But looking now at the hunger in his expression, he realised that this was a new low.

'Lily didn't want to hear a word I said. What makes you think I could convince her to open up?'

'She seemed to like you. I thought maybe you'd—'

'What? That I'd convince her to speak to you? Are you serious?'

'Come on, Theo—'

'Even if I thought she might listen, do you really think I'd help you after what you did?'

Justin frowned. 'Do you have some kind of problem with me?'

Theo took a deep breath, doing all he could to restrain

himself. 'As it happens, Justin, I do. Your review. That bloody review you wrote of *An Inspector Calls*.'

The frown intensified. 'Are you really sour about that?'

'Sour?' Unable to hold it back any longer, Theo let his fury surface. 'Sour doesn't even cover it. Do you have any idea of the damage you caused? Of what that review cost me?'

'What are you talking about?'

'A role. A national, touring production. A chance to get out of this place and actually make a real stab at an acting career. And your review screwed it all up.'

Justin scowled. 'How could my review—'

'The director saw it! If you hadn't . . .' Theo stopped and took a long, deep breath. 'We were getting on well. I went to Bristol, gave the best audition of my life. Then they saw your review.'

'Well, *I* didn't give it to them.'

'You might as well have done. You put it on your bloody website for all the world to see.'

'All the world?' Justin gave a short laugh. 'We're the *Hamlet Herald*. Nobody in Bristol cares about what we write. Nobody outside Hamlet even knows we exist!'

Theo paused, momentarily knocked off guard. 'What are you saying?'

'I'm saying that the chances of someone in Bristol just stumbling on my review are slim to none.'

'You think someone might have given it to them?'

'Must have done. Nobody in *Hamlet* reads our paper, let alone Bristol.'

Theo turned away, his mind racing. In all the months since

the audition, it had never occurred to him that someone might have deliberately shown the review to the director.

He tried to think of who might do it. One of the other actors going up for the role? It was, after all, a cut-throat profession. If they'd googled him frantically enough, they might just have stumbled across Justin's review. But then how would they have known his name? He hadn't known any of theirs.

'Listen to me,' said Justin, rising from the sofa with a squeak of green leather. 'We're after the same thing. You talk about getting out of this dump; that's exactly what I want too. I'm sitting on the story of my life. A murder right under my nose. A *murder*, Theo, and I'm the only reporter here! All I need is for Lily to talk to me, to give me the interview that I can finally use to approach a *real* paper.'

'Why should I care?'

'Because I can help you.' There was something feverish in Justin's eyes now. 'Please, let's help each other. You convince Lily to talk to me. Get me an interview and I'll find out who sent that review to your director.'

'And how would you do that?'

Justin broke into a broad grin. 'I'm a journalist. Asking questions is what I do.'

For several seconds, Theo looked at him. Could he be right? Could someone really have sent the review on purpose? If it were true, it would certainly be useful to have help pinning down the culprit. Even if he had to accept it from the likes of Justin.

But they were still Justin's words. It was still, ultimately, his fault.

He took a step closer. Then another, until the two of them were just inches apart. At last, when they were so close he thought he might choke on the stench of that cheap aftershave, he dropped his voice low and muttered just three words.

'Piss off, Justin.'

25

Edward watched as Lily White shrugged half-heartedly, her eyes glazed over.

'It was a champagne bottle. A small one. The kind you'd get on a plane or in a minibar.'

Sylvia wrinkled her nose. 'Why would Carl need to show the police something like that?'

'I'm sure it's nothing, darling,' said Nigel.

'If it was nothing, he wouldn't want to show it to her, would he?'

Edward barely heard Nigel's reply. Since PC Fay had confined them to the restaurant, all Nigel and Sylvia had done was bicker. By the time Gwen and Lily came back from the library, their wittering had become little more to Edward than white noise; a dull whine that chimed relentlessly in his ears.

He glared down the table at them, his frustration brewing like a kettle on the boil. 'I can't listen to this,' he said, standing abruptly to his feet.

Martha frowned at him from the neighbouring chair. 'Where are you going? That police officer said we were to stay here.'

'She's right, Edward,' Hugh chimed in. 'We really ought to—'

'I know what she said. I just . . . I'm sorry. I need space. Somewhere to think.'

'Edward,' Martha called after him. 'Edward, please.'

But he wasn't listening. He trembled with rage as he stalked into the hallway, and for a split second, he almost turned right, towards the main door. He wanted to inspect it for himself; to go to the shop and see just how much damage they'd done this time.

Begrudgingly, he held himself back.

When Fay broke the news to them, he'd wanted to go over there. Just a few minutes and then he would come straight back to Hamlet Hall. Even that had been too much to ask. There might be evidence to recover, she'd said. Fingerprints. DNA samples. If he wanted the culprits found, the best thing he could do was steer clear until the police had been.

He stood there in the hallway, clenching his fists. He might not be able to leave Hamlet Hall, but he couldn't spend another moment sitting in the same room as Nigel and Sylvia Cobb. He needed somewhere else to go. Somewhere quiet, where he could just rest his mind.

The lounge wasn't a possibility; that was where the actors had been told to wait. Neither was the library. It might well be vacant, now that Gwen and Lily White had rejoined the group, but there was only a single wall between it and the restaurant. Right then, Edward wanted to put as much distance between himself and the Cobbs as he possibly could.

Turning on the spot, he looked towards the staircase.

Regardless of whether anyone believed Sylvia had been seeing to her make-up, it seemed she *had* managed to get into one of the guestrooms during the interval. Surely, that suggested at least one of them was unlocked.

Fay would disapprove, of course. Perhaps she'd even ask if he was trying to sneak a look at White's body. But in that moment, Edward didn't care.

As he climbed the stairs, the boards creaking beneath his feet, his thoughts returned to the shop. It had to be one of those thugs Nigel Cobb had recruited to work on the lighthouse. He'd claimed they were spending New Year's Eve with their families, but Edward had seen them. Even served a couple of them reluctantly over the counter. Men like that didn't have families, and those who did weren't the type to go home to them. They'd still be skulking around Hamlet Wick somewhere.

Reaching the top of the stairs, he shot a glance left. The door to Damien White's room, at least, would surely be locked. For a brief moment, Edward thought it was a pity. He wanted to see the scene that Will had described for himself. To see White's body dumped upon the floor.

Because he'd deserved it, after all. And didn't Edward deserve to see it? He felt no shame as these thoughts began to fill his mind. Not even as he pictured Lily, the young woman who had lost her father. If she knew the sort of man he truly was, she might very well agree.

Why had White come back? Gwen's plans for the lighthouse would have done so much good. Why, now that someone was finally stepping in to sew up the wound, was he returning to rub salt into it?

With a tremendous effort, he turned his thoughts to Martha.

She had suffered all those years, just as he had. And yet, he knew she wouldn't think this way. He might not owe it to White, or even to his daughter, but he owed it to Martha to show a shred of decency. Even if he knew that the man lying dead on the floor would never have done the same for him.

With a sigh, he tried the handle of a guestroom at the top of the stairs. Finding it unlocked, he stepped inside.

The first thing that struck him was the cold. The room was freezing, and when he flicked on the light Edward immediately saw why. The window was wide open, thin curtains fluttering gently in the breeze.

Initially, he was confused. Perhaps it had been opened that afternoon, to air the room, and not since closed. But surely Ian had more sense than that on a day so bitingly cold. And even if it had been left open by accident, why air a room in which nobody's staying?

As Edward stood there in the doorway, surveying the scene, he settled on a second anomaly. Something he should have noticed the moment he stepped inside, but was only just seeing.

A vase of flowers had been knocked off the desk. A large puddle stained the carpet, petals and stems scattered across the floor.

With a sudden flash of realisation, Edward knew what must have happened. Someone had been in this room. For some reason, they had come to the window. And whoever it was had been in a hurry.

26

In a way that was profoundly unsettling, the guestroom in which Will was about to be interviewed gave him exactly the same feeling as the offices of the last three therapists his parents had insisted he visit.

Without a word, PC Fay waved him into one of two chairs that had been positioned in the centre of the room. He wished something had been placed between them. He felt painfully exposed, the open space making it considerably more difficult to hide his trembling hands.

'I think you should speak to Carl,' he said. 'I heard him, downstairs. He was saying that he needed you. It sounded important.'

Fay was unmoved. 'Mr Gifford can give his statement next, if he has something to share. Right now, I'd like to hear from you.'

She took out a Dictaphone, clicked it on and set it beside her on the desk. Will watched as the wheels began to slowly rotate behind the plastic screen.

'Could you please state your name for the recording?'

'Will Hooper.'

'Would you mind speaking up?'

He cleared his throat, forcing as much energy into his quivering voice as he could muster. 'Will Hooper.'

'Mr Hooper, did you and Ian Davies discover the body of Damien White this evening?'

Will nodded.

'Could you please answer aloud for the recording?'

He swallowed back a lump in his throat. 'Yes.'

'When did this happen?'

'A couple of hours ago. Maybe quarter-past nine.'

'And can you describe how you came to find him?'

Will closed his eyes, picturing the scene. 'We'd gathered the guests in the restaurant, but there'd been no sign of Mr White. Lily, his daughter, was starting to worry, so Ian and I went to check on him. That was when we found . . .' He paused and took a breath. 'That was when we found him.'

Fay took a notepad from the desk and began to study some scribbles she'd presumably made while speaking to Ian. 'I understand a short interval took place after dinner. Between half-past eight and nine o'clock. And it was during this time that you believe Mr White was killed. Can you explain why?'

'Well, it was at the beginning of the interval that he went upstairs to his room. Lily then heard him speaking with Justin—'

'Justin Fletcher?'

Will flinched. 'That's right. I think he was asking for an interview about the lighthouse.'

Fay looked again at her notes. 'You've mentioned already this

213

evening that Miss White heard someone leaving her father's room.'

'Footsteps,' said Will. 'She says that she heard footsteps.'

Fay nodded. 'You've also said that Gwen Holloway heard these footsteps.'

'Yes. Some of the other guests had been . . .' He paused. 'They'd been less than hospitable to Mr White over dinner. I think Gwen had gone to make sure Lily was all right.'

'So I hear.' Fay flicked back a page in her notepad. 'Mr Davies has told me about the grievances that were aired over dinner. Mr Cobb resigning his work on the lighthouse and the accusation of his workers breaking into the Finns' shop. Mr Fletcher pestering Mr White's office in London for an interview. The suggestion of a sexual relationship between Mr White and Mrs Holloway.' She looked up from the notes. 'Could it have been Mr Fletcher who was heard leaving Mr White's room?'

'No. At least, I don't think so. They heard it at the end of interval, but it sounds like he'd turned Justin away after just a few minutes.'

Fay made a fresh note in her pad. 'If I've understood this correctly,' she said, 'at the beginning of the interval, Miss White hears Justin Fletcher asking her father for an interview. She hears the two of them speaking, and is therefore able to confirm that, at this moment, Mr White is still alive. Two things then happen: Gwen Holloway comes to Miss White's room and Mr Fletcher returns to the restaurant; although it's unclear in which order these two events take place, as Miss White appears not to have heard Mr Fletcher leaving. Towards the end of the interval, Miss White and Mrs Holloway both hear someone leaving Mr

White's room. They assume at the time that it's Mr White himself, but now believe it must have been his killer.'

'That's my understanding,' said Will quietly.

Fay paused. Then those cold eyes locked with Will's. 'Where were *you* during the interval, Mr Hooper?'

There it was. The question he'd been dreading.

'I was in the lounge.'

'For the entire half-hour?'

'Yes,' he stammered. 'I mean, no. Not for the whole half-hour. I was in the restaurant first. Then I went to the lounge.'

'Is there anyone who can confirm this?'

'Theo. Theo Bloom. He was with me the whole time. Claire was there too, at least for the first few minutes.'

'Claire is one of the actors?'

Will nodded. 'Yes,' he said hurriedly, glancing at the Dictaphone. 'I was feeling a little unsteady after what had happened over dinner. She went to see if she could find me a glass of whisky.'

Fay sat still for a moment. 'Mr Hooper, could you please explain what's taking place this evening at Hamlet Hall?'

'It's a murder mystery party.'

'And how, exactly, does the party work?'

'I'm sorry?'

She shrugged. 'I'd imagine there's a murder the guests need to solve.'

'Yes.'

'So how do they go about doing that?'

Will cleared his throat nervously. 'There are clues hidden around the hotel. One in the lounge, another in the library and

215

the last is in the restaurant. The guests are divided into groups and given half an hour in each room to solve a puzzle that will lead them to the clue.'

'And they'd use these clues to identify the murderer?'

'Yes. The actors were going to be there with them. Theo in the lounge, Jack in the restaurant and Claire in the library. Once the guests found the clue, the actors would give them a piece of information. If they managed to gather all three, they should be able to tell which of them is the murderer.'

'It sounds very elaborate,' said Fay. 'Could you please explain your role in organising this event?'

Suddenly, Will found himself wishing once again that some kind of barrier had been placed between them. 'I wrote the story.'

'It's an original story?'

'Yes.'

'So the murder is of your own creation?'

'Yes,' he said again, barely able to manage anything further.

'Could you please describe how this murder takes place?'

Surely she knew this already. Ian must have shared it just minutes earlier in his own interview.

Will glanced at the tape recorder on the desk, the little wheels continuing to spin. She needed to hear him say it. She needed it on tape, in his voice. He had the feeling of standing over his own grave, a shovel thrust into his hands, and being told to dig.

He took a deep breath. 'A character I've invented, Lord Ashcombe, is struck around the head.'

'And where does this murder take place?'

'On the beach.'

'Which beach?'

'The one outside.'

Fay paused, peering at him closely. 'Mr Hooper, are you aware of how closely the murder in your story resembles that of Rory Holloway?'

'It's a story,' he rasped, his imaginary shovel plunging into the earth. 'It's just made up.'

'I understand that you've made it up. My question is whether you recognise the similarity it bears to the murder of Rory Holloway.'

Will nodded.

'Could you please answer for the—'

'Yes.'

She stopped, her eyes narrowing again. 'You've seen Mr White's body,' she said.

'Yes.'

'Could you describe how he appears to have been killed?'

Will thought of the wound on the back of Damien White's head. 'I didn't kill him.' His voice quivered. 'I was with Theo. In the lounge.'

'And I'll be speaking with Mr Bloom in due course,' she said calmly. 'But my question wasn't where you were. It was how Damien White appears to have been killed.'

'Someone hit him around the head.' The words were like treacle on Will's tongue, each one dragging him down even further.

'My thoughts exactly. And do you see the resemblance that this *also* bears to the murder of Mr Holloway?'

Will couldn't answer. His mouth hung open, his lips

twitching but no sound emerging. Fay simply waited, leaving the silence to linger uncomfortably between them.

'Mr Hooper,' she said at last. 'Twelve years ago, it would have been absurd for you to be considered a suspect in Rory Holloway's murder. You were far too young to have beaten a grown man to death and your involvement in the case required you to be treated only as a witness.' She leaned forward an inch. 'You don't have either of those luxuries this evening. Nor do you seem to have any reasonable explanation for why you have quite clearly based the enactment of a fictional murder on the death of Rory Holloway.'

She leaned in further still. 'What you do, apparently, have in your favour is a single witness to attest that you weren't near Mr White at the time he appears to have been killed; a murder which appears also to have been committed in a strikingly similar manner to that of Rory Holloway.' She paused. 'Is there anything you'd like to tell me before this goes any further?'

Will couldn't speak. He couldn't even look away, her eyes locking him into place. 'No,' was all he managed.

For what felt like a lifetime, she fixed him with a stare. All the while, his mind raced. What could he tell her? The truth? She wouldn't believe it even if he did.

His hands were trembling violently, his jaw clamped shut. If he opened his mouth, he knew he'd be sick. Fay took a breath and he braced for what he was sure would be the most clinical question yet.

But it never came.

Just as she was about to speak, the door was flung open, striking the wall with a crash that made Will leap halfway out of his seat. Pure malice flickered over Fay's face, and Will turned to see a startled Edward Finn bursting into the room. He was pale, his eyes wild.

'It's the room,' he said. 'The room at the top of the stairs. Someone's . . . I think someone's been inside.'

27

Lily stared at her phone, the screen filled with a picture from the summer.

That had been a good day. She'd been home for a week, between an internship in Edinburgh and a music festival in Europe, and while her dad had been off overseeing a new development, she and her mum had happily filled the time with cocktails and spa afternoons. The moment this particular picture had been taken, an Italian waiter in Covent Garden had just mistaken them for sisters. Or at least, he'd pretended to. Her mum had loved that. She was laughing, teeth gleaming and blonde curls bouncing.

But as hard as she tried, Lily couldn't take any comfort from it. With just twenty minutes until midnight, it had been well over an hour since she'd left her message. Even if her suspicions were correct, and her mum had picked up last-minute tickets to a show, she would be out of the theatre by now. She must, surely, have looked at her phone.

Lily's eyes flickered to the corner of the screen. Still not a single bar of signal. Perhaps her mum had tried to reach out and just hadn't got through. Perhaps she'd been calling frantically since picking up the message. But Lily had told her to call the landline in Ian's office. She'd said, specifically, that she wouldn't pick up a call to her mobile.

She tried to distract herself by searching for information on Rory. There would have been news articles published at the time. There might even be something that expanded on her dad's role as a suspect.

Having failed, when visiting the office, to find a router, she asked Ian if there was Wi-Fi she could use. He nodded solemnly and slipped from the restaurant, before returning with a pass-word scrawled upon a slip of paper.

Quite where he'd fetched it from, Lily couldn't guess. Wherever he'd gone, though, he needn't have bothered. The connection was painfully slow, taking a whole minute to open an old *BBC News* article announcing Rory's death. When it did finally load, Lily couldn't even say that it was worth the wait. The article mentioned a body on the beach, but there was nothing about her dad.

By the time Will joined them, she'd all but given up on her search. Seating himself at the head of the table, he explained that the police officer was now questioning Edward Finn; something about an intrusion in one of the guestrooms.

Martha rose to her feet. 'I shouldn't have let him leave,' she murmured, panic in her voice. 'I should have made him stay put.'

'He'll be fine, Martha,' said Gwen. 'Let the constable speak to him. I'm sure he'll be—'

'No, Gwen. The shop, the lighthouse . . . It's all hit him a lot harder than I think you realise. I'm going to find him, and I'd like you not to stop me. I want to sit with him. Make sure he's all right.'

Gwen hesitated, clearly uncomfortable with yet another of their group leaving. But in the end, she nodded sadly, making no attempt to stop Martha as she hurried from the room.

Lily felt a sudden flash of guilt. How could her dad not have cared about what he was doing to these people? She knew he was ruthless, but this was different. How could he have been so heartless? So . . . cruel?

After Martha had left, Gwen turned to Will. 'What did Edward see?'

Propping his elbows on the table, Will ran a hand through his hair. 'I'm not sure. He just came barging in, saying something about a window being open and a vase knocked over in one of the guestrooms.'

'What was he doing in the guestrooms?' asked Hugh.

Will gave a little shrug.

Gwen shot Hugh a worried look. 'You don't suppose . . .' She paused, bracing herself. 'Whoever's responsible – for what's happened to Damien, that is – you don't suppose they could have escaped through the window? They'd be in a hurry. They might knock over a vase on their way past.'

Hugh grimaced. 'Those windows are narrow. And the drop must be at least twelve feet. You couldn't escape that way without drawing some attention.'

'What if it's the other way round, then? What if someone climbed in and they're now hiding in the hotel?'

'How? Again, that window's twelve feet off the ground, if not more. And if someone came in through one of them, wouldn't they think to close it again?'

Gwen looked pained. 'So why go into the room at all? Why

open the window and why in such a hurry that you'd knock over the vase?'

Hugh didn't answer. Instead, he swept a glance around the restaurant, looking carefully at each of them in turn. 'That's it,' he announced. 'Nobody else is leaving this room alone. Not until the police have said explicitly that we can go. If you have somewhere to be, you go in a group.'

In the corner of the room, Lily saw Ian press a hand to his face. Hugh, meanwhile, looked at Sylvia. Catching his eye, she sat bolt upright.

'You can't think I had something to do with it?'

'You still haven't told us why you were upstairs during the interval.'

'I have. I was fixing my make-up.'

Hugh raised his voice, addressing everyone at once. 'Does anyone believe that in the thirty minutes Sylvia spent upstairs, she did nothing but fix her make-up?'

Nobody responded. Nigel started to raise his hand, but with a single stern look from Hugh, quickly put it down again.

'Sylvia.' Hugh's voice seemed calm enough, but Lily could hear it straining. 'Whatever you were *actually* doing while White was killed – regardless of whether it has anything to do with Edward's window – now's the time to come clean.'

They locked eyes, each challenging the other to stand their ground. Finally, Sylvia stood, a scowl on her face, and strode promptly from the room. Lily watched her go, then saw Nigel let loose a great sigh and hurry after her.

She felt a small flicker of satisfaction. While she certainly had no love for Hugh, she couldn't help but enjoy the sight of Sylvia so flustered.

'Did you really need to do that?' said Gwen. 'These are questions for the police to be asking, not us.'

Hugh's eyes remained fixed on the door. 'They'll have their turn. But right now, I've had enough. Enough of being lied to. Enough of wondering just what it is we're actually doing here.'

His expression darkening, he looked towards the table. Following his gaze, Lily saw him settle on Will.

'Hugh, please . . .' Gwen put a hand on his arm, but he paid her no notice.

'We all know what happened to you, Will,' he said. 'We all know how young you were and we can all imagine how horrifying it must have been to find Rory on that beach. But it's time you explain why you've done this tonight.' He took a step forward. 'Why are we playing out a story about my brother's murder?'

Will cowered beneath him, terror written plainly across his face. 'We aren't . . .'

'Are you trying to solve what happened to him? Trying to relive it?'

'Of course not. No, I wouldn't—'

'Or are you trying to accuse someone?' Reaching the table, Hugh gripped the back of the nearest chair. 'Is that what this is? You think you know something about Rory that the rest of us don't, so you've gathered us here to reveal who killed him?'

'No!' Will sprang to his feet, putting the table between himself and Hugh.

Gwen tightened her grip on her husband's arm. 'Hugh,' she said firmly. 'Hugh, please . . .'

'Who is it, Will?' he growled. 'Who's your murderer? Which of us have you chosen?'

'It's a game,' Will protested. 'It's only a game . . .'

There was a heavy silence as Hugh loomed over the table.

'The envelopes,' said Lily. 'The ones that were in our places.' She held up the paper that identified her as Jane Ashcombe. 'Will said it himself. Whoever's playing the murderer, it'll say so in their letter.'

'Lily . . .' Gwen looked at her desperately. 'Please don't encourage this.'

Hugh seemed to think for a few seconds, staring at the letter in Lily's hand. 'You've read yours,' he said. 'I suppose it isn't you?'

Over his shoulder, Gwen fixed her with a pleading look. Lily could see what she was trying to say. That she could stop this. Prevent it from getting any more out of hand.

For a moment, she considered it. She thought of all the pain her dad had caused these people. She thought of the lighthouse, and the memorial to Teddy that it ought to be. She thought of the Finns, the harmless old couple whose shop had now been broken into three times. And she thought of Rory, betrayed by his oldest friend in his hour of need.

She should stand down. Let the police investigate this properly. With all that she'd learned, she wasn't even sure her dad deserved to be defended.

She entertained the thought for just a few seconds before she remembered the sight of his body, heaped on the floor. She thought of Rory, and how he, too, had been killed in Hamlet Wick, his life ended by a blow to the head. And she thought of how Gwen could have told her about him from the start, but had forced her to barter it out of Justin and Theo.

In that moment, all the frustration that Lily bore for her dad – for the secrets he'd kept and the people he'd hurt – gave way to a burning anger. She realised that she didn't want to hold Hugh back. She wanted to understand what the hell was going on.

'No. It isn't me.'

Hugh tugged his arm roughly out of Gwen's grip, took his own envelope from the table and ripped it open. His eyes flickered back and forth as he read the letter. 'Nor me,' he said. 'Justin?'

Since speaking to the actors in the lounge, Justin had barely said a word, scowling as he loitered by the sideboard. But as Hugh rounded on Will, he seemed to come alive. 'I opened mine earlier,' he said eagerly. 'Nothing in there about being the murderer.'

Lily watched as Hugh scooped up Edward and Martha's envelopes, tearing each of them open and quickly scanning the letters.

'It isn't the Finns.'

'Hugh,' said Gwen. 'Darling, please stop this.'

But Hugh wasn't listening. The mist had completely descended as he snatched up Nigel and Sylvia's envelopes.

'Ian.' Gwen turned to the bay window, where Ian was quietly watching the unfolding chaos. 'Ian, please. Do something.'

Lily saw Will flash Ian a desperate look, begging him to help. It might be his story that they were acting out, but the two of them had organised the evening together. If anyone was going to stand up for him, Ian would surely be the one.

He looked at Gwen, then let his eyes drop to the floor.

Hugh placed both hands on the back of the nearest chair. 'That leaves just two,' he said, fixing Gwen with a cold look. 'You . . .'

'And my dad,' Lily finished.

Before anyone else could speak, Gwen lunged for the table, seizing the remaining envelopes.

'You're angry,' she said, clutching them close as she retreated to the mantelpiece. 'I understand. But whatever Will intended for tonight – whatever connection there might be to Rory – it's for the police to deal with. Not us. Please, Hugh. I can't let this continue.'

Hugh stared at her, fury in his eyes. Then he turned to Will. 'Who is it?' he asked, his voice low. 'Which one have you chosen?'

Will said nothing.

'Is it Gwen?' He took a step forward. 'Or is it Mr White?'

At the sound of her dad's name, Lily saw Will's face finally crumple.

'It is, isn't it?' Hugh pointed towards Gwen. 'If we opened those envelopes, the letters inside would tell us that White is your murderer.'

'It's a story.' Will's voice was hoarse. 'That's all this is. It's just a story.'

'But you admit to choosing White.'

'I didn't know he was even coming! Ask Ian. It was Lily who booked them in and all she said was that she was coming with her father.'

Hugh paused, a hint of uncertainty suddenly flickering in his expression. He turned to Ian, who seemed to consider for a moment, before giving a stiff nod.

'He's right, Hugh. I hate to say it, but he's right. We had no idea.'

'There,' said Gwen, her shoulders slumping. 'You see? How could all of this be some dramatic way of accusing Damien of killing Rory, if Will didn't even know that he was coming?'

For a split second, Hugh had looked as if he might be convinced. But at the sound of his wife saying 'Damien', his nostrils flared and he rounded again on Will.

'Prove it,' he snarled. 'Prove to me that this isn't all about Rory.'

Will's eyes flittered around the room, searching for help. Some way to save himself. 'The clues,' he said breathlessly. 'When the game began, you would have looked for three clues, which reveal why Lord Ashcombe was murdered. Look at those, and you'll see it's all just a story.'

He hurried to the sideboard. At first, Lily thought he was going for the gramophone, but instead, he stopped at a wooden globe. Tipping it open to reveal a hidden drinks cabinet, he drew out a bottle wrapped in a dark label.

'What's that?' she demanded.

'Medicine. Jack would have given the group in here a riddle. Solve it, and it would have brought you to this.'

'Why?'

'Jack's character was the village doctor. Once you'd found the medicine, he would explain that Lord Ashcombe was terminally ill.'

'Why would you murder someone who was already dying?'
said Justin.

'The other clues would answer that.'

Lily looked at Hugh. He was peering at the bottle. It might
have helped Will's case, but she could see he wasn't yet wholly
convinced.

'What else?' Gwen urged. 'Where are the others?'

Will was almost hopping now from one foot to the other,
fizzing with nervous energy. 'The library,' he said. 'There's one
in the library, and the third is in the lounge.'

He hurried into the hallway, shoes clicking on the tiled floor
as the group followed. Scurrying into the library, he flicked on
the light and went straight to a shelf in the far corner, from
which he withdrew a cloth-bound book.

'*The Murder of Roger Ackroyd*,' he said. 'Solve the second
riddle and the answer would lead you to this. There's a note
inside.'

Hugh snatched the book from Will's hands and opened it. A
few pages in, he paused and lifted out a slip of paper.

'You see?' said Will. 'It's gossip, passed between two members of the household. Once you'd shown it to Claire, she would
have explained that Lord Ashcombe had an affair with one of
the maids.'

Hugh didn't reply at first. Instead, he stared at the page, the
look on his face turning first to surprise, then to stone-cold fury.
'Is this a joke?'

Slowly, he lifted the page from the book and turned it around
so the others could see. As he did, Lily heard the faint chiming
of a clock striking somewhere in the hotel.

229

Midnight. The start of a new year, although the thought of it being cause for celebration seemed laughable now.

Transfixed, she watched as with each toll the light faded from Will's eyes. The note certainly contained a message, but it was not a rumour about an affair with a maid. Instead, it consisted of just four hastily written words. Four words which, as Lily read them, caused her stomach to turn:

For Rory and Teddy.

Midnight

28

Justin no longer cared about Lily turning down his interview. Just as he realised he no longer cared about Damien White sending him away or Theo telling him to piss off. As he stood there in the library, staring at the note in Hugh's hand, he knew he was still sitting on the story of his life. More than that, it was developing before his eyes.

For Rory and Teddy.

It was scrawled in large text, filling the entire page, as if to drive home each letter.

'You need to explain this, Will,' said Hugh. 'And you need to explain it now.'

Will shook his head, his eyes like floodlights. 'I can't.'

'Will, I swear to God—'

'I can't! I'm telling you, I didn't put that there.'

'Then who did?'

'I don't know.' Will's voice was rising, panic taking hold. 'The note I'd planted was part of the game. It was about Lord Ashcombe; about him having an affair with the maid.'

Justin watched as Hugh rifled through the book. 'There's no sign of any other note. Only this one.'

'Then someone's taken it.'

'Who?'

'I don't know!' Will spun around on the spot, searching desperately for help. He turned to Ian, but it was immediately clear he'd find no support there. The older man glared back at him, a ferocious expression on his face.

'You'd better work it out quickly,' said Hugh. 'Because as far as I'm concerned, this is all you. And unless you can come up with a convincing explanation, the police will feel exactly the same.'

Will sank into a dusty leather armchair and pressed his hands to his face.

'Where's the third clue?' asked Hugh. 'You said it was in the lounge.'

'It's hidden inside the grandfather clock. A rolled-up copy of Lord Ashcombe's will.'

Hugh pressed the book into Justin's hands, the note resting on top, and stalked into the hallway.

After he'd gone, Gwen turned to Will. 'Could anyone else have known about this? Is there anyone you've told?'

At first, he didn't answer. He didn't even move. But when he did, finally, raise his head from his hands, it was with a look of wide-eyed realisation. 'The actors,' he breathed. 'They had to know where all the clues were.'

Justin brandished the note. 'Why would they swap out your clue for this? None of them have anything to do with Rory. Or, for that matter, with Teddy.'

Before Will could scramble for an answer, Hugh returned

with a thick brown envelope. Tearing it open, he withdrew a sheet of cream-coloured paper.

'Nothing about Rory in here,' he said. 'Or Teddy.'

'So it's just the note?' said Lily. 'Why not swap out the others too?'

'Because they were being watched,' said Justin. 'Think about it. We've been in the restaurant all evening, so nobody could have done anything with that bottle. And the actors have barely left the lounge. But the library's been empty. If you knew where to find it, this would be by far the easiest clue to get your hands on.'

'Is there any way someone else could have found it, Will?' asked Gwen. 'Someone besides the actors? Was it written down anywhere that the note was hidden in this book?'

Justin felt a smile spreading across his face. He was enjoying every moment of this. Each delicious second.

'The ring binders,' said Will, his voice becoming more frantic by the second. 'I made three ring binders; one for each of the actors. If you got hold of one of those, you'd have instructions for the whole evening. Lines of dialogue, backstory for the characters and the location of all the clues.'

'There you have it.' Gwen turned to Hugh. 'Five people who knew already that there was a note hidden in this room and three separate ring binders in which it was written down.'

He frowned at her. 'Five?'

'Will, the actors and Ian.'

'Me?' Ian protested.

'You've helped Will organise this evening,' said Gwen. 'You might not have written the story, but surely you knew where he'd put the clues?'

235

Justin swept Ian a glance. He suddenly looked sheepish, shuffling on the spot.

'I suppose,' he said. 'Yes, I imagine I'd have known there was one in here.'

'You're suggesting it could have been any of us,' Hugh said quietly. 'Nigel or Sylvia. Or the Finns.' He paused. 'Or me?'

'All I'm saying,' Gwen replied, 'is that until the police have had a chance to properly investigate, we can't simply assume this was Will.'

'But why? He's the one who planned this. The one who's made a game out of Rory's death. What does it matter if the rest us could have found out where this note was? What reason would anyone have to do this, apart from *him*?'

From the corner of the room, there came the sudden sound of breaking glass. Turning to investigate, Justin saw the shattered remnants of a champagne flute scattered at Ian's feet. He swore under his breath, then crouched down and began to gather the broken fragments.

Gwen hurried to his side.

'It's fine,' Ian muttered. 'Honestly. I can do it.'

She ignored him, kneeling down to help scoop up the shards. But after a moment, she stopped, a quizzical expression on her face. 'Ian,' she said. 'Your hand.'

Justin followed her gaze. Quite how he'd missed it before, he had no idea, but Ian's hand was wrapped in a bandage. More than that, the linen was stained red. He'd cut himself, and however he'd done it, it must have been fresh.

He tried to whip it away but Gwen caught him by the wrist. 'Ian, you're bleeding.'

'It's nothing,' he said. 'An accident in the kitchen. It'll be fine.'

She shook her head. 'This needs to be changed. Do you have a first-aid kit somewhere?'

Forcing a weak smile, Ian tugged his hand away again and stood abruptly to his feet. 'You really don't need to. I wouldn't want to waste the linen.'

'Gwen,' Hugh growled. 'For God's sake, leave him be. If he says he's all right—'

'It's in the office.' Will leaned forward in his armchair. 'The first-aid kit. I saw it in the office. I could fetch it, if you like.'

'You stay right there.' Hugh snatched the book from Justin's hands. 'Until we get to the bottom of *this*, you aren't leaving my sight.'

Deflated, Will sank back into his chair.

'He's right, Will,' said Gwen. 'You'd best stay here. Justin can go.'

Justin recoiled. 'Absolutely not. I need to be in here. Someone has to report all of this!'

Ian looked similarly unhappy. 'You really don't need to—'

'It's bleeding through, Ian.' There was suddenly an edge to Gwen's tone. 'Will, give him that chair, please. Justin will fetch the first-aid kit and we'll change the bandage.' She turned to Hugh. 'It'll only take a minute. Then we'll show Will's note to Constable Fay.'

Reluctantly, Ian allowed her to take him by the elbow and guide him into Will's armchair. 'Fine,' he said, fixing Justin with a glare. 'It's in the top drawer of my desk. The *top* drawer. Fetch it and come straight back.'

Stinging with resentment, Justin opened his mouth to protest, but a stern look from Gwen held him back. There was no point arguing. If he was quick, he could be back before he missed anything more.

With a scowl, he scurried from the library, almost jogging as he crossed the hallway and entered the little corridor at the foot of the staircase. Finding the door to Ian's office, he hurried inside and flicked on the light. It was a depressing scene, the magnolia walls, bottles of booze and dusty old computer almost making him feel better about his own desk at the *Hamlet Herald*. He supposed he should know better than to be surprised. Hamlet Hall put on a good show, but this was its heart. Old. Faded. Done.

Eager to get back, he opened the top drawer of the desk and lifted out a green plastic box, marked with a large white cross.

How could Ian even have cut himself? He hadn't done anything *that* exciting during the interval, had he?

Justin paused. Thinking about it, he had absolutely no idea what Ian had done during the interval. He'd said nothing about where he'd been and virtually nothing about how he'd hurt himself. The one thing he'd been clear on was that Justin should look only in the *top* drawer of the desk for the first-aid box. He'd been pretty insistent on that.

Perhaps a little too insistent?

Justin looked at the lower drawer. As he did, he thought of the dozens of unanswered applications he'd sent to other newspapers. *Real* newspapers. He thought of Damien White, Lily and even Theo all denying him an interview, and a sudden determination overcame him. Screw Ian. He was going to get his story, even if he had to unearth it for himself.

He slid open the bottom drawer, and rooted around inside. Nestled among a stack of invoices and receipts, an object, a little larger than a cricket ball, was wrapped in newspaper. It had a weight to it, settling with a thud as Justin placed it on the desk.

Carefully, he began to unwrap the little parcel. As he did, and the truth of what Ian was hiding within the drawer became clear, it was all he could do not to cry out with joy.

29

'How have you done this, Ian?' Gwen knelt beside him, peering at the bloodstained bandage.

He shook his head. 'I was helping Carl in the kitchen, clearing the crockery after dinner. I wasn't paying enough attention and I suppose I must have slipped.'

'During the interval?' asked Hugh.

'That's right.'

Will was barely listening. Instead, he was trying desperately to calm himself, thinking of how he could explain the note to PC Fay.

Gwen had been right, of course. If they'd somehow got hold of one of the actors' ring binders, any of the guests could easily have swapped out a clue. But who? And why do it at all?

Feeling his chest tighten, he took a deep breath on his inhaler. All the while, he was aware of Lily glaring at him from across the library.

'Can I see it?' she asked.

At first, Hugh didn't reply. Then, reluctantly, he tucked

the scrap of paper inside the book and pressed it into her hand.

Will watched helplessly as she flicked through the pages. She seemed not to be looking for anything in particular, barely glancing at each page before moving on to the next. But towards the back, she stopped.

'It's been ripped out,' she said.

Hugh frowned at her.

'The page,' she explained. 'The one the note's written on. It's been ripped from the back of the book.'

Leaving Ian in his armchair, Gwen went to see for herself. 'So somebody came in here,' she said, 'ripped out the page in order to write this note and then swapped it for Will's.'

Hugh scowled. 'It could still have been *him*. Wouldn't he do that deliberately; make it look like it was done in a hurry?'

'That's for the police to decide,' said Gwen.

Unable to hold back his frustration any longer, Hugh rounded on her. 'Why are you defending him?'

'Because he might be telling the truth. If he's really written down in three separate ring binders where this note would be—'

'Or he might be lying,' Hugh snapped. 'Who knows how long he's been planning all of this? Who's to say he didn't make sure it was written down in three different places as another way of covering himself?'

Gwen opened her mouth to protest, but Hugh spoke over her before she had the chance.

'Take his side if you like. But as far as I'm concerned, he still has a lot of explaining to do.'

'He isn't the only one.'

At the sound of Justin's voice, Will turned to see him standing in the doorway, his hand outstretched. He was holding something, although it took Will a moment to realise exactly what. The longer he peered at it, though, the clearer it became.

In Justin's hand was a rock, its edges jagged and its surface stained dark with blood.

'You little shit,' Ian breathed. 'I told you that the first-aid box was in the top drawer. The *top* drawer!'

He leapt to his feet, and for a split second, Will thought he was about to cross the room and attack the young reporter. Apparently having the same thought, Justin took a sudden step back, before Hugh sprang into Ian's path and grasped him by the shoulders, holding him at bay.

Once she seemed certain Hugh had him securely held, Gwen turned to Justin. 'Where's that come from?'

'Ian's desk,' he replied. 'Hidden in the bottom drawer.'

Relinquishing his grip on Ian, Hugh went to inspect the rock. 'Will,' he said quietly. 'How, exactly, has White been killed?'

Will couldn't reply. He stared at the rock – at the dried blood that coated it – and tried not to picture Damien White's motionless body on the floor of his room. Nor the gaping wound at the back of his head.

'He's been hit around the head,' said Lily, her voice laced with venom. 'Just like Rory.'

Hugh turned back to Ian. 'Explain.'

Ian shook his head. 'I can't.'

'No?' Hugh jabbed a finger into his chest so aggressively it sent him staggering backwards. 'Then perhaps you could explain instead where you were during the interval? Or, for that matter, why you're wearing that bandage? Because let me tell you, I was in the kitchen with Carl for the full half-hour and I didn't see you in there once. Edward came in at one point, but there was no sign of you. So, you can give up this story about cutting yourself on the crockery.' He shook his head. 'I've been laying into Sylvia all evening for not telling us where she was, but it seems you've been just as secretive.'

'All right!' Ian held up his hands in surrender. 'You're right. I made a mistake. I wasn't in the kitchen. I was in my office.'

'Your office?'

'Yes.'

'And how did you come to have a rock in your desk? A rock which, if I'm not mistaken, is covered in White's blood?'

Will saw the fear in Ian's eyes. Could it be him? Could he have slipped away during the interval, struck Damien White around the head and then hidden the murder weapon in his office?

Ian composed himself. 'It was thrown from an upstairs window,' he said. 'Into the garden. I saw it land and went out to see what it was.'

'Not on your life,' said Justin. 'I've just been in that office and it's pitch black outside. With the light on, you can't see a thing in the window but your own reflection.'

'He's right,' Lily added. 'I hate to admit it, but I thought exactly the same thing when I tried to call home.'

Will felt a sudden burst of resentment. Had Ian set this up?

Set *him* up? He'd known where all of the clues were. Was he trying to throw Will to the wolves, just to save his own skin?

'Try again, Ian,' said Hugh.

Ian sighed, the tremor in his voice becoming even more pronounced. 'I'm telling you, I saw it being thrown from an upstairs window.'

'Which window?' said Hugh.

'The middle room, at the top of the stairs.'

'How could you tell?'

Ian glared at him defiantly. 'I own this hotel. I know which room is which.'

'It makes sense,' said Gwen. 'That's the room Edward went into. With the vase of flowers. What if someone hit Damien around the head with this rock, then went in there to throw it away before going back downstairs? They'd have been in a hurry; panicking, even. It's possible they'd rush out again without closing the window properly.'

'Perhaps they did,' said Hugh. 'But if Justin and Lily are right, it doesn't change the fact that Ian couldn't have seen it happen from the office.'

Gwen grimaced. She had no answer.

Will, meanwhile, was mentally retracing each step he and Ian had taken together that day. He remembered setting the table and placing the clues that afternoon. Greeting the guests and sitting down for dinner. Then discovering White's body, meeting Fay and showing her the CCTV footage.

'The window,' he said. 'Ian and I took PC Fay to the office to look at the security cameras. When we arrived, the window was open a crack.'

244

'Is that it, Ian?' said Hugh. 'Had you been in the garden?'

'Adds up to me,' Justin chimed in. 'Much more feasible that he'd see it being thrown from upstairs if he was lurking in the garden.'

Ian rounded on him. 'I wasn't *lurking* anywhere.'

'Think about this, Ian,' said Hugh. 'Think carefully. You've got what looks like a murder weapon in your desk and no explanation of where you were when White was killed. No one would blame you if you did it. We all know how much you're struggling with this place; perhaps you were worried the tourists would stop coming altogether once he'd finished at the lighthouse. But this will go better for you if you come clean.'

Ian took a deep breath. 'I'm telling you, I was in the office.'

Hugh nodded. 'So I suppose when you were sitting in your office, with the window open to let in a pleasant December breeze, and you saw this rock being thrown into the garden, you went out of the back door to fetch it?'

'Obviously.'

'Then you'll have passed Nigel. He was smoking by the back door for the whole half-hour. He'll have seen you coming and going. If this is true.'

Ian's shoulders sank.

'Do you want to know what I think?' Hugh continued. 'I think that for some reason, you'd slipped out of your office window into the garden. While you were out there, you saw this rock being thrown from upstairs and you went to pick it up. You climbed back inside, saw in the light what it was and you panicked. None of us knew yet that White was dead, but you could guess something terrible had happened.

245

'You hid the rock in your desk. And somewhere along the way, you injured your hand.' He leaned in close. 'The question is how. What were you doing out there that meant you cut yourself?'

It was at that moment that Martha Finn stepped into the library, followed by Edward. She looked from the desperate expression on Ian's face to Hugh, and then to the bloody rock in Justin's hand.

'I think I can explain.'

30

After Theo had sent Justin away, Jack followed Claire back into the lounge without a word. He trudged to the far side of the room, settled himself in the same tartan armchair that a few minutes earlier he'd vacated, and began once again to gaze, wide-eyed, towards the bay window.

It was a curious sight. In all the years Jack had been his drama teacher at Hamlet High School, and later his cast mate in the Hamlet Players, Theo had never seen him sit so still. Nor heard him go so long without speaking. Whatever he'd been doing during the interval, it had taken a toll.

He turned to Claire. 'Where did you go? While I was speaking to Justin.'

'I just waited in the hallway.'

'And Jack?'

She gave a little shrug. 'He's had a lot of champagne. He needed the loo.' She leaned forward, dropping her voice to a whisper. 'He was in there a few minutes. I think he might have been doing his hair.'

Theo wasn't surprised. He knew that Jack made a point of

always carrying a comb in his pocket. It was a piece of advice he'd tried several times to bestow on the Hamlet Players, saying it was tricks like these that they would need to make it in the world of theatre. So far, it was a habit Theo hadn't taken up. Instead, he'd focused on the advice given to him by the various other members of the group. Invest in some decent head shots. Learn how to take direction. Record lines on your phone, so you always have someone to rehearse with.

Taking his glass from the coffee table, he tipped back the small amount of remaining champagne and rose from the sofa.

'What are you doing?' asked Claire.

'I need to speak to him.'

'He doesn't seem in any mood for talking.'

Theo looked towards Jack. She was right, of course. He seemed far from hospitable. But he had to try. Since speaking to Lily in the hallway, he had been silently nursing a theory. One which he had decided he was now ready to test.

Claire took his wrist. 'Please, Theo. I really think you ought to—'

'I need to speak to him. You can come with me if it makes you feel better. But please don't try to stop me.'

He spoke more harshly than he'd meant, but it had the required effect. For a moment, Claire hesitated. Then she slackened her grip on his wrist and stood up.

Together they crossed the room, Theo seating himself in the

armchair opposite Jack, while Claire took one beside him. He looked up as they approached, gave them a little frown, then returned his gaze to the window.

Once he was settled, Theo took a deep breath. He was keenly aware of Claire watching him, waiting nervously. 'Jack,' he said, as firmly as he could manage. 'There's something I need to ask you. Something important.'

'At your leisure, dear boy.'

'Where were you during the interval?'

Jack's eyes narrowed slightly. 'The interval?'

Theo nodded, letting the question hang in the air. Behind him, the grandfather clock was ticking softly.

'I told you at the time. I was going for a cigarette with Nigel.'

'I know. But that wasn't true, was it?'

Jack's eyes narrowed even further.

'Claire went to find a drink for Will,' Theo explained. 'Something to steady his nerves before he went back into the restaurant. She saw Nigel smoking at the back door, but says there was no sign of you.'

A puzzled expression lingered on Jack's face. 'I might have stepped away for a moment to visit the loo. But I assure you, I was otherwise there the entire time.'

Unconvinced, Theo said nothing.

'For pity's sake,' Jack said irritably. 'What are you asking, exactly? If I went upstairs and killed Damien White?'

Theo took another deep breath, bracing himself. 'Were you with Sylvia Cobb?'

For the first time in all the years Theo had known him, Jack looked genuinely stunned. He didn't answer the question. But then he didn't need to. The truth was written plainly across his face.

'I was speaking earlier to Lily White,' Theo continued. 'She says that Sylvia won't tell anyone what she was doing during the interval. Only that she was upstairs.' He paused, dodging a nervous look from Claire as he prepared for the accusation that he was about to make. 'She's the woman you've been seeing, isn't she?'

Jack didn't move. His mouth hung open, eyes wide with surprise. Then he pursed his lips, breathing heavily like a bull about to charge, before ultimately giving a long sigh.

'Not any more. You're right, we spent the interval together. But not in the way you might think.' His eyes dropped down to his lap. 'She broke things off. Nigel's grown a spine and resigned the project on the lighthouse, so she's giving him another chance.'

He shook his head. 'I know what you're thinking. Both of you. I can see it in your faces. You think it was just an affair. Something cheap and dirty. But it was more than that. We had a connection – a *real* connection. And we were going to do so much. We were going to visit London together. Edinburgh. Perhaps even New York. But what's she chosen instead? With *him*? A life of mundanity.'

Theo wasn't sure whether to feel sympathetic or repulsed. He thought of Nigel, his wife meeting Jack behind his back, and quickly made up his mind.

'How long's this been going on?' he asked.

250

'A few months. Since Nigel's work on the lighthouse began to go south.'

'So she's only going back to him because the business is improving? Because he can provide again?'

Jack scoffed. 'Have you *met* Nigel Cobb? A provider is all he is. All he'll ever be. He doesn't excite Sylvia. Not in the way that I do.'

Theo grimaced, making no effort to hide his distaste. 'Are you going to come clean?'

'Of course. When that police officer gets round to me, I'll tell her. I'm sure you won't be the only one wondering where I was. Better she knows the truth than suspects I had anything to do with Mr White.'

'That's not what I meant. Are you going to tell *Nigel*?'

Jack snorted, an unpleasant smile flickering across his face. 'Sometimes I forget just how young you are.'

'You don't think he deserves to know?'

'I hardly think it matters. If Sylvia's decided she wants to patch things up, letting him know isn't going to help.'

'He might feel differently.'

'Theo,' said Claire gently. 'I don't agree with what Jack's done. Not in the least. But he's right. It's Sylvia's marriage. It's for her to work out.'

Jack nodded curtly. 'There you are.'

'But—'

'But nothing. I'll tell the police, but nobody else is going to know. All *you* need to know is that Sylvia and I spent the interval talking things out in one of the guestrooms. We had nothing to do with Damien White.' He rose abruptly to his feet. 'Now, if you'll excuse me, dear boy, I'm going to see if Carl will be so kind as to pour me a fresh glass of champagne.'

He strode across the lounge and swept into the hallway, slamming the door behind him as he went.

31

The fire had died while they'd been in the library, causing Lily to shiver as the group returned to the restaurant. Hugh tossed a log into the hearth, the embers rekindling slightly, while Gwen drew up a chair for Martha.

'Mrs Finn,' said PC Fay. 'I insist that we speak in private.'

'I'd like to do it here,' Martha replied. 'It's right they all know.'

Lily saw Fay grimace. It was the third time she'd asked, and the third she had been refused. She seemed to relent, though, positioning a chair of her own so that she and Martha were facing one another. Edward fetched one too, seating himself beside his wife.

The others had formed something of an audience, Will, Justin, the Cobbs and the Holloways all seated at the table. Ian loitered by the bay window, pacing a little and fidgeting nervously with his injured hand.

Lily, however, hovered by the sideboard. She wasn't prepared to sit calmly with them at the table, but there was also an advantage to the spot she'd chosen. From where she stood, she was looking straight over Fay's shoulder. Whatever it was that Martha had to confess, she wanted a clear line of sight.

'Did you play any part in murdering Damien White?' asked Fay.

'Heavens, no.'

'Did Mr Davies?'

'No.'

'But you know where he was when Mr White was killed.'

Martha shot a glance at Ian. Then she turned to Edward, sitting beside her. He was looking at her intently, his concern written plainly across his face. She drew a deep breath.

'Ian was breaking into our shop. Just as he's done twice already.'

At the table, Lily saw Sylvia raise a gloved hand to her mouth. Even Justin, who'd been furiously taking notes on his phone, paused to look up.

Fay was the only one who seemed unaffected. It looked to Lily as if she'd barely even flinched.

'How do you know this?'

Martha didn't reply at first. Her eyes were now fixed on the constable, as Edward gawped at her from the neighbouring seat. When she spoke again, the defiance seemed to be slipping from her voice.

'Because I asked him to.'

This proved too much for Edward. He stood and moved to the bay window, where he dropped into an armchair and buried his face in his hands. Gwen hurried over to him and put an arm around his shoulders.

'That's how he was able to access your safe this evening,' said

Fay, barely noticing Edward's distress. 'You'd given him the combination.'

Martha nodded.

'So you knew all along.' It was Nigel who spoke this time, his hands bunched into fists on the table. 'You knew it wasn't one of my boys. But all these months, you've let me take the blame.'

'I never meant to—'

'Do you have any idea what this has done? The damage to my business? My reputation?'

'Mr Cobb,' said Fay. 'If you could please calm yourself—'

'Calm myself?' Nigel jabbed a finger at Martha. 'This has nearly ruined me. And you, Ian. You could have stopped this. You could have said something—'

'Mr Cobb,' Fay snapped. 'Calm yourself or I'll remove you.'

With what looked to Lily like a tremendous effort, Nigel managed to restrain himself. Sylvia put a hand on his arm.

'I'm sorry, Nigel,' said Martha. 'Truly I am. I never thought you'd be blamed. And I certainly never meant for you to be.'

'Then what *did* you mean to happen?'

She swallowed, her resolve failing.

'Mrs Finn,' said Fay. 'I can't allow us to speak in this way. I'm going to insist that we continue in private.'

'No,' Martha protested. 'I won't speak to you elsewhere. I need them to hear. I need *Edward* to hear.' She looked towards the far corner of the room, where her husband still held his head in his hands.

'I'd been wanting to do something for a while,' she continued. 'Not this, necessarily. But something. I'd come to the hotel to

255

deliver some shortbread biscuits that Ian had ordered for the guestrooms when I overheard him on the telephone. He sounded so upset, and when I asked if everything was all right, he broke down. He told me all about his money troubles. What a mistake buying Hamlet Hall had been. How trapped he felt.

'The idea didn't occur to me immediately. It was a few days later; one evening, actually, when I was lying in bed.'

'You asked him to break into your shop,' said Fay.

'I did. I told him what I wanted and said that if he helped me, I'd make sure there was some money he could take. I knew it wouldn't be enough to solve his problems, but I couldn't do it by myself, and . . . Well, even if what I could give him only helped a little, I was sure he wouldn't turn it down.'

Even with her confidence dwindling, it seemed to Lily that there was no remorse in Martha's voice. She might well be frightened, but she believed in what she'd done.

It occurred to Lily that her dad would have been impressed.

'I thought tonight would finally be the one,' she continued. 'It was perfect. We were here, so the shop was empty, and Edward was so worried about another break-in that he'd moved everything into the safe. All Ian had to do was find a convenient time to slip away.'

'Is that when you cut your hand?' asked Gwen.

Ian nodded sheepishly. 'Martha gave me a key to the front door. But it needed to look convincing. So I broke the window.' He looked down at his feet. 'I was careless; in such a hurry to get back that I slipped and cut myself on the glass.'

'That's what you were doing in the garden,' said Lily. 'When you saw the rock being thrown from upstairs.'

Ian nodded again. 'I'd sneaked out through my office window. Less chance of being seen. But when I came back, Nigel was smoking by the door. I couldn't risk him spotting me as I climbed into the office, so I waited until he'd gone. While I was out there, something was thrown into the garden from upstairs. After Nigel had left, I went to see what it was. I brought it inside, and saw . . .'

He tailed off, but Lily knew exactly how that sentence ended. He saw that it was covered with her dad's blood.

'I panicked,' he explained. 'I didn't know about Mr White, but something terrible had obviously happened. And now it had my fingerprints on it. Perhaps even some of my blood. I didn't know what to do, so I hid it, thinking I'd deal with it later.'

'Could you see who'd thrown it?' asked Hugh.

Ian shook his head. 'I was pressed up against the wall, so that Nigel wouldn't spot me. All I could see was an upstairs window opening and something being flung out.'

'You should have told me this,' said Fay. 'You should have shared it the moment I arrived.'

'I wanted to. But I had no way of explaining myself – how I'd found it or managed to get my blood on it – without admitting where I'd been.' His voice began to quiver. 'I'm sorry, Edward. I'll return the money. Pay for the damage. I just . . . I needed it so desperately. And when Martha told me how much she wanted to leave . . . When she came to me with this idea, I couldn't turn it down.'

Edward looked to Martha. 'You really want to leave?'

'I've wanted to for so long.'

'And where would we go?'

'I don't know. Somewhere else. *Anywhere* else, so long as I don't have to look at that lighthouse every morning. That's what I want, Edward. To never see it again. But you just won't part with this place. Even after all the heartbreak it's caused us, you only ever see the same Hamlet Wick you loved as a boy. That's why I've done this. Why I've lied to you. I thought that if I could make you believe this place was something else – something ugly – you'd change your mind. We could finally leave.'

Her voice broke, tears forming in the corners of her eyes.

For a long while, nobody spoke. Nobody even moved. Then Lily saw Edward's face soften. He rose from the armchair, moved to the fireplace and put his arm gently around Martha's shoulders.

'I don't understand,' she said, taking advantage of the silence. 'Why would you want to leave so desperately? Is what my dad's been doing to the lighthouse really so terrible?'

An uncomfortable hush descended.

'Lily,' said Gwen. 'There's something you need to—'

'Gwen!' Hugh hissed at her from the table.

'It's all right, Hugh,' said Martha. She was dabbing the tears from her cheeks, her voice now steadier. 'It doesn't seem right she be the only one who doesn't know.' She looked Lily in the eye. 'This isn't to do with your father. It goes back quite a bit further than that. This is to do with Teddy.'

She turned to Edward, but he couldn't meet her gaze. His head was bowed, tears in his own eyes now. She squeezed his hand and drew a deep breath. 'Teddy was our boy,' she said. 'He was our son.'

Lily felt as if her feet had been kicked from beneath her. She looked around, but nobody came forward this time. Not even Gwen could look at her.

Martha's eyes began once again to well with tears. 'I can't do it any more, Edward. I can't look at that lighthouse every day and not know what he was doing up there. I can't keep seeing his room and thinking about all the things he never did; how the two of you never built the boat you'd always talked about, how he never had the chance to deliver that card . . . I have to leave. *We* have to leave.'

Edward pulled her close. 'We will,' he said. 'We'll go. I promise.'

Lily looked in turn at each of the others. Of course, they all knew this already. Gwen was crying now too, Hugh trying to look anywhere other than at the Finns.

'Card?' she said.

Hugh looked at her quizzically.

'What card?'

He shrugged, and she turned to look at the Finns.

Edward handed Martha a handkerchief from the pocket of his jacket. She dabbed at her eyes, then said quietly, 'We never told anyone about that.'

Lily tried to press further, but Fay stepped in first.

'Was it significant?'

Martha glared at her. 'There was nothing *insignificant* about my boy.'

'I only meant, Mrs Finn, do you think it might support some explanation as to why he'd climbed the lighthouse?'

Edward took Martha's hand and gave it a squeeze. Her expression was still one of malice – not that Fay looked at all deterred – but the gesture seemed to soothe her enough that she could at least answer the question.

'I wouldn't have thought so,' she said. 'But it's always stayed with me. It was a whole year after he died before I could go into his room. And another after that before I could bring myself to start taking away his things. We were clearing out the wardrobe when I found it. Hidden away under a jumper.'

'Who was it addressed to?' asked Fay.

'Nobody. He hadn't written it yet. But it was clear what he meant to do with it. A great big heart on the front, and a pink envelope.' Martha's eyes softened and she managed a sad smile. 'It would have been someone from school, I suppose, although I've no idea who. Either way, Teddy must have had a crush.'

Before Fay could press her any further, the door was flung open and Jack barged into the restaurant. He was panting, his eyes wide.

'It's Carl,' he said. 'In the kitchen. He's dead.'

One o'clock

32

Hugh was the first to react. Before anyone could stop him he bolted towards the door, pushing past Jack into the hallway. Gwen called after him, but he was already gone. Will heard his footsteps on the tiles as he made for the kitchen, PC Fay hurrying to catch him.

'Mr Holloway,' she cried, shoving Jack aside. 'Mr Holloway!'

Justin was next, and then Lily, neither of them wasting any time in rushing to investigate.

It all happened so quickly that Will was only vaguely aware of what was going on. As he went with the remaining guests to the foot of the staircase, and gazed down the little corridor towards the kitchen, a numbness overcame him. He saw Fay standing in the doorway, doing her best to keep Lily and Justin at bay. Hugh was behind her, crouching down on the floor. He was saying Carl's name over and over, begging him to get up.

Gwen clutched his arm. 'Come away,' she said. 'Please, Will. Come back to the restaurant. We shouldn't see this.'

To Will's right, the door to the lounge opened and Theo appeared, his brow creasing into a frown.

'What's happening?'

'It's Carl,' said Nigel. 'He's . . . Jack says he's dead.'

Before he could say any more, Fay managed to clear Justin and Lily from the corridor, ushering them back into the hallway.

'Mr Bloom,' she said, her voice like iron. 'Take Mr Marshall and go back into the lounge. Everyone else, return to the restaurant.'

Pale-faced, Jack allowed Theo to usher him away, and Gwen steered Will towards the restaurant. All around him, he caught fleeting snippets of frantic conversation. He heard Hugh still urging his friend to get up, while Justin argued with P C Fay that he should be allowed to see the body. He caught Martha and Edward discussing who would possibly want to hurt Carl, Nigel and Sylvia asking each other when he was last seen.

He didn't engage. He couldn't bring himself to. Guided by Gwen into a chair at the table, he fetched the inhaler from his jacket pocket and took a deep breath. Then he just sat staring into space.

Another murder. Another life snuffed out at the event he had masterminded.

Could Hugh be right? Could all of this be his fault? If it weren't for him, would Carl still be alive? Would Damien White?

He felt himself slipping. Felt the all-too-familiar sensation of the shale under his feet, the breeze upon his skin and the sound of seagulls cawing. He didn't fight it this time. He didn't have the strength to. He allowed the memory to pull him under, and watched in his mind's eye as the gulls took off one by one, revealing the sodden body of Rory Holloway.

By the time Fay and Hugh joined them, Will had lost all grasp of time. He glanced up at them, heart pounding.

'Well?' Sylvia demanded. 'What's happened? An accident, surely?'

Hugh was the first to reply. 'He's been shot.'

Sylvia paled at the news, although Fay seemed to have no interest in offering words of comfort.

'Mr Davies,' she said, 'are there any firearms on the premises?'

Ian looked mortified. 'Obviously not.'

'Then a weapon has been brought into the hotel. Everyone will be searched. The actors, too.'

'But this is ridiculous,' Sylvia protested. 'Nobody here has a gun. I don't even know anyone who does!'

'I do.'

Will turned, following the sound of Lily's voice.

'You've brought a firearm into the hotel?' Fay asked her.

'Not me. My dad.'

Hugh fixed her with a look so hateful it could have shattered marble. Lily didn't seem to see it, though. It looked to Will as if she was trying very deliberately to avoid the other guests, her eyes fixed firmly on Fay.

'Do you know where he kept it?' the constable asked.

'Yes.'

'Show me, please.'

Without a word, Lily crossed the room and led her into the hallway. With every step, Hugh followed them. Then, barely a second after the door had closed, he snatched a champagne flute from the table and hurled it into the fireplace. The ensuing crash rang from the walls, causing Will to jump in his seat and sending shards of broken glass ricocheting onto the wooden floor.

Breathing hard, Hugh gripped the mantelpiece with both hands. 'Of course it would be them,' he hissed. 'Of course it would.'

Slowly, Gwen approached and laid a hand on his back. 'You heard Lily,' she said gently. 'If there is a gun, it's Damien's.'

'You're defending *her* now too?'

'You can't think she has anything to do with this?'

'Why not?' Hugh jabbed a finger at Will. 'I suppose you think we shouldn't suspect him, either?'

'I hardly think Will would—'

'Wouldn't he? He's the one who's brought us all here. *He*'s the one who's made a game out of Rory's death. How do we know he isn't responsible for this, too? How can we be sure this wasn't part of his plan from the beginning?'

'Hugh!'

At the sound of Gwen's raised voice, Hugh seemed finally to stop. He took a deep breath, and when he spoke again his own voice was low and deep, like that of a wounded animal.

'Well,' he muttered. 'Whoever's responsible, it seems to me we're playing a different game now. Killing White is one thing. He was an outsider. A bastard who caused nothing but hurt and deserved to die.'

'Stop,' Gwen breathed. 'Please stop this—'

'I'm not ashamed of it,' he snapped. 'If any of you had told

266

me you'd killed him, I'd have shaken you by the hand. But Carl was decent. More than that, he was one of us.' He weighed up each of the guests in turn. 'Whoever's done this – whatever their reasoning – they've crossed a line. They've shown that they aren't afraid to murder one of our own.' He shook his head. 'We're all in the firing line now.'

33

While she was determined not to show it, as Lily went with PC Fay to the Range Rover she was silently beginning to panic.

She'd had to mention the gun. In the interest of self-preservation, if nothing else. She couldn't imagine how any of the guests would even know it existed, but a man had been shot. If it came out that a gun had been in her dad's glovebox – one which she had known was there but had failed to mention – there'd be no explaining herself.

'You have your own key?' Fay asked her.

'We all do. It's the family car.'

Fay raised an eyebrow at the idea of a gleaming white Range Rover being used as a family runaround, but she didn't pass comment. Instead, she took Lily's key, opened the passenger-side door and popped the glovebox.

In a strange sort of way, Lily was beginning to think her dad would have approved of this police officer. It first occurred to her during Martha Finn's confession. From where Lily stood, Fay had been cold. Clinical. To look at her now, she might just as easily have been searching for a handkerchief as a murder weapon.

She tucked her hands under her arms. A sharp breeze was rolling in from the sea, the waves hissing against the shore. She looked towards the water, but it was a dark canvas. Still, she could just about make out the shale beach.

She supposed that was where the rock would have come from.

For Rory and Teddy.

If whoever left that note in the library had been sincere – if her dad really had been murdered in Rory's name – they must feel it was pretty poetic to have killed him not only in the same way, but with a stone from the same beach.

She turned away, her gaze settling on the little shop, and then, high on the hill behind it, the lighthouse. She thought of Martha Finn, living in its shadow. Gazing up at it, day after day, never knowing why her son had climbed it. Never understanding why he'd needed to die.

She felt herself overcome by a sudden sense of frustration. How could one little village at the bottom of the world be the site of so much misery? And what had compelled her dad to return here? By all accounts, the lighthouse had been left to rot for twenty-five years. Why, when it should so rightly have been given over as Gwen's memorial for Teddy, had he decided he now wanted it?

More than ever, she wished she'd never agreed to visit Hamlet Wick. Wished she could clear her memory of all the pain her dad had wrought. She couldn't even bring herself to grieve for him. She tried to summon the fury that had burned inside her when she found his body, but it was no use. As she stared at the lighthouse, it was shame that caused her heart to pound.

Fay emerged from the Range Rover. 'There's no gun here, Miss White. Are you sure you saw it?'

Lily felt her heart sink. 'I know I did. It was definitely there when we parked up.'

Fay locked the car and instructed Lily to follow her back into Hamlet Hall. Together, they climbed the oak staircase, turning right at the top and making for a room in the back corner of the hotel.

Lily didn't go inside straight away. Instead, she hovered in the doorway and looked back the way they'd come, towards the far end of the corridor. There was nothing to see, of course. Even if his door had been open, she wouldn't glimpse him from this angle.

With a deep breath to steady her nerves, she stepped into the room. Two chairs faced each other, Fay motioning for her to take one.

'Where would Mr White keep his own key to the Range Rover?'

Lily thought for a moment. 'His jeans. Front-left pocket.'

Instructing her to remain where she was, Fay slipped back onto the landing, leaving her alone. Lily was grateful. It gave her a moment to steel herself. The gun might be missing, but *she* hadn't killed the chef. As increasingly repulsive as it was becoming, she had to approach this the way her dad would have done. She had to control the room.

She took several deep breaths, trying hard to slow her thumping heart. Her palms were clammy, a sense of nausea building in her stomach. She screwed her eyes shut, concentrating hard on the forced rhythm of her own breathing. She would not allow this to get the better of her. Not this place, nor these people. Shock, grief . . . There would be time for all of that later. Right now, she had a job to do. She had to survive. But more than that, whatever game was being played in Hamlet Hall, she had to win.

When Fay returned, she sat a little straighter, adopting the sternest expression she could muster.

'Well?' she asked.

Fay didn't reply. Instead, she slipped a Dictaphone from her pocket and placed it on the desk. 'Miss White,' she said, settling into the other seat. 'Why does your father keep a gun in his glovebox?'

Lily glanced at the Dictaphone, the little wheels rolling behind the plastic window. 'He was mugged. In Italy. He keeps it as a means of protecting himself if something similar happens again. But he's never used it. I've never even seen him hold it.'

'Does he have a licence for it?'

'I doubt it.'

Fay took out a pad and jotted down a note. 'You're sure you saw it today?'

'As we were parking up. Dad fetched a phone charger from the glovebox.'

'Could you describe it?'

'It's a gun. I'm hardly an expert.'

Fay cocked an eyebrow, prompting Lily to sigh.

'It's a handgun. Black. Quite small, I guess.'

'And by telling me about this weapon, you're suggesting someone took it from the car in order to murder Carl Gifford?'

271

Lily looked down at the Dictaphone again, her confidence dwindling at the thought of this conversation being recorded – being listened to over and over. 'The gun was there when we arrived. Now it's gone and someone's been shot.'

'Could Mr White not have removed it? Perhaps he brought it into the hotel when you arrived?'

'Well, if he did, I didn't see him. And I don't know how he could fetch it without me noticing. He was the first out of the car when we parked up, and he didn't take it then.'

Fay nodded. 'Then the question, if we're agreed Carl Gifford has been murdered with your father's gun, is how it's been taken from the car. The doors haven't been forced, nor the windows broken.' She paused. 'How many keys are there?'

'Three,' said Lily. 'His, mine and Mum's.'

'Your mother is at home in London?'

'That's right.'

Fay looked at the Dictaphone. 'I've inspected Mr White's body and confirmed that his key is in the pocket of his jeans. The door to his room is locked and I, according to Ian Davies, am carrying the only key.' She turned back to Lily. 'I saw you fetch your own key out of your pocket just a few minutes ago. Has it been there all evening?'

'Yes.'

'Is there any point at which it could have been taken?'

'And returned to my pocket?'

Fay raised an eyebrow.

'No,' said Lily.

'You're sure?'

'You tell me. I've worn this hoody since we arrived, and the

272

pockets are zip-up. How would anyone take the key and then put it back again without me noticing?'

'So one of the guests has somehow taken Mr White's key? Then, after murdering Carl Gifford, they put it back. All while the door to his room has, itself, been locked?'

Lily spread her hands.

'Did Mr White mention it to the other guests?'

'No.'

'Might anyone have already known it was there?'

'How should I know?'

Fay leaned forward in her seat. 'Miss White. I understand you've suffered a terrible loss this evening. You're a long way from home, surrounded by strangers who have been less than accommodating—'

'Accommodating?' Lily's voice rose. 'One of those *strangers* has killed my dad!'

'But I must ask' – there was suddenly steel in Fay's voice – 'that you give this a little more thought. Because until you can provide any evidence that one of the other guests has stolen your father's gun – or, for that matter, that any of them even knew it existed – it seems considerably more plausible that your own key was used.'

'But my key's been with me.'

Fay said nothing. Silence hung in the air, until Lily realised just what she was suggesting.

'You're asking if I took it.'

'Did you?'

'Obviously not. Why would I?'

'After what's happened to your father, you might want some protection of your own.'

273

Lily glared at her. 'If I took Dad's gun, why would I kill the chef?'

'Perhaps you suspected him of murdering your father.'

'I don't even know him! I've been sitting down there all night with the likes of Hugh and Sylvia. People who seem to *actually* want my dad dead. Why would I suspect Carl?'

A glimmer of uncertainty flickered over PC Fay's face. It lingered for just an instant, her stoic expression returning as quickly as it had left. But it was enough to pique Lily's curiosity.

'Did something happen between them?'

Fay sat back in her seat. 'If you aren't aware, it isn't for me to say.'

'Was Carl involved in what happened to Rory?'

'Miss White, it isn't for me to say.'

Lily took a deep, shuddering breath, her hands bunched into fists as she fought back a rising wave of fear. She would not allow herself to be overwhelmed. Gritting her teeth, she thought of her dad, sprawled on the floor of his room, and imagined what he would do. How he would turn the situation his way.

'Fine,' she said, her voice trembling slightly. 'Sylvia enjoys gossip. And Hugh still seems pretty cut up about his brother. I'm sure one of them will be only too happy to tell me.' She folded her arms, looking Fay in the eye. 'Or you could do it. Save us both some bother.'

Her heart thumped in her ears. She wondered if her dad had ever felt so frightened when he tried to bully a situation into going his way. If he did, he never showed it. Perhaps that was the point. You don't need to be the strongest person in the room. Just the bravest.

Fay grimaced. 'When Rory Holloway was murdered, your father was briefly the prime suspect. Mr Holloway had made no bones about the disagreement they'd had before he left London; how he'd fallen on hard times and Mr White took advantage of his misfortune. By the time he was killed, he must have told half of Hamlet about how much he hated your father.'

'But he had an alibi,' said Lily. 'My mum.'

Fay nodded. 'Your mother told CID he'd been with her in London. Shortly after, fresh accusations were made against Carl Gifford. Accusations that carried considerably more weight.'

'What accusations?'

Fay's nostrils flared. She wasn't enjoying this shift in control. But she couldn't stop now. Lily knew just enough that she could cause real trouble with the others. She would have to finish this story herself.

'Rory Holloway was reportedly seen with Mr Gifford's girl-friend on the beach, here in Hamlet Wick. First, they were seen kissing, then arguing. Word got back to Mr Gifford, who found Mr Holloway drinking in a nearby pub that same afternoon and very publicly assaulted him.'

'And that was enough for Carl to be suspected of murdering him? A fight in a pub?'

Fay looked her in the eye. 'The following morning, Rory Holloway's body was found on the beach.' She didn't seem the type, to Lily, for dramatics. Even so, she paused, as if for effect. 'Mr Gifford was taken into custody,' she continued. 'But the autopsy placed Rory Holloway's death at around midnight, when multiple eyewitnesses had seen Mr Gifford drowning his sorrows at a lock-in, in a pub on the opposite side of Hamlet.'

'Could the girlfriend have been involved?'

'She was discounted entirely. She'd been at work when the sighting took place, and a search of Rory Holloway's apartment also gave us a blonde hair. She provided a sample of her own, and a DNA test confirmed it wasn't a match. Whoever Mr Holloway had been seen with fit a very similar description – blonde hair, pale complexion. But she was never identified and she never came forward.'

Lily paused to take it all in. 'I suppose the folks here think none of this should have been necessary. They'd probably say you should have locked up my dad and been done with it.' She frowned. 'That's why you think I'd accuse Carl of killing my dad? Why I'd want to kill *him*?'

Fay gave a little shrug. 'First, your father is murdered. Then Carl Gifford. Now a gun which only you could feasibly have access to is missing. If you'd already known about Mr Gifford's involvement in Rory Holloway's case, it would be remiss of me not to ask.'

Lily said nothing. There was something threatening in Fay's tone. She wasn't in the clear yet. She was still a suspect.

'Which returns us to the question of who else could have killed Carl Gifford,' she continued. 'The last confirmed sighting seems to have been when you spoke to him in the hallway, just before eleven o'clock. After that conversation took place, did you see anyone from the restaurant go to the kitchen?'

This knocked Lily off balance. It hadn't occurred to her that she and Theo might have been the last people to see Carl alive. That his final words might very well have been spoken to her.

She cleared her throat, shaking herself back into focus. 'People have been in and out of that restaurant all night.'

'What about Mr Gifford himself? What exactly did he say to you?'

'Not much. He asked where you were. We told him you were interviewing Ian and Will, so he went back to the kitchen.'

'He didn't say anything else?'

Lily shook her head, before being struck by a sudden thought. 'Wait,' she said. 'Wait, he was holding something. It looked like a single serving of champagne. The kind you get on a plane.'

Fay paused. 'I've seen the champagne that was served with dinner. There were full-sized bottles in the kitchen. Several of them.' She frowned. 'Did anyone say anything to suggest they'd asked for a different kind to the rest of the group? Something that would require a smaller bottle, just for them?'

'Not that I heard.'

Fay nodded. 'There's an EpiPen in your father's room. I presume he had an allergy of some kind.'

'He couldn't eat nuts. I told Ian about it when I made the booking.'

'Could anyone at the table have known about it?'

'I don't know. He always tries—' Lily stopped, catching herself. 'Always *tried* to keep it a secret. Like he was embarrassed by it.'

Fay clasped her hands. 'I think it's possible someone at that table knew. I think the bottle Carl Gifford meant to show me may have been spiked, and that he'd been told to serve it to your father.'

'But what would be the point? His allergy was never severe enough that it would have killed him. And even if it had been, his EpiPen was just upstairs.' She stopped, the realisation dawning on her. 'You think it was to get him away from the table?'

Fay leaned forward in her seat. 'If I'm correct, then whoever supplied that bottle knew Mr White would need to leave the table to fetch his EpiPen. I'd go so far as to say they knew he would go upstairs and close himself in his room in order to use it without being seen. In short, they knew it would allow them to catch him alone.'

'And Carl . . . If this is true, they killed him because . . .'

'Because he'd started to suspect it too. Because it looked like he wanted to show me the bottle and tell me who'd given it to him. Carl Gifford was killed because he knew who'd murdered your father.'

Lily's resolve immediately vanished. 'But that means it's my fault Carl's dead. I told the others that he was looking for you. I even told them he was carrying a bottle.'

Fay's expression softened slightly. But if Lily expected words of comfort, she was to be quickly disappointed.

'This would have taken preparation,' she said. 'Of the people in Hamlet Hall right now, who could have known that you were coming here tonight?'

'Nobody. I booked the rooms myself and I didn't give Dad's name. Just said I needed one for him and another for me.'

'But surely you gave your surname.'

Lily shook her head. 'I only gave my first name. I didn't know the full extent of it, but I knew Dad had something of a reputation. I thought if I gave the name White, word might get around.'

Fay leaned back in her seat again, her lips pursed. 'It didn't seem strange to you that Mr Davies didn't insist on a surname?'

'I don't know. I guess it seemed odd. But having seen this place . . . I get it now. Ian was hardly going to turn down the business.'

Fay took a deep breath. 'Miss White,' she said at last. 'I need to ask you again. Did you take the gun?'

Lily glared at her. 'I've already told you I didn't. Why ask me again?'

'Because our killer is someone who knew your father was coming to Hamlet Hall, who was aware of his allergy and who not only knew of the existence of his gun, but also had the means to retrieve it from the car.

'While we've been in this room, you've told me that you were the one who booked the two of you into Hamlet Hall, taking care to keep his identity concealed. You've told me that he keeps his allergy a secret and you've told me not only that he didn't mention his gun to anyone in the restaurant, but that you saw it in the glovebox earlier today and have been carrying a key to his vehicle all evening.'

Lily gawped, wondering if, somehow, she had misheard. When Fay made no effort to correct herself, though, and Lily realised that she had indeed understood her correctly, she found herself overcome with a white-hot fury.

'So you're not only asking if I killed Carl. You're asking if I killed my dad, too?'

'I'm sure you understand why I'd need to.' She looked Lily in the eye. 'Miss White, did you kill your father this evening?'

For a long while, they simply stared at each other. When Lily replied, it came as a snarl, low and guttural, as primal as any sound she had ever made.

'*I haven't killed my fucking dad.*'

'Then I think we're finished,' said Fay. 'But before you leave this room, it's imperative you understand how dangerous this situation continues to be. If your father's killer has also murdered Carl Gifford, we can be certain they're still inside Hamlet Hall. And if they suspect they're on the cusp of being unmasked, it seems they won't be afraid to act again.'

34

Will took a breath on his inhaler. Then he gave it a shake. It was almost empty.

He thought of his rucksack hanging in Ian's office, and wished he'd let Claire fetch his spare during the interval. He wasn't relishing the thought of asking Hugh if he could go and retrieve it himself.

In the time that P C Fay and Lily had been away, the atmosphere in the restaurant had changed. While the guests had certainly been troubled by the prospect of a killer hiding among them, Will couldn't help wondering how many shared Hugh's opinion that Damien White had deserved to die. Carl's murder, however, was something else entirely. Suddenly, they were looking at each other with fear in their eyes. They weren't just questioning who was responsible. They were wondering who might be next.

He was staring at the surface of the table when the chair beside him was drawn and Justin sat himself down. Clasping his hands, he looked Will in the eye, a kindly expression on his face.

'How are you holding up?' he asked quietly. Before Will could answer, he leaned in close and dropped his voice even further. 'I know you didn't do it.'

'You believe me?'

'I do. Or at least, I know you can't have killed Carl. Someone's had eyes on you the whole time. But the others . . .' He hissed through his teeth. 'They'll take more convincing.'

Will swept a glance around the restaurant, looking from face to face. Justin was right, of course. He'd seen it already in the hateful glares that Ian and Hugh were casting him. The fleeting, fearful glances from Edward and Martha Finn. Even the quizzical looks from Nigel and Sylvia, like he was a horrible exhibit in a museum.

He saw it, plain as day. They thought it was him.

His gaze settled the longest on Hugh. Gwen had just about managed to calm him down, but he still looked as though he was standing on a knife edge. One nudge in either direction and he'd topple. Will supposed he understood. Rory had been his brother, Carl his friend. If anyone was going to be the most badly wounded, it would be him.

Reaching inside his jacket, Justin slipped out his phone and placed it carefully on the table. 'Talk to me,' he said. 'Tell me why you've done it.'

'You just said you believed me.'

'I believe you didn't kill Carl. Probably not Damien White either. But Will . . .' He shook his head. 'It's so clear what you were trying to do tonight. That story of yours. Lord . . .'

'Ashcombe.'

'Lord Ashcombe. He *is* Rory Holloway, isn't he?'

Will didn't answer.

'Look,' Justin pressed. 'Even if the police work out who's murdered Carl and Mr White, the others will still talk about what you've set up here. The story. That note in the library – "For Rory and Teddy".'

'That wasn't my note!' Will's voice rose slightly, prompting Justin to throw up a hand to silence him.

'All right,' he said gently. 'All right, it wasn't your note. But what were you trying to achieve? Why don't you just tell me that? I can run it in the paper. It'll be your chance to explain. Because when tonight's through, and everything that's happened gets out, it won't just be the people in this room asking why you did it. It'll be everyone.'

'But Hamlet—'

'I'm not talking about Hamlet. Someone like Damien White . . . His murder will make the national papers. Perhaps even TV. This time tomorrow, there'll be thousands of people – up and down the country – all asking why you've set this up.' He leaned in a little closer. 'Were you trying to solve it? Is that what tonight was about? The letter you'd given White said he'd murdered Lord Ashcombe. Were you saying he'd murdered Rory, too?'

'I've told you,' Will replied, his voice quivering. 'I've told you all. I didn't know Mr White was coming. I had no idea who would get that envelope.'

'OK.' Justin paused, apparently reconsidering his approach. 'Perhaps you were trying to commemorate it, then? I can't imagine what it must have been like, finding Rory on the beach. Were you trying to relive it, somehow? To—'

283

From across the room there came the sound of a chair scraping against the floor.

'I'm going for a cigarette,' Sylvia declared, standing abruptly to her feet.

Nigel squinted at her. 'The police said that we were to stay—'

'I don't care,' she snapped. 'I need a cigarette.'

'Please, Sylvia . . .' Gwen flashed her a desperate look. 'At the very least, let someone go with you. We need to stay in pairs. Maybe even groups of three.'

'Why?'

Gwen opened her mouth to reply, but the words didn't seem to come.

'Because there's a killer in here.' Hugh looked around the restaurant, his eyes settling on each of them in turn. 'I'll say it if nobody else will.'

'*Jesus*,' said Sylvia, her voice rising. 'All I want is a cigarette!'

'All right.' Gwen put a hand on her shoulder. 'We'll go together. One cigarette at the back door, then we'll be straight back.'

Will watched them go, Sylvia muttering and grumbling to herself with every step. He turned back to Justin. The young reporter was still wearing a kindly smile, the phone resting in his hand.

For several seconds, Will looked at it. Could Justin be right? Should he be leaping at this chance? An opportunity to explain himself?

His heart thumped, and in his mind he became a child again, running onto the beach with his bucket in his hand. He saw the familiar, shapeless huddle of damp clothes and pale skin, dumped upon the shale. A mop of thick hair, crusted at the back with blood. Rory Holloway's wide, lifeless eyes.

He thought of how that moment had stayed with him ever since; twelve long years, reliving it over and over. He remembered the way his classmates tormented him. Screaming and crying at him in the playground, trying every day to push him over the edge. Then, once they'd eventually lost interest, leaving him so frightened and jittery that he'd tried just to fade into the background, often hoping that he wouldn't be noticed. He thought of all the friends he'd never had, all the things he'd missed out on. He imagined a lifetime of feeling this way, held in the grip of something he wanted simply to forget.

How could he explain? Where would he even begin? He knew how he felt; knew deep in his gut what he had wanted to achieve. But if there were words that would put it in a way that made sense, he didn't seem to possess them.

He looked up from the phone and met Justin's eye. 'I'm sorry,' he said. 'But I can't speak to you about this.'

Immediately, that gentle smile gave way to a scowl.

'Fine,' Justin said briskly. 'Suit yourself. But don't say I didn't try to help you.' He lurched forward, grasping Will's shoulder, and hissed in his ear. 'No one in here believes you, Will. And when the police let us go, no one out there will either.'

35

As she stalked through the hallway, back towards the oak doors, PC Natalie Fay did all she could to maintain the calm, steely front with which she'd just interviewed Lily White.

But inside she was screaming.

What the *fuck* had she been thinking? It had seemed like such a good idea; keeping the scene to herself. And she was getting close, too. Hearing what Will Hooper had done, recreating the death of Rory Holloway . . . He must be involved. And if he hadn't killed Damien White himself, he'd know exactly who had. A little more time and she would get a confession out of him.

But now . . . It was all going wrong. She'd been cocky, waiting far longer than the hour she'd agreed to give herself before calling it in, and now another murder had been committed right under her nose.

She threw open the doors, the cold air enveloping her as suddenly as if she'd plunged into the sea. She could pull this back. If she was convincing, her handler might believe two hours of radio blackout. Just. And if she was lucky – *very* lucky – they might not yet have noticed that she hadn't checked in. Thank God for New Year's Eve.

Closing the door behind her, she took the radio from her jacket and clicked it on. 'PC Natalie Fay, reporting in. Two suspicious deaths confirmed at Hamlet Hall. Immediate assistance required.'

She waited for the response. But the radio was completely silent.

She shook it, trying desperately to fight back a rising wave of panic. 'PC Natalie Fay,' she said again, straining to keep the fear from her voice. 'Two suspicious deaths at Hamlet Hall. *Immediate* assistance required.'

Still there was no response.

'Come on,' she pleaded with the little device. 'Come *on* . . .'

She looked back at Hamlet Hall, the old house looming over her. She'd never been so frightened in her life. Or so far out of her depth.

If she drove back down the Lane, she could pick up some signal in Hamlet. But there was no way she could leave the scene. Damien White was locked in his room, but she couldn't secure the kitchen. If she left Carl's body unattended, CID would crucify her.

What about a landline? There must be one, for Ian to have called her out in the first place. But then how would she explain why she hadn't used it before?

Her mind raced. Perhaps she could say that she hadn't realised her call didn't come through on the radio. Why would she use the landline if she thought help was already coming? But they'd never believe it. Any call she placed would have received

287

an acknowledgement – why would she think it had gone through if she'd had no response?

She stared out at the beach. The wind was so cold she could feel her eyes beginning to water, her breath starting to come in short gasps.

She could wait it out. If they hadn't already, they'd soon notice her silence. If they couldn't get in touch, they'd assume something had happened. Support might be on its way already. But then how would she explain the landline? Ian had called them easily enough. Why hadn't she?

She swore, her breath steaming in front of her as she hissed into the wind. Finally, she turned back towards Hamlet Hall.

She had to use the phone. Two people were dead; one on her watch. Whatever the consequences – whatever it meant for her career – she couldn't wait any longer.

Of course, it would still take time for them to mobilise. She could keep interviewing the guests while she waited for her support to arrive. Gather more evidence. Perhaps, if she squeezed just hard enough, she could even get a confession from Will. If CID arrived to find she had the murderer in custody, she might *just* save herself.

But for now, at least, her time had run out. There was no more waiting to be done. She had to make the call.

36

Theo knew he'd heard her. At the far end of the hallway, smoking a cigarette while she nattered to Gwen Holloway, was Sylvia Cobb.

A grimace was fixed upon her face, but Theo was undeterred. He had to speak with her, telling Claire that he needed the loo in order to slip out into the hallway. He wasn't proud of having lied but it was for the best. If he'd told her where he was actually going, she would only have urged him to stay put in the lounge.

Taking a deep breath, he made his way towards the back of the hall. The two women turned to face him, hearing his footsteps on the tiled floor.

'Gwen,' he said. 'Would it be all right if I spoke to Mrs Cobb for a moment?'

She shuffled uncomfortably. 'I'm not sure, Theo. Hugh's adamant we stay in groups.'

'Please. It's important.'

She looked to Sylvia, who gave a lazy shrug.

'All right,' she said, still wearing a nervous expression. 'But I'll stay out here. I'll stand by the reception desk, give you some privacy.'

Theo thanked her. Then, when she'd backed far enough away that they wouldn't be heard, he turned to Sylvia. For all intents and purposes, she looked to Theo as if she might not have realised he was even there. She stared through the open French doors, taking another drag on her cigarette.

'I'm sorry to bother you, Mrs Cobb—'

'Don't,' she snapped. 'Don't call me that.'

He frowned at her, no idea how he was supposed to respond.

'What's your name?' she asked him.

'Theo.'

'Theo *what*?'

'Bloom.'

She gave a little snort. 'How would you like to be called Cobb, Theo?'

'I can't say I've ever thought about it.'

'Nobody's ever thought about it. Because nobody's ever wanted to be called Cobb.'

Theo swallowed back a lump, his heart thumping in his ears. 'Can I call you Sylvia?'

She grunted in response.

'Then, Sylvia, there's something I need to tell you. Something about Jack.'

This time, she looked at him. Her eyes flicked up and down, taking him in. 'Who's Jack?'

For several seconds, neither of them moved.

'Sylvia,' Theo said quietly. 'I know about the two of you. I know that you're together. *Were* together.'

She said nothing, her eyes narrowing.

'I noticed he was missing during the interval,' Theo continued. 'Lily told us that you were unaccounted for too.'

'Why should that mean anything?'

'It might not. It might just have been a coincidence. But when I asked Jack about it a few minutes ago, he admitted that he'd been with you.'

Sylvia's lips drew back into the most vicious scowl Theo had ever seen.

'I'm sorry,' he said. 'He'd been bragging about seeing a married woman, and I just—'

'Idiot,' she hissed. 'That *fucking* idiot.' She dropped her cigarette onto the tiled floor and crushed it beneath her heel. 'And what is it that you want? To get back at him, I suppose?'

That was exactly what he had wanted. But now he was faced with it, he felt foolish. Could he really use this woman's marriage – however frayed it might be – as a weapon to hurt Jack? For causing him to forget some lines?

No, Theo reminded himself. It was more than that. It was the audition in Bristol. His chance to leave Hamlet Wick and make something of himself. That was what Jack had taken. Justin too. Between them, they'd cost him his future.

'He's told me about you, you know,' said Sylvia. 'He's told me all about how he's mentored you. How much he's taught you. He says it'll make you a star one day.'

Theo restrained a sudden swell of resentment. Before he had

291

a chance, though, to point out what sort of mentor Jack had actually been, she looked away and gazed, wide-eyed, through the French doors.

'I warned him this would happen,' she muttered. 'I told him how furious you'd be if you ever found out what he'd done.'

Theo frowned. What did she mean, *if he ever found out*? A crowd of sixty people had seen him fluff their scene. Was she suggesting it might not have been an accident? That Jack had somehow done it maliciously?

'I told him it was petty,' she continued. 'Warned him you'd be furious if you ever found out he'd sent it. If I'd known *I* was the one you were going to punish for it, I wouldn't have bothered.'

'Sent what?'

She glared at him, her nose wrinkling as if she'd caught an unpleasant aroma. 'That bloody review of Justin's.'

Theo had the distinct feeling of having been punched in the stomach.

'He should never have told me he'd done it,' she wittered on. 'I saw straight through it, of course. I told him he was only doing it because he was jealous. Because he couldn't stand that you were going to land the sort of role he'd never managed.'

'Are you sure?' Theo pressed. 'You're *certain* it was him?'

Sylvia scowled. 'He told me himself. Did you really not know? Honestly, who else would it have been?'

Theo didn't reply. He wanted to deny it. To tell her she was wrong. But he couldn't. Instead, he was cursing himself for being so naive. As Sylvia said, who else?

'Now,' she said sharply, yanking the French doors closed with such force they rattled in their frame. 'You aren't using me as some tool to get back at Jack. Not now Damien White has gone and Nigel can get things back on track with the firm. You can take this to him if you like and the two of you can fight it out to your hearts' content. But you'll do it without involving me. Jack and I are done.'

Without another word, she slipped away. Over his shoulder, Theo heard her heels on the tiles and then the creaking of the restaurant door.

For some time, he simply stood there, staring at his own reflection in the glass. He became so lost in his own thoughts that he barely noticed Gwen approaching,

'Theo,' she said gently. 'Is everything all right?'

He didn't answer. Truthfully, he didn't think he could. A numbness had overcome him. A sense of pure disbelief.

Sylvia was wrong. She *had* to be. Perhaps she'd been confused. Or could it even have been a lie, to keep him distracted until she could say something to Nigel? She'd been lying to *him* proficiently enough. Her own husband. Perhaps she'd managed to pull the wool over Theo's eyes, too.

'Theo . . .' Gwen stepped closer and placed a hand on his shoulder.

Her touch planted him firmly back in the moment, and in an instant, he knew that Sylvia had told the truth. She hadn't been bluffing. Not simply trying to deflect his attention.

Jack was the one.

He took a deep breath, trying to calm himself, but it wasn't enough. As the cold sting of reality took hold, he felt himself tremble with fury.

37

As she scanned the restaurant, taking in each of her fellow guests' faces, Lily was beginning to accept that she had no way of determining which of them could have taken the gun from the Range Rover.

She was still adamant that nobody could have slipped her own key from her pocket, only to put it back without her noticing. But then they couldn't have taken her dad's either – at least, not without first stealing the key to his room from PC Fay. And even if one of them had somehow managed it, there was no way they'd have known the gun was even there.

And yet, it had happened. The gun *had* been taken, although there seemed to be no trace of it now. After sending Lily back to the restaurant, Fay had gone to the office and called again for support. Then, she'd searched each of the guests in turn, patting them down and turning out their pockets and bags. She'd even gone across the hall to the lounge and done the same with the actors, but all to no avail. Whoever had shot Carl, the gun had now gone.

Getting nowhere, Lily thought instead about the spiked

bottle of champagne. That had required planning. Someone had known they were coming, known about her dad's allergy and known it would force him from the table to fetch his EpiPen.

Probing the room, she looked first towards the bay window, where Gwen was deep in conversation with the Finns. Her dad's high school girlfriend; she would surely have known about the allergy. They would have been on dates. Had dinner together. And if Gwen knew, then by extension, Hugh could know as well.

As for the Finns, it seemed to Lily they weren't close to her dad. But she couldn't rule them out. Learning that they had been Teddy's parents – that the lighthouse had been intended as a memorial for their own son . . . If they'd somehow managed to uncover the allergy, Lily wouldn't be at all surprised to learn they were the murderers Fay was hunting.

She turned next to Sylvia, who sat alone at the table, Fay having chosen Nigel as her next interviewee. Lily pictured him, sweating in that guestroom as she grilled him on his work at the lighthouse. Had he and her dad ever met to discuss the work in person? Nigel might have offered refreshments. Even lunch. If so, he would need to be told about the allergy. And if he'd discovered it, might he have then gone home with that information to Sylvia?

Justin was next. He'd gone straight upstairs at the beginning of the interval; to ask for an interview, he'd said, only to be sent away with his tail between his legs. Or perhaps not. Perhaps he really had been the one Lily and Gwen had heard hurrying from the room. The one who she was so sure had been her dad's killer.

He did seem obsessed with the idea of his story. Even now,

he was seated at the head of the table, furiously typing what Lily guessed must be his report of the evening's events into his phone. Her dad had always taken pains to keep his allergy a secret, but if there was some nugget of information out there on the internet – a juicy detail for Justin to include in his exposé – she could certainly imagine the young reporter tracking it down.

Finally, there was Will. He'd planned the story. The clues. *For Rory and Teddy.*

Martha's confession and Carl's murder might have provided a compelling distraction, but Lily hadn't forgotten the note in the library. Nor had she forgotten that she'd told Ian about the allergy. She'd been sure he wouldn't work out from her first name alone who her dad must be. But if she was wrong – if he'd somehow managed it – then surely Will had known, too.

He even looked guilty, huddling in the corner of the room.

And yet, as she looked at him, Lily noticed something curious. He was wheezing slightly, taking slow, pained breaths, as if struggling for air.

Gwen noticed it too, her brow creasing with concern. 'Will,' she said. 'Are you all right?'

Panic sparked in his eyes. 'I'm sorry. It's nothing. I just . . . I need my spare inhaler.'

From his seat by the fireplace, Hugh muttered something under his breath.

'It's OK,' Will said hurriedly. 'I don't need it right now. I can wait until they let us leave.'

He sounded eager enough, but even from the opposite side

of the room, Lily could hear the wheeze in his voice. It was becoming more pronounced by the moment.

Gwen gave him a gentle smile. 'Is it here? In the hotel?'

Apparently recognising that Gwen, at least, was on his side, he nodded. 'My rucksack's hanging up in Ian's office.'

'It's all right. Come on. I'll go with you.'

'No.' It was Ian who spoke this time. 'I'll go.'

Since Carl's body had been discovered, Ian had barely said a word. He'd sat at the table, drawing nauseated glances from Sylvia as he fidgeted with the bandage around his hand. Now, as he pushed back his chair and climbed to his feet, he seemed suddenly determined.

Clearly uncomfortable, Gwen looked towards the fireplace, where Hugh was nudging at the flames with an iron poker. But there was no longer any sign of his earlier insistence that they all stay in the restaurant. If he was even listening, he didn't show it.

'I'll go with him,' Ian repeated. 'We'll be straight back.'

Seeing that Hugh wasn't going to protest, Gwen relented, giving Will a reassuring nod. Lily watched as he trudged after Ian into the hallway. After they had left, and stillness had once again settled on the room, she turned her attention to Hugh.

An hour earlier, she wouldn't have been the least bit surprised to learn that he had murdered her dad. The way they'd spoken to each other over dinner, she would barely have flinched if he'd openly admitted it. But Carl's death had changed things. Watching him now, a look of wide-eyed bewilderment on his face, she was certain he couldn't be the one.

With a deep breath, she crossed the room and took the seat

opposite him. He watched her warily, and as she sat down, she could have sworn she saw his grip tighten on the poker.

She nodded towards the door, as if following Will. 'Do you really think he did it?'

Hugh returned his gaze to the fire. 'You tell me. You're the one who brought a gun into the house.'

She thought about protesting but decided against it.

'I'm sorry about Carl,' she said.

He didn't reply.

'And I'm sorry for what happened to your brother.'

Hugh looked up sharply, his eyes locking with hers. She met his expression, just as she knew her dad would have done. But as she did, she saw something that puzzled her. He seemed to soften slightly, confusion in his eyes.

The look vanished before she could give it much thought. He shook his head, like snapping from a daydream. 'They worked with me for a little while,' he said. 'The pair of them. Carl was training to be a chef. And Rory . . .' He tailed off, and for a split second, Lily thought she heard a slight tremor in his voice. He cleared his throat before continuing. 'He spoke about you sometimes. Said how much he'd like to see you again. Your mum, too.'

Lily wasn't sure what to say. Since learning of Rory's death, her questions had focused on why he'd been killed; whether her dad could really have been involved. It hadn't occurred to her that Rory might have thought of her after returning to Hamlet Wick.

'I never knew that Rory was from Hamlet,' she said. 'But I suppose I couldn't have. Dad never brought me here. He never even spoke about this place. If you'd asked me before, I'd probably have assumed he and Rory met in London.'

Hugh scowled. 'They grew up together. All the way through their teenage years, they were inseparable.'

'And then my dad screwed him over.'

Something dark simmered in Hugh's eyes.

'The constable told me,' Lily explained. 'She said Dad bought Rory's half of the firm and then sent him packing back to Hamlet. That doesn't sound like something you'd do to your best friend.'

Hugh glared at her. 'What do you *want?*'

She paused, steeling herself. 'I want to know if you really think he murdered your brother.'

Hugh fixed her with a look of such malice it became an effort to hold his gaze.

'I know you hate him,' she said. 'Listening to all of you speak – learning about the lighthouse – I even think I can understand why. But you can't really believe he would kill someone. Least of all someone he was apparently so close to.'

Hugh turned away. He stared at the crackling flames, and it was only when Lily began to wonder whether he might be planning simply to ignore her that he finally spoke. 'Rory never should have gone to London,' he said wearily. 'He wasn't cut out for it. He had dreams, just like your dad. But you need to be a certain kind of ambitious to make it in the city, and that just wasn't him.'

Lily sat quietly, thinking of what Gwen had told her in the library.

Rory had all of Damien's ambition but none of his charisma. He was never as witty. Never as clever. If you want the truth, he was never as ruthless.

'Don't get me wrong,' Hugh continued. 'He lasted a while. After he and your dad finished university, they were in business together for the best part of ten years before things got too much.' His expression softened slightly. 'I don't know what it was exactly; whether it was the pressure of the job or just the pace of the lifestyle. Either way, we didn't see how bad it was until he was too far gone. Until he'd racked up so much debt that there was no way anyone here could have helped him. So he went to your dad. His best friend. His business partner.'

Lily noticed Hugh's knuckles pale as he gripped the poker a little tighter.

'You say White bought Rory's half of their firm. That's not how I'd describe what happened. Their whole lives, they'd been like brothers. Then, when Rory needed help, your dad saw a chance to fill his own pockets. By the time he was done – when he'd taken what he wanted – Rory didn't even have enough to his name for a train ticket home to Hamlet.'

Lily had to force herself not to look away. The fire spat, filling the silence until she worked up the courage to ask her next question. 'But why would my dad want to kill him?'

Again, Hugh made her wait for a reply, his eyes narrowing. 'When the police took Rory's body away, they found a photo inside his jacket. It was a picture of your dad's stag party, taken the night before he married your mum. All of the lads lined up in a bar somewhere.'

300

'You don't think he just had it as a keepsake? A reminder of better times?'

Hugh shook his head. 'There was a receipt in his pocket, from the chemist in Hamlet. When the police followed it up, they said he'd visited that afternoon to have it run off. He didn't buy anything else. Just that one picture.'

Lily almost laughed at him. 'You think my dad killed Rory because he bought a picture?'

Something awful played upon Hugh's lips, midway between a smile and a grimace. 'A picture of your dad's stag night,' he said. 'And Rory was the best man.' He leaned in close, dragging out each word. 'But Rory wasn't in it.'

Lily fought back a sudden flicker of uncertainty. 'Perhaps he took it.'

Hugh shook his head. 'The police tracked down all the lads in the photo. It took some time but they each confirmed the same thing: Rory hadn't been there. Food poisoning. That was what he'd told them. Nobody set eyes on him until your parents' wedding, the following morning.'

He paused, still gripping the poker tightly. 'So you explain that to me. Explain why Rory would run off a photo of a party he wasn't at, for a man he'd grown to hate, then turn up dead the next morning.'

Lily felt her heart beat a little quicker. She could almost sense the anger building in Hugh. 'A photo of his stag night doesn't prove that my dad killed Rory,' she said, hoping she sounded more confident than she felt. 'Besides, he had an alibi.'

'From his own wife. Hardly convincing.'

301

'Well, what about the woman Rory had been seen with? The blonde woman?'

'They never found her.'

'But don't you think she might have been involved? They were seen arguing on the beach, then what, twelve hours later he's killed? Doesn't that seem suspicious?'

Hugh waved the poker, swatting her question away. 'Unless the police ever work out who she was, we'll never know.'

Lily looked away, settling eventually on the bay window. In the corner of the glass, she could just make out the faint glow of the distant floodlights. 'I can't understand why my dad would come back here,' she said. 'There doesn't seem to be much he isn't blamed for. Even Teddy.'

Hugh glowered at her. 'He told you about Teddy?'

'He didn't tell me anything. It was Gwen who warned me what had happened, when she came to my room.' Lily shook her head. 'How can nobody have known what he was doing up there? There must have been a reason. He must have been doing *something*.' She frowned at Hugh. 'You were with them that night. They were at your house, weren't they? With Gwen?'

'Why should that mean anything?'

'I thought Teddy followed them everywhere; my dad and Rory.'

'Well, that night he *fucking didn't*.' With a clang that filled the entire restaurant, he tossed the poker onto the floor and stood up so abruptly he almost knocked over his chair.

Lily watched as he turned his back on her. There was no denying she'd touched a nerve. But why would it be Teddy who seemed to push him over the edge?

She looked towards Martha Finn. The older woman was still in the far corner of the restaurant, where she had, until Hugh's outburst, been speaking quietly with Edward and Gwen. They locked eyes, Martha giving her a quizzical look, and for a few precious seconds Lily deliberated over what she was about to do.

Could she be imagining things? Had she just worn Hugh down with all her questions about Rory?

No. There was something else. She felt sure of it. More than that, she wanted to pursue it; wanted to uncover at least one more truth.

'Hugh . . .' Martha peered across the restaurant. 'What's going on?'

'Nothing,' he called back. 'It's nothing, Martha.'

In that moment, Lily was certain. She heard the tremor in Hugh's voice; she saw the panic in his eyes and knew that something wasn't being said. Watching Hugh's discomfort grow, she thought of what her dad would have done. She pictured him lying on the floor above their heads and knew exactly what his advice would be.

Control the room. Seize your opportunity and bleed it dry.

'I was asking about Teddy,' she told Martha. 'About the night he died. I was asking where my dad was.'

'Why would you want to know?' Edward Finn demanded.

'Because earlier this evening, Gwen told me that on the night Teddy fell, she had been with Hugh, my dad and Rory. She said that Teddy wasn't there.'

'I've just told you the same thing.' Hugh shot Gwen a nervous look.

'Lily,' she said gently. 'I told you, we were drinking. Teddy was so much younger than us . . . He was only thirteen. We weren't going to give him alcohol.'

'I think this has gone far enough.' Hugh raised his voice, but Lily put out a hand, holding him at bay.

'Who was the card for?'

He looked at her blankly.

'The Valentine's card that Martha spoke about. When she was clearing out Teddy's things, she found it hidden in his wardrobe. Who was he saving it for?'

'I don't know.'

Lily paused, trying frantically to connect the loose threads before the situation got away from her. She heard her dad's voice in her mind, urging her to keep going. To stay in control.

She looked around the restaurant, taking in the Finns, Gwen and Hugh, even Justin. She fumbled through the details in her mind, turning them over and over until, finally, a solution began to reveal itself. An image that slowly took form.

'Lily,' said Gwen. 'I really think you ought to stop this. Perhaps I should fetch you some water. You must be in terrible shock.'

Lily didn't reply. She was still sifting through the clues in her mind. 'A blank Valentine's card,' she said quietly, her eyes narrowing. 'Martha never knew who it was for. But I'm willing to bet that you do. Don't you, Gwen?'

'Lily.' All of a sudden, Gwen's voice was like granite. 'This is extremely inappropriate.'

'Teddy followed my dad and Rory everywhere,' Lily

continued, her heart thumping in her ears. 'Like a lost lamb. That's what Martha said. And all this time that's what everyone's believed. But I don't think they were the ones he was following. The ones he idolised. I think it was *you*. You're who the card was for. You were the one he was trying to be close to.'

'Martha.' Gwen seized her hands. 'You mustn't listen to this. Lily's not thinking straight. Damien's been murdered and she thinks one of us is responsible. She doesn't know what she's—'

'I'm right, aren't I?' Lily cut across her, turning to Hugh. 'If Teddy had written that card, it would have been Gwen's name that Martha found inside.'

'I . . .' Hugh floundered, completely out of his depth, until a glance from Gwen seemed to provide all he needed to get a hold of himself. 'Of course not. It's absurd.'

He recovered well, clearing his throat and puffing out his chest. But it was too late. Lily had seen his fear and it was enough.

'There's only one reason I can think of for covering that detail up,' she continued. 'For leaving it unspoken all these years. And that's to hide what really happened the night Teddy fell.' She turned to Gwen. 'He *was* with you, wasn't he? What was it, a dare? Or were you just testing the boundaries? Seeing how far he'd go to impress you?'

Gwen glared at her. 'I didn't send Teddy up the lighthouse.'

'Perhaps not. Perhaps he volunteered. But here's what I believe – if it was Teddy's idea, you didn't stop him. I think he wanted to impress you, and after a few drinks you were only too happy to let him try. So he climbs to the top, loses his footing and falls. Then the four of you agree a story about how you'd been partying at Rory's the entire time, with Teddy nowhere in sight.'

Lily turned to Hugh. 'Tell me I'm wrong.'

He said nothing, his eyes wide with panic. His lips parted but no sound emerged. He glanced from face to face, looking desperately for some kind of escape. But there was nowhere to run. And the terror in his expression told the group all they needed to know.

'There you have it, Martha,' said Lily. 'You want to know who sent Teddy up that lighthouse? I think she's standing right in front of you. She has been all along.'

38

Will and Ian crossed the hallway in complete silence, passed the foot of the staircase and stepped into the little corridor. At the far end, the kitchen door had been closed. Will noticed Ian lingering for a moment to stare at it as they reached the office.

'Will,' he said quietly. 'If it *was* you . . . Carl. Damien White. You know things will go better if you just admit it.'

Will had half-expected a conversation like this. Why else would Ian have been so insistent on walking him to the office himself? But he'd imagined his tone would be hard. Cold, even. Instead, he looked defeated. In the dim light that seeped from the hallway into the corridor, Will could see that he just wanted this all to be over.

'I promise,' he said. 'I swear it wasn't me.'

'Then what was it for? That story you came up with . . . Lord Something-or-Other?'

'Lord Ashcombe.'

'Whatever his name was. It was so clear you'd based it on Rory Holloway. Why did you do it? Why bring all of that back up?'

Will said nothing. Not because he lacked the courage to explain, but because he couldn't find the words.

What could he say? Justin had asked him the same question and he hadn't been able to articulate the truth. Hadn't been able to say just what he'd intended, without fear of sounding completely deranged.

He took a deep breath. 'It was something my therapist said.'

'Your therapist?'

Will nodded. 'I've seen quite a few since the morning I found Rory. I've spent all these years trying to find a way of forgetting it; of just getting the sight of him out of my head. But nothing's ever worked. I've tried hypnotherapy. Sleep therapy. I've probably tried every kind of therapy going, but none of it helps. I still dream about him. I still go back, every day, to that moment on the beach.'

He closed his eyes, although he was still aware of Ian watching him closely. 'I haven't been to a session in a long time,' he continued. 'But the last therapist I saw said something that's stayed with me. She said the key to overcoming a fear is often to face it. Tackle it head on and understand that the thing you're scared of can't hurt you. You can hardly do that with a murder, though. Least of all one that was never solved. There's no explanation for what you saw. No reason for it. No culprit to blame it all on. Even so, that advice stuck.'

He hesitated, all too aware of how carefully he had to choose his next words. Ian was listening, but if there was a moment when he'd lose him, Will knew this would be it.

'You know already that I work at the relic shop on the high street. There isn't always much to do, so I read some of the books to pass the time. That's where I came across an old murder mystery. It had everything. The grand house, the body in the library, all the guests with their secrets . . . And then, at the end, the detective rounded everyone up, unmasked the murderer and explained exactly how they'd done it.

'At first, I couldn't say what it was that affected me so much. But after a while, it struck me. It was a sense of pure closure. Every loose thread was tied up. Every secret was revealed. Everything just *made sense*. Then the murderer was arrested and everyone else went back to their lives.

'I knew it was just fiction. But even so, I couldn't shake the feeling that maybe this was what I was missing with Rory. They never caught his killer. They never worked out why he was on the beach that day. Perhaps if they had – if it had all just made sense, like in this book – I would have been able to put it behind me.

'I knew I wasn't about to solve his murder. But I remembered what my therapist said, about facing your fears, and I thought maybe I could do that. If I could turn Rory's death into something else, and if I could live it out – see it through to the end – then perhaps I could get that closure too. Even it wasn't real. Even though *I*'d been the one to make it up. Maybe it would be enough.'

Ian pressed his hands to his face with such pressure that when he lifted them away his eyes were bloodshot.

'I thought about changing the story when I heard that Hugh was coming,' Will explained. 'Having the murder take place in some other way. In another place. But that would have defeated the entire point. I'd changed the names, set the story in the 1920s, made up all of the supporting characters . . . I hoped it would be enough. That by being in Hamlet Wick, it would be close enough to Rory for me to still believe it was him, without the others seeing through it.'

'Well, it wasn't.' Ian replied so sharply that Will took a step backwards. 'It's mad. Completely mad. And I *wish* you hadn't done it here. But I suppose I understand.' He looked towards the restaurant. 'If it wasn't you that killed Carl and Damien White, which of them was it?'

Will was silent. Or at least, as silent as he could be. He was wheezing badly now, desperate for his spare inhaler.

Ian sighed and nudged his head towards the office door.

Without a second's hesitation, Will hurried into the little room, flicked on the light and reached for a hook on the back of the door. Unzipping his rucksack, he rummaged frantically inside, searching for the spare inhaler. Instead, his fingers brushed against something he didn't recognise. Something cold.

'What is it?' Ian asked, following him inside.

'Nothing,' Will replied. 'It's nothing. There's just . . .' He wrapped his fingers around the object and lifted it from the bag. In the sharp light that filled the office, there was no denying what it was.

In his hand was a gun.

At first, they both stared at it. Then Ian's face twisted with pure fury.

'You little shit,' he growled. 'You little *shit*!' Grasping Will by the lapels, he dragged him back into the corridor and thrust him hard against the wood-panelled wall. The gun tumbled to the ground, clattering against the tiled floor. 'What is this?' he snarled. 'What the hell is this?'

310

'I don't know,' Will gasped. 'I swear – I've never seen that before.'

'To think I believed you! That fucking sob story about your therapist inspiring you to do all of this. You were just setting the scene, weren't you? Getting ready to say this gun isn't yours. That someone's set you up!'

'They have! Please, I've never seen that gun before. I've never even *held* one!'

'Enough!' Ian's breath was hot on Will's face. 'Enough lies! There's no getting out of this now. We're showing this to the police and then that'll be it. The story about Rory, the note in the library, this gun in your bag . . .'

Panicking, Will did all he could to hold back tears. Ian was right. There'd be no convincing them now. He couldn't even rely on the gun being fingerprinted; his own would surely be all over it.

He took a deep breath, trying desperately to calm himself. Then came a sound that caused his heart to stop.

Footsteps on the stairs. Fay was coming.

39

Theo stormed into the lounge, the door crashing against the wall with such force that Claire gave a small shriek.

'Theo?'

He heard her, but he didn't stop. Instead, he went straight to the far end of the room and loomed over Jack's armchair.

'The review,' he said. 'Justin's write-up of *An Inspector Calls*. You were the one who sent it to the *West Side Story* director in Bristol.'

Nobody spoke. Nobody even moved. Theo stood, waiting for his defence.

'Oh, Jack,' Claire whispered. 'You didn't . . .'

'Of course I didn't.' He stared up at Theo. 'Where would you get such an idea?'

'Sylvia.' Theo was breathing hard, barely managing to restrain his fury. 'She told me. Just now in the hallway.'

Jack opened his mouth to protest, but nothing came. There was panic on his face now. He knew he'd been caught.

'Theo,' said Claire gently. 'I think we all just need to stay calm. I'm sure there's a rational explanation.'

'I don't need an explanation,' Theo spat. 'I know exactly why he did it. He was jealous that I was going to land the sort of role he never had.' He glared at Jack. 'I always knew that you were a loser. Even at school, we could all see how pathetic you were. But I never knew you were so petty.'

Jack sprang to his feet, his nose inches from Theo's. 'Fine,' he growled. 'Yes. I did it. I had a moment of weakness, Theo. *A moment of weakness*. That's all.'

'That's all?'

Jack softened slightly. 'You don't know what it's like. To strive for something for years – to dedicate yourself to a dream – only for it never to happen. And then I see you. Not even twenty years old, and about to land a role on a level I'd never come close to. You can't imagine how that feels. I'm not proud of it, but my jealousy got the better of me.'

He faltered and gazed out of the bay window. 'I felt dreadful after I'd done it,' he said, defiance slipping from his voice. 'Truly dreadful. I knew that I'd made a terrible mistake, but it was too late to take it back.' He turned to face Theo again. 'I'm sorry. Truly I am.'

It was some time before Theo was able to reply. He was aware of Claire hovering at his shoulder, watching him expectantly, and of the endless ticking of the grandfather clock.

'All this time, I've blamed Justin,' he said quietly. 'But it was you. You ruined the best opportunity I've ever had. Maybe the best I'll *ever* have.' He felt his eyes narrow. Heard his own voice turn cold. 'Well, two can play that game. Let's see how Nigel Cobb takes the news about you and Sylvia.'

Jack's eyes flew wide, filled with sheer, unbridled terror. 'No!' he cried. 'Theo, you mustn't!'

Even Claire was trying to talk him down, but it was no use. Theo didn't hear them. Already, he had crossed the room, thrown open the door and stepped into the hallway.

Two o'clock

40

'You bitch,' Martha whispered. 'You evil bitch. All these years, you've said you wanted to support us. Spoken about turning the lighthouse into a memorial, when *you're* the one who sent him up there!'

'Please, Martha,' said Gwen. 'You have to believe me. It isn't true!'

She tried to reach out, but Martha wrenched her hand away.

'The memorial's a good point,' said Lily. 'I understand why you wanted it, Gwen. I'm sure it's done wonders for your reputation. But why did my dad want it? What was so terrible about creating a memorial for Teddy?'

Gwen turned on her, eyes burning. 'You have to stop this, Lily. You really have no clue what you're talking about.'

'Is that what tonight's all about?' she continued, undeterred. 'Were you the one who killed him? To get the lighthouse back? To finish your memorial?'

'If I killed Damien, who did we hear leaving his room? Who did Ian see throwing the rock out of the window?'

Lily faltered, scrambling desperately for an answer. But she had nothing. No ingenious explanation or biting response.

'Now,' said Gwen breathlessly. 'If we're all finished with this lunacy, can I suggest we—'

Before she could go any further, Theo thundered into the restaurant. He stood in the doorway, sweeping the room until he finally settled on Nigel Cobb.

'Jack's been sleeping with Sylvia,' he announced.

At first, nobody moved. Even Nigel, it seemed to Lily, had no idea what to make of this bizarre interruption. He squinted at Theo, his mouth hanging slightly open.

'Jack,' Theo repeated, breathing hard. 'Jack Marshall. He's been sleeping with your wife.'

Nigel turned to Sylvia, and in an instant, Lily recognised that Theo was telling the truth. She had suddenly turned very pale, her eyes bulging.

'Theo!' Jack ambled into the room after him, breaking the silence. 'Listen to me, boy. You have it all—'

He didn't finish. In a heartbeat, Nigel had sprung to his feet, cleared the length of the restaurant and punched him squarely on the jaw, sending him tumbling to the ground.

The room erupted. Nigel roared at Jack, while Sylvia shrieked and Hugh bellowed at him to stop. Martha screamed at Gwen – Lily could just about make out the word 'Teddy' – while Edward tried desperately over the clamour to calm her.

Lily watched, dumbfounded by how quickly she had lost control.

She looked from face to face, until at last she found herself locking eyes with Justin. He was sitting at the table, his phone resting in front of him and the little red light blinking as he surveyed the commotion. He lifted a fresh glass of champagne, toasting her from across the room, before raising it to his lips.

41

Will was panicking.

He was seated in Ian's chair, the harsh light overhead and the Dictaphone on the desk making the little office feel like an interrogation room; the kind he'd seen in dozens of tacky American crime dramas. But there was no witty back and forth over thick case files and paper cups of coffee. Instead, he felt only a sense of helplessness as Fay took command of the room with her usual silent efficiency.

He watched, heart pounding in his ears as she slipped on a pair of latex gloves and lifted the gun from the desk.

He stared at it, still struggling to comprehend the very sight of it.

Several of the farmers in the surrounding countryside would have shotguns, and he'd even seen an antique pistol for sale once in the shop. But the weapon in Fay's hands was different. It was pitch black, the barrel gleaming, and small enough that Will imagined it could easily be hidden inside a decent-sized pocket.

Even to an untrained eye like his, it was clear this wasn't a trinket. It was a tool. An instrument designed for efficiency. But more than that, he was certain he was looking at the weapon with which Carl had been murdered.

Turning the gun over in her hands, Fay expertly slipped out the magazine. 'One shot fired,' she said. 'Five left.' Delicately, she set it down. 'I take it this is the gun from Damien White's car?'

Will took a deep breath, trying desperately to calm his nerves. 'I don't know. I've never seen it before.'

'Then what's it doing in your bag?'

'Someone must have put it there.'

'Who?'

'*I don't know.*'

Fay loomed over him. 'Mr Hooper,' she said slowly. 'Think for a moment about how severe your situation is. You told Mr Davies, just a few minutes ago, that you organised this evening in such a way as to mimic the murder of Rory Holloway. Damien White, who none of the other guests could have known was attending, has been found murdered in his room, beaten around the head in what appears also to be in the same fashion as Rory Holloway. A note has been discovered in the library, declaring that what's taken place has been in Mr Holloway and Teddy Finn's names—'

'That wasn't mine,' Will protested. 'Someone swapped it out. My note read—'

'Carl Gifford has been shot dead,' Fay continued, raising her voice. 'Most likely because he had realised who killed Mr White. And now a gun has been discovered in your bag.'

Will couldn't speak. He was completely paralysed, the words refusing to come.

321

'There's one detail in particular that I don't understand,' said Fay, a hint of malice creeping into her voice. 'How did you get the gun? How did you know it was even there? It was kept secretly inside Mr White's personal vehicle. How did you take it?'

'I didn't know,' Will stammered. 'I didn't—'

'Have you paid someone for information? Mr White will have cleaners. Personal assistants. Someone close to him must have known the gun was there. Did they help you plan this?'

Will screwed his eyes shut, forcing back tears. When he opened them again, Fay had crouched down, bringing herself to his level.

'Shall I tell you what I think?' she asked. 'As you well know, Damien White and Carl Gifford were the two lead suspects in the murder of Rory Holloway. It's crossed my mind this evening that you might have recreated that murder in an attempt to solve it. But perhaps I was wrong. Perhaps you think you already have. And what you're actually trying to do is avenge him. You're punishing the two men you believe to be responsible.'

Will risked a glance at his own reflection in the window. He looked terrible. He was deathly pale, his hair a mess, the over-sized dinner jacket hanging from his shoulders.

He lifted his inhaler and took a deep breath. Then he closed his eyes, steeling himself for a moment, before looking back at Fay. 'I'm telling you,' he said slowly. 'I didn't have anything to do with Damien White's—'

'Enough!' She brought her palm down so forcefully on the desk that it caused the whisky bottles in the far corner to clink together like the keys of a xylophone. 'Enough lies,' she hissed.

'Tell me the truth. Tell me *exactly* what that gun is doing in your bag.'

Will had no answer for her. He looked helplessly around the room, taking in the cleaning rota, the dusty computer and the still-trembling bottles of whisky on Ian's desk.

He paused.

Staring at the bottles, he watched as the surface of the amber liquid gently rocked back and forth.

'Mr Hooper,' said Fay. 'Mr Hooper, are you listening?'

Will barely heard her. He was missing something. Something crucial. He clawed through his memory, like trying to recall a half-forgotten dream. Then, at last, the realisation struck him.

'I know . . .' he whispered, more to himself than to Fay or Ian. 'I know who did it.'

They both looked at him, aghast. But before Fay could say another word, there came the sudden sound of wood crashing upon wood.

42

In the restaurant, the guests continued to shriek at each other. Hugh tried to force Jack and Nigel apart, while Edward did all he could to keep Martha away from Gwen.

Neither was having much success. Jack cowered behind Hugh, blood streaming from his nose as Nigel roared about stealing his wife. Martha, meanwhile, was screaming at Gwen. For the most part it was unintelligible, although Theo could make out two words which she kept returning to. The first was 'Teddy'. The second was 'liar'.

He hadn't known exactly what reaction the news of Jack and Sylvia would prompt, but he hadn't expected anything as explosive as this. Seeing Nigel land a punch on Jack's jaw had seemed appropriate. For a few seconds, it had even felt good. But he had no clue what was happening between Martha and Gwen. Looking at the chaos before him, he had the feeling of having tossed a match onto a box of fireworks.

The noise was so overpowering that he didn't hear the footsteps behind him. But from his position by the door, he did feel a sudden gust of cold wind sweep down the hallway, as someone fled Hamlet Hall.

Straying from the restaurant, he moved cautiously towards the open doors, arriving just in time to see Claire clambering into the driver's seat of a gleaming white Range Rover.

Before he had a chance to consider what, exactly, he was watching, Fay barged past him. 'Stop!' she yelled, leaping down the steps and climbing into her own car as the Range Rover's engine rumbled into life.

Will appeared at Theo's shoulder, with Ian just a few paces behind.

'What's happening?' asked Theo.

'It's her,' said Will, staring at the Range Rover. 'It's Claire.'

Theo returned his attention to the two cars.

Could it be true? She certainly seemed eager to get away. When Fay had arrived, she'd parked tightly in front of the Range Rover, which was now forcing Claire to back up in order to get free. If she hoped it might stop the cumbersome vehicle from pulling out, though, she had no such luck. By the time she'd started the Vauxhall's engine, Claire was free, and was already turning around in a broad circle.

There was no denying where she was headed. The Lane; the narrow track that served as the one route out of Hamlet Wick.

The Range Rover's tyres crunched on the shale as it strayed clumsily onto the beach. At the same time, Fay put the Vauxhall into reverse, the car shrieking as she lurched backwards towards the mouth of the Lane. Realising what she was attempting to do, Claire gave a sudden burst of speed, engine roaring.

Fay made it first.

With a squeal of brakes, the Vauxhall backed into the narrow gap between the hedges, barely a second before Claire collided with her. Stampeding into the driver-side door, Theo watched as the Vauxhall's airbag burst, the window shattered and the side of the car crumpled inwards. The impact tipped it sideways, lifting briefly onto its passenger-side wheels before crashing back down.

With Will and Ian still hovering at his shoulders, Theo watched, astonished, as Claire opened the driver's door and climbed down from the Range Rover. Blood trickled from a small cut on her head, but she was in considerably better shape than Fay. Through the Vauxhall's shattered windscreen, Theo saw her slumped against the airbag.

'I'm calling an ambulance,' said Ian, before turning away and hurrying back into the hotel.

For a few seconds, Claire stared at the crash, as though she was trying to decide if there was any way of getting past the ruined Vauxhall. Then she looked up towards Hamlet Hall and her eyes locked with Theo's.

'What's going on?'

Theo wasn't sure who had called out, but as their voice echoed down the hallway behind him, Claire seemed to snap abruptly back into focus. She broke into a run, sprinting, not past the cars and into the Lane, but past Hamlet Hall, towards the harbour.

It was Hugh who appeared first, the sound of the crash apparently proving enough to break up the commotion in the restaurant. Squinting into the darkness, he swept his gaze towards the

Lane. 'Oh, God,' he murmured, before running towards the wrecked cars.

The remaining guests followed, Gwen and Nigel rushing to help Fay while the others lingered in the doorway.

'Who's that?' Martha asked, pointing at Claire. She was still running, having just about reached the little shop on the harbour wall.

Theo watched as she fled, before turning to Will. He was fixed on Claire, a look of ferocious determination upon his face.

Too late, Theo saw what was about to happen. He tried to call out, but Will had already gone. Breaking into a run, he took off after her, his feet pounding as he sped into the night.

43

Will heard Theo calling out his name, but he didn't stop.

He had to know why Claire had done it. Why she'd murdered Carl and Damien White. Why she'd positioned him as the killer.

But more than that, he had to know if she'd been connected to Rory. He'd invented Lord Ashcombe's murder to make fiction out of Rory's. To find a way of seeing it through a different lens. Perhaps, if he could catch up with Claire, he would get *real* answers instead.

His feet pounded, his lungs beginning to burn. She had already passed the Finns' shop, reaching the edge of Hamlet Wick. Will had hoped she might stop, realising there was nowhere else to go. Instead, she'd turned back, seen him pursuing her and carried on. By the time he reached the shop, passing the sailing boats as they bobbed in the harbour, she was halfway up the hill, sprinting towards the lighthouse.

He urged himself on, legs groaning as he began to climb. When he reached the top, there was no sign of her, although there was also no question of where she must have gone. The barbed wire that adorned the fences spoke for itself, but between the gates, there was a gap just large enough for a slender person to squeeze through.

He threw himself towards it, paying no notice as the metal raked against his chest and back. Struggling through to the other side, he emerged so haphazardly that he tumbled heavily to the ground. He picked himself up and took in a digger, several bags of cement, skips full of rubbish and two Portakabins branded with *Cobb Construction Ltd*.

He felt a flash of panic. When he saw Claire running towards the lighthouse, he'd been sure he would have her cornered. There was certainly nowhere else to run. But he hadn't considered just how many places she would have to hide.

His eyes darting around the site, he settled on the keeper's hut, adjoining the lighthouse's tower. The door was swinging gently on its hinges.

Hurrying into the hut, he found it to be completely bare inside, presumably gutted by Nigel's workers. There was no chance of Claire hiding in there. Instead, he looked towards a second door at the far end.

He flew across the hut, barging through the door, and found himself standing at the base of the tower. A rusty, spiralling staircase was built into the wall. And at the top, there was Claire, visible for just a second before she disappeared from view.

Panting, Will began to climb. This was it. There was nowhere to go at the top of the tower; only a narrow platform that ringed the light like a dirty old crown. The same platform from which, all those years ago, Teddy had fallen.

Will's legs seared, the staircase rattling beneath his feet, but he didn't care. He was going to catch her. To have the answers he'd waited so many years to hear.

He burst onto the platform, only to find himself dropping to his knees as something hard was swung into his stomach.

Badly winded, he looked up to see Claire holding a rusty piece of old pipe. A handrail circled the edge of the platform, though it was in dire need of repair, with several lengths of metal tubing either scattered about or missing completely.

He cursed his own foolishness. She must have been hiding just out of sight, listening to him clattering up the stairs. It had probably been the easiest thing in the world to pick up one of the fallen sections of handrail and wait beside the open doorway.

Trying to recover his breath, he looked out to sea. Moonlight glittered on the surface of the water, and to his right, the Finns' shop and even Hamlet Hall were now so small they could be doll's houses. There was a void of impenetrable darkness that he knew must be the Lane, and in the distance, Hamlet itself was a cluster of even smaller lights.

In any other moment, it might have been beautiful. But this was not the time to admire the view. He returned his attention to the killer looming over him.

'The whisky,' he managed to say. 'During the interval. You tried to fetch me a glass of whisky. You said that you'd looked everywhere. The kitchen, the lounge, Ian's office . . .'

He climbed to his feet, his stomach groaning from the blow she'd dealt him. She took a step forward, the pipe still clutched in her hand, and he backed hurriedly away. He must have only made it a couple of feet before he met the wall, his back pressed against the cold metal.

'If you'd really looked in Ian's office, you would have seen it straight away, sitting on his desk. But you didn't. Because you were upstairs, murdering Damien White.'

Claire glared at him, hatred in her eyes.

'You went into one of the other guestrooms,' he said. 'You threw the rock that you'd used to kill him out of the window, into the garden. And then you murdered Carl. Lily told us that he was looking for PC Fay. She said he wanted to show her a little bottle of champagne. I guess Theo must have said something too, and you realised that he knew. That he'd worked out it was you.'

He tried to stand upright, gasping with pain from the impact of the pipe. 'Fay found an EpiPen in Mr White's room. Did you spike him with something? I'll bet that's what happened. You gave that bottle to Carl at the beginning of the evening and told him that Mr White had asked for it specifically.'

He shuffled a step to the side, keeping his back pressed to the tower as he tried desperately to put some distance between them. He had to keep talking, though. He needed these answers.

'How did you get the gun?' He took another nervous step away from her, his eyes glued to the pipe in her hand. 'How did you know it was in Mr White's car? How did you know he would be here at all? Even we didn't know!' His voice rose, a note of hysteria creeping in. 'And why me? That note in the library, the gun in my rucksack . . . Why try to pin this all on me?'

For a long while, Claire just looked at him, the wind blowing strands of hair in front of her face. He let the silence linger this time, panting on the cold air.

'It shouldn't have happened,' she said at last. 'There was no

need for Carl to die. Or for you to take the blame. I was supposed to leave the moment Damien was dead – lure him away
from the table during dinner and be long gone before your game
even had a chance to begin. But I couldn't get to the front door
without being seen from the restaurant. Then that police officer
arrived and I just had to make do. If I couldn't leave, I needed
to make sure I wasn't caught. Just until I could get out. Until
everyone's attention was elsewhere.'

With her free hand, she brushed the hair from her eyes. 'It
wasn't personal, Will. It could have been any of you – whoever
kept Fay distracted long enough for me to get away – and when
I read that script of yours, in those damn ring binders . . . You
want the honest truth? You put *yourself* in the firing line.'

Will felt anger stir in his gut; white hot, like he'd never felt
in his life. Before he could reply, though, he heard footsteps
coming from within the lighthouse. Someone else was climbing
the tower.

Claire looked towards the doorway, panic skirting across her
face, and Will saw an opportunity. He sprang forward, hoping
to reach her while she was distracted. But he was too slow. She
swung the pipe around again, catching him this time with a
savage blow to the ribs. He collapsed against the tower, the
antique platform rattling beneath him as he tumbled away.

The footsteps, meanwhile, were coming closer. Whoever
was climbing the lighthouse was almost at the top. Knowing he
might have just seconds left, Will abandoned all other questions,
leaping straight to the one that he needed answering most. The
question that had tormented him for twelve years.

'Did you kill Rory?'

Claire's eyes blazed. 'I loved Rory. This was all *for* Rory.'

Will frowned, completely baffled. He opened his mouth to reply, but before he could, Lily White appeared in the doorway. She looked at Claire, the moonlight glittering in her eyes, and spoke a single word.

'Mum . . .'

44

Standing in the doorway, Lily couldn't take her eyes off the woman in front of her.

She'd dyed her blonde hair dark and was wearing, bizarrely, what seemed to be a maid's uniform. But there was no denying it. In the glow from the floodlights at the base of the tower, Lily immediately recognised her mother's face.

'Mum,' she said again. 'What are you . . .?'

She looked closer, taking in the rusty length of pipe in her hand, and Will, heaped against the side of the tower, his face twisted in pain as he clutched his ribs.

Immediately it was clear why she had been so insistent they attend this murder mystery party. And why, all night, she hadn't answered her phone. Lily realised now how the murderer had known they were coming. Known about the allergy. How they'd managed to get inside the Range Rover.

'You killed Dad?' She spoke the words breathlessly, refusing to believe they could be true. 'And the chef? You killed him too? Mum, what have you done?'

Her mum stepped forward, eyes wide with panic. 'Lily . . . You shouldn't be here. You shouldn't *see* this. Please . . . Come back down with me and we can—'

'No!' Lily recoiled, the platform creaking beneath her feet. 'I'm not going anywhere until you explain what's going on.'

'I had to do it. For us. For you.'

'For me? How can any of this be for *me*?'

'Please, Lily. Not here. Just come down with me—'

'Mum! You've killed two people. You've killed *Dad*. Tell me, right now, what this is about. Or when they catch us up, I'll hand you over to the police myself.'

She flinched. Then her shoulders slumped. 'Damien did terrible things. Things that we've tried to make sure you knew nothing about.'

'I know what he did. He stole this lighthouse. Stole Teddy's memorial—'

'I'm not talking about the lighthouse.'

'What, then? What else did he do?'

Her mum closed her eyes. 'Do you remember your Uncle Rory?'

Lily didn't answer straight away. Instead, she felt a sense of dread begin to stir, deep within her gut. She knew where this was going; what was coming next.

'Damien murdered him. He did it right there, on the beach. Hit him around the head with a rock and then left his body like a sack of rubbish.'

Lily followed her gaze towards the water and immediately wished she hadn't. Realising for the first time just how high she'd climbed, she turned back towards the tower and saw Will. He was still heaped upon the floor, clutching his ribs and gasping with pain.

'Why?' she asked. 'He'd already ruined Rory's life. Screwed him out of his half of the firm and sent him packing. Why follow him here? Why murder him?'

Her mum stared at her, the wind tugging at her hair. 'How could you—'

'And why did you cover for him?' Lily pressed. 'You helped him get away. *You* told the police he'd been at home. Why do any of that if the truth was that you wanted to kill him for it?'

'Because I couldn't tell the police where he'd really been.'

'Why not?'

She didn't answer, her face twisting into a grimace.

'*Why not*, Mum?'

'Because I was here too.'

Lily stared, her breath steaming in front of her face as she tried frantically to connect the threads she'd uncovered in Hamlet Hall. 'The blonde woman,' she said. 'Who was seen with Rory on the beach. The one who everyone thought was Carl's girlfriend. That was you?' She hesitated. 'Is that why Dad murdered Rory? Were you having an affair?'

Her mum gawped at her, completely lost for words.

'And the photo,' Lily continued. 'Rory had a photo of Dad's stag party printed the day he died. Was he with you that night too?'

Her eyes were wide with disbelief. 'How do you know this? How can you possibly—'

'*Just tell me!*'

Her mum flinched, fear creeping into her voice. 'Yes. Rory came to me the night before I married Damien. He begged me not to go through with it. Said he'd loved me since university; since the moment we all met in that drama society.'

'All that time, you'd been seeing Rory behind Dad's back?'

'No! No, of course not. When Rory came to me, I'd been having doubts. About the marriage. About Damien.' She seemed to be yearning now, pleading with Lily to believe her. 'I let him in, but it was a moment of weakness. That was all. A single moment. The next day, I pulled myself together. I told Rory it couldn't happen again and that I was going through with the wedding.'

'So when *did* you start seeing him again?'

'After he'd moved back here, to Hamlet.'

Lily looked down at the platform, unable to meet her eye but reluctant to look out to sea. 'I suppose it must have been easy. I was at boarding school. Dad was always away. What happened, then? Dad found out somehow, and he killed Rory?'

'Lily . . .'

'But what was the photo of the stag night for?'

'Lily, please.'

'Did you *tell* Dad? Were you going to leave him and be with Rory?' She felt the cold prickling her face, tasted salt on her lips. But she didn't stop. 'Is that why he had the photo? As proof? To rub Dad's nose in it?'

'There was more to it than that. There are things you don't know—'

'And why did Dad come back here? He murdered someone

337

on that beach and got away with it. Why would he ever come back?'

Her mum sighed, shoulders slumping. 'He couldn't let Gwen have the lighthouse.'

'He couldn't *let* her? Gwen might be awful, but a memorial's still a memorial. Why couldn't Dad let her build it?'

She didn't speak. Instead, she raised the pipe and pointed it towards Will. Panic erupted on his face, but Lily saw that it wasn't him she was looking at. Just above his head, there was something engraved on the side of the tower. Something carved roughly into the panels.

Fingers going numb with cold, Lily took out her phone, using the light to see exactly what had been written. It was a crudely drawn heart, with the word *Gwen* scratched into its centre.

'This is it,' she said, more to herself than to her mum or Will. 'This is what Teddy was doing up here.'

She imagined a thirteen-year-old boy, egged on by four older teenagers as he scrambled up the tower. She pictured him, crouching where she was now, eagerly carving Gwen's name with a nail or a pocket knife.

The wind tugged at her hair, drops of moisture peppering her skin.

Had it rained that night? Was that how he fell; stood up too quickly and just slipped? Or perhaps he really had drunk some of their booze. Gwen had lied about everything else. Didn't it make sense she would lie about that too?

She thought of them on the ground; her dad, Gwen, Rory and Hugh. She heard them calling up to Teddy with words of encouragement, bottles of cider in their hands. Then she saw the horror on their faces as he tumbled over the railing, plummeting towards the ground.

'Damien told me they'd closed this place off,' her mum explained. 'After Teddy fell, it was just left to rot. Nobody came up here. Nobody even came near. But when Gwen announced she was reopening the lighthouse – preserving it as a memorial – Damien panicked. If this was found, he was convinced it would come back to him. Everything he'd built, everything he'd worked for . . . It would all be taken away.'

Lily's mind raced. She understood her dad's fear. The card Martha had found in Teddy's wardrobe hadn't been written, so nobody had ever known about his feelings for Gwen. Instead, the people of Hamlet had known only that Gwen was Damien's girlfriend, and Lily could imagine what they would ultimately assume. That *he* must have dared Teddy to come up here. To carve Gwen's name into the lighthouse on *his* behalf. Nobody would believe the younger boy had done it of his own accord. One way or another, Lily was certain that the blame would come to rest on her dad's shoulders.

'So he bought this place,' she murmured. 'Why? To hide this?'

'To make sure it was destroyed. He couldn't trust Gwen to do it properly. But then Damien was never very good at trusting people.'

Lily glared at her. 'He was right not to. How long have you wanted to kill him? His own *wife*?'

Something changed in her mum's expression, malice flickering in her eyes. 'Since the moment he told me he'd killed Rory. Since the moment I had to lie to the police and help cover it up.'

'And I gave you the chance to finally do it. I asked him to bring me here; to this quiet place in the middle of nowhere. And I let you talk me into spending the night at this party. All you had to do was follow us down here, kill him and then run back to London before anyone caught you.'

Lily stood, squaring up to the woman before her. 'To think that you were there the whole time. I needed you – I tried to *call* you – and you were in the next *fucking* room, hiding with the actors until you could slip away. How did you even get inside? Are the others in on it? Did you pay them or something?'

She paused, looking at how her mum had dyed her hair; the desperate escape she'd just attempted; Will, wounded against the side of the lighthouse. 'No . . . You've had to sneak your way in. Convince them somehow that you're an actress. If they'd been in on it too, Carl wouldn't have tried to show the police the champagne bottle. You wouldn't have needed to . . .'

She tailed off, her voice breaking slightly. 'This is your fault. You get that, don't you? If you hadn't gone back to Rory, he'd never have been killed. None of this would ever have happened.'

Her mum floundered, the fury fizzling out as quickly as it had surfaced. 'I never meant for any of this. I never meant to go back to Rory.'

'Then why did you?'

'Because you started to look like him.'

Lily frowned, caught completely off guard. 'Why would I look like him?'

340

'Please,' she said. 'Not here. Not like this. You must see, I did all of this for you.'

But Lily didn't relent. Her dad was dead – murdered by her mother – and she had to understand why.

Her mum turned away, looking out towards the dark water. 'It was like clockwork. Nine months after the wedding – nine months exactly – you came along. I only spent the one night with Rory, so I thought it couldn't possibly have been . . . But as you grew up, it became so obvious. It was all over your face.' She turned back, meeting Lily's eye. 'Damien isn't your dad. He never was. *Rory* was your father.'

45

Theo had never been so close to the lighthouse.

All his life, the place had been fenced off, to avoid a repeat of the tragedy that had befallen Teddy. As Nigel unlocked the gates and heaved them open, it somehow felt wrong. Like treading on sacred ground.

Brushing Nigel and Sylvia out of the way, Hugh marched towards the keeper's hut, Justin bounding at his side. The Finns had stayed with Gwen to watch over PC Fay until the ambulance arrived, although Theo suspected that even without the mangled police car in the mouth of the Lane, they would never have come to the lighthouse.

He looked towards the top of the tower.

Even now, he couldn't fathom it. They might only have met that evening, but Claire had been so kind. So supportive. He couldn't believe she would murder two people. And yet, nor could he deny the brazen escape she had attempted right before him.

'Wait,' he called, hurrying to catching them up. 'Hugh, wait!'

Hugh ignored him, striding ahead. Theo broke into a run, catching up just as he reached the door to the hut.

'Let me go first,' he said. 'Just me. I might be able to talk her down.'

Hugh grimaced, as if this were most absurd suggestion he'd ever heard. But Theo didn't budge.

'Five minutes,' he said. 'I've spent all night with Claire. If it really is her – if she's really the one – I might convince her to give up. Please, just let me try.'

Hugh considered for a moment, his scepticism painted plainly across his face. At the sound of shoes crunching upon dirt, he turned to see Ian hurrying to catch them up.

'The ambulance is on its way,' he said, panting slightly from having jogged up the hill.

'And the police?'

'They're coming as quickly as they can. They've put out a priority call, now PC Fay's down, but it's chaos out there. Resources stretched, officers scattered across the county . . . They say it'll still be some time before anyone makes it.'

'They won't even get through,' Sylvia added. 'The cars are blocking the Lane. And the ambulance will be stuck there too, when it arrives. Any police will have to park up and get here on foot.'

Hugh swore loudly, his breath pluming in front of him.

'Please,' Theo said again. 'Let me try. She's already trapped up there. If she makes a run for it, you'll be right here waiting.'

Hugh glared at him, evidently unhappy. But eventually, he stepped away from the door. 'Five minutes,' he said. 'But if you can't talk her down, we're coming up.'

46

Lily felt as if the ground itself had vanished from beneath her.

She couldn't speak. She couldn't even move. She simply stood, going numb with cold as the wind clawed at her skin.

'My dad?'

Her mum nodded, her face creased as she tried, it seemed, to hold back tears. 'You were so young when Rory left London that I couldn't tell. But as you grew older, it became more and more obvious. The resemblance . . . I must have spent a couple of years wondering if it was really there or if I was just imagining it. But once I was sure, I came down here to tell him. To ask him what I should do. I never expected a relationship to start from it and I certainly hadn't planned for it. But it did.'

She shook her head, her hair whipping in front of her eyes as the wind picked up. 'You're right. I used to come while you were at school and Damien was on business. Never for long; just a night or two. But every time I came, I was more certain that if it weren't for you, I wouldn't have gone back to London.

'Rory tried for months to convince me to leave. He wanted to tell Damien the truth – to bring you here, so the three of us could be together. A *real* family, he used to say. And I wanted it too, Lily. A quiet life for the three of us by the water. You, me and Rory. I wanted it more badly every time he spoke about it.'

Lily glared at her. 'So why didn't you do it?'

She paused, her voice straining, and Lily felt her shock turn to anger. Was she really expecting her to just accept this? To thank her for murdering her dad, for the sake of a man she barely remembered?

'You never knew Damien,' her mum said. 'Not really. By the time I realised the truth about you, I'd known for years that marrying him was a mistake. He'd always been cunning. Wily. But when he sent Rory away – bought him out of the firm for a fraction of what he should have been owed – I realised just how ruthless he was.

'I was desperate to leave. I thought about it every day, but I knew I couldn't. Damien might have let me go, but he'd never have let me take you. So I told Rory no. I told him again and again, until he finally decided to take things into his own hands. The next time I visited, he called Damien. He told him I was in Hamlet and that there were things the three of us needed to talk out.'

Lily thought back to her conversation with PC Fay, recalling the story of the blonde woman Rory had been seen with the day he was killed. 'You argued,' she said. 'On the beach . . .'

Her mum frowned, but she didn't bother to ask this time how Lily could know what had happened. 'I tried to talk him out of it but he was insistent. He was going to tell Damien the truth about us. About you. I couldn't be here for that; couldn't bring myself to go through with it. So I left. I drove straight back to

345

London and didn't hear anything more until Damien came home the following morning. Just as the sun was coming up, he told me Rory was dead.'

A tear finally trickled onto her cheek, the wind catching it and tugging it towards her ear. 'If I ever told you the truth, he said, he'd cut us off. Both of us. If we wanted to be Rory's, we could fend for ourselves. A few hours later, the police called. They asked if I knew where Damien had been the night before, and I made my choice. I chose to protect us. To protect *you*.'

This time, Lily didn't even try to reply. She didn't have the words. She found herself grateful for the thin layer of drizzle that was beginning to fall. It masked her tears as she looked at this murderer, masquerading as her mother.

'So you did the same to Dad,' she said. 'The same place, in the same way, with a rock from the same beach.'

Her mother took a step forward. 'I was so tired, Lily. Tired of seeing him every day, knowing what he'd done. Tired of knowing you weren't his. I had to do something. For you. For us. And then you told me he was bringing you here. You asked me for help and I found the party at Hamlet Hall. I saw an advert online – saw that they were looking for an actress – and I thought . . . Could I do it? Could I finally shake him loose?

'I've seen Damien's will. If I could slip into the party, do what I needed to and slip out again before the game began – before you and I had any chance to cross paths – we'd be free. All of the money would come to us. We might not be with Rory, but we could do whatever we wanted. Just the two of us.'

'And you really thought you'd get away with this?'

346

'Why not? Will told me how this evening would begin – the guests having dinner in the restaurant while the actors waited in the lounge. I knew I'd have hours to get to Damien before the game began; before there was any chance of you and I seeing each other. If I'd only managed to get out before the police arrived, I could have been halfway back to London by now, ready to receive the news that my husband had been murdered in Hamlet Wick. Nobody here knows me, and nobody knows about us and Rory. Why would they suspect me?'

She looked at Lily pleadingly. 'Can you really not see why I've done this? I couldn't let things go on as they were, not when I have the rest of our lives to think about. Can you not see how much better everything would be if it had all just worked?'

'It doesn't matter. The police will be coming. They'll arrest you—'

'No. We can get out of this. Together.' She sprang forward, her shoes squeaking on the damp platform, and grasped Lily's arms. 'This is why I invented Claire. If we can get away without them realising who I am – leave them looking for some actress who doesn't exist – we can still make this work.'

Lily saw a wild look gleam in her eyes.

'We'll pretend you're my hostage. We'll tell them I'm taking you with me and I'll kill you if they follow us. I'll drop you off somewhere and drive back to London. When they pick you up, you can tell them . . . Tell them I didn't need you any more. Tell them you fought back and I left you on the side of the road. They'll call me to break the news about Damien and everything will be back as it should be.'

For several agonising seconds, Lily didn't know what to say.

She was horrified – repulsed, even – by the woman who stood before her. The woman claiming to be her mother.

Looking away, she saw Will, still slouched against the tower. He was watching the pair of them, his eyes wide with terror.

'What about him? He's heard all of this. He'll tell the police who you are.'

Her mum nodded and took a deep breath. 'People have fallen from this lighthouse before. That poor boy, Teddy. All those years ago.' She looked Lily in the eye. 'Just one more. One more death and then we can start again. We'll take all the money and we'll run. What do you say?'

47

Will tried to scramble to his feet. He had to get away. Had to escape.

Seeing him begin to stir, Claire – or whatever her name might actually be – swung the pipe again, catching him this time with a vicious blow to the knee. He tumbled onto his belly, landing so close to the edge of the platform that his head and shoulders jutted out into space. He saw the hill looming below him, and even further still, the black waves crashing against the base of the cliff.

Feeling terror begin to take hold, he scrambled backwards, doing his best to ignore the pain. The platform was wet, his shirt soaking through as he wriggled away. Rolling onto his back, he saw Lily grasp her mother's arm, holding her at bay.

'We have to,' she urged, trying to wrench herself free from Lily's grip. 'I won't let Damien ruin our lives. If this is what it takes – if this is how we'll finally be free of him – we have to do it.'

Lily shook her head. 'Please, Mum. Please don't.'

In an instant, her face changed. 'Do you think Damien hesitated when he murdered Rory? He'd have done this in a heartbeat if it meant saving his own skin.'

Will watched, shivering, as he tried to gauge what could be going through Lily's mind. She must have been silent only for a few seconds, her face pale in the glare of the floodlights. But to Will, they were the longest seconds of his life. As he lay there, his ribs throbbing and knee searing, he was all too aware that he was watching her decide whether this moment would be his last.

'You're right,' she said quietly. 'Dad wouldn't have given it a second thought. But that's the point, Mum. Look at this place. Everyone here has a reason to hate him. He hurt people. He hurt *you*.' She relaxed her grip. 'Please talk to the police. If you explain everything to them, like you have to me, maybe they'll understand. Maybe they won't sentence you quite as harshly. Please, Mum . . . Don't take both my parents away.'

Will watched, allowing himself to feel a warm flicker of hope as Lily's words caused the expression to soften on her mother's face.

'You're still so young,' she said. 'I forget sometimes. There's so much you don't understand yet. Well, I won't let this happen to us. I won't let Damien ruin our lives. If you won't help, I'll do it myself.'

She turned on Will, and once again he felt the fear take him. He shuffled away, crawling on his back, but almost immediately reached the edge of the platform. Lily was pleading now, trying desperately to hold her mother back, but she wasn't listening. She took a step forward, murder in her eyes.

'I won't tell anyone,' he whimpered. 'I promise. Just let me go. Let me—'

'Claire.'

A new voice rang out, causing her to stop dead. Over her shoulder, Will watched as Theo stepped through the doorway.

48

If Theo had still harboured any doubts about the woman he'd known to be Claire, the sight that greeted him quickly laid them all to rest.

He'd climbed the spiral staircase as carefully as he could manage, wary of it creaking beneath his feet. When he reached the top, he hid to the side of the doorway, his phone in his hand as he hovered just out of sight.

He'd wanted to listen as she explained herself. Now he'd heard enough. And so he stepped onto the platform to find Will, the drop looming behind him while Lily tried desperately to hold her mother back.

'Lily's right,' he said. 'The police are coming and the others are all waiting for you on the ground. Just come down and talk to them. There's no getting out of this.'

She glared at him. 'Walk away, Theo. Go back down and tell them all to leave. You haven't heard everything. You don't need to be involved.'

'I've heard enough. I know that you murdered Carl and Mr White. That you're going to murder Will.' He glanced down at the phone in his hand. 'Just stop. If you do this properly – if you explain what happened with Rory – they'll all listen. The police might be lenient.'

She seemed to consider for a moment. From the corner of his eye, Theo saw Will looking up at him hopefully.

'I can't,' she said, the defiance returning to her voice. 'They won't listen. They won't understand. It's too late for that now.'

Theo nodded sadly. He held up the phone. Just as he'd hoped, up here, on the hill, he had a single bar of precious signal.

49

On the ground, Justin was becoming impatient.

He shuffled on the spot, his hands stuffed into the pockets of his chinos to stave off the cold. Every so often, he looked towards the top of the lighthouse, his resentment building.

He should be up there. *He* should be the one learning what had happened to White.

He wasn't the only one growing restless, either. Hugh had been pacing outside the lighthouse keeper's hut since Theo disappeared inside, glancing at his watch every few seconds.

Surely Theo's time must be up, Justin thought. Had it really been less than five minutes? From where he was standing, it could just as easily have been an hour. At this rate, even the police would arrive before Theo managed to talk Claire down.

He felt his phone buzz inside his blazer. As he slipped it from his pocket, the screen lit up.

'It's Theo,' he said.

'What does he say?' asked Hugh.

'Nothing. He hasn't said anything. It's just an audio file.'

50

'What have you done?' Lily's mother stared at Theo, her eyes bulging. Then she launched herself at him, her voice rising to a shriek as she let the pipe clatter to the ground. '*What have you done?*'

Seizing him by the lapels, she spun him around and thrust him with startling force against the railing. The rusty bars strained under his weight. He felt rain on his face and heard the water crashing against the cliffs below. He was vaguely aware of Lily crying out, but it was no use. Her mother held him fast at the edge of the platform.

'I recorded you,' he said, doing all he could to restrain his rising panic. 'I've been recording you since I climbed the staircase. And I've sent the file to Justin.'

'You're lying!' She shook him violently, causing the barrier to give an alarming creak.

'I wanted to hear you explain. I was going to prove to the others that they were making a mistake. That they must be looking for someone else.' He turned his head a fraction, risking a glance at the drop that awaited him. Immediately, he wished he hadn't. He tried to wriggle free, but his shoes slipped on the damp platform and he almost lost his footing. It was only her grip that kept him upright.

'You'll see for yourself when you come down,' he said hurriedly. 'They're probably all listening to it right now. Hearing you admit to murdering Damien White.'

Their faces just inches apart, he saw sheer terror in her eyes. But still she continued to hold him firmly in place against the antique barrier.

'Please, Mum,' said Lily. 'This has gone too far. Please, just come down.'

'Listen to her,' said Theo. 'The police are on their way, and knowing Justin, he's probably uploading your confession to the *Herald*'s website as we speak. There's no way out of this. Everyone knows what you've done.'

The sound of a distant siren drifted on the air. Turning his head once more, Theo saw the blue lights, pulsing in the darkness between Hamlet and Hamlet Wick.

'They're here,' he said. 'The police.' He turned back to face her. 'Come down with us. There's nothing else to be done now.'

But the woman he had known as Claire simply watched, terrified, as the lights inched closer.

'Please, Mum,' said Lily. 'You said everything you've done tonight was for me. Do this for me too.'

For a long while, she seemed to think. Then, slowly, she let go of Theo's jacket. Relief washing over him, he lurched away from the edge, throwing himself against the side of the tower and slumping onto the platform beside Will.

Lily flicked him a quick glance, as if making sure he was clear, before returning her attention to her mother. Neither of them said a word. Together, they simply gazed out at the flashing lights, the siren growing louder as it crept closer.

At last, as a desperate, pleading expression took form on Lily's face, her mother turned and gave her a single nod.

51

Will struggled to comprehend the feeling that overcame him as they made their way down the spiral staircase.

He was still in pain from the blows he'd been dealt with the pipe. His ribs throbbed and his knee burned so badly that Theo had to help him on the steps. The staircase was too narrow for them to walk side-by-side, but he stayed just one step in front, allowing Will to grasp his shoulder like a crutch. He was quaking, too, his entire body trembling at the prospect of being thrown from the rusty platform.

As for 'Claire' . . . She and Lily walked ahead. Despite all she'd done, Will would have been lying if he'd said he didn't feel at least a small measure of sympathy for her. She was a murderer; one who'd been willing to add his own name to her list of victims if it meant escaping. But having heard her story, he hoped Theo had been right; that the police would, as he'd urged, be sympathetic.

And yet, despite the threat of death, or the curious cocktail of sympathy and bitterness that he bore for his would-be killer, the feeling that ultimately overcame him was one of elation.

He wasn't going to be blamed for the murders of Carl and Damien White. But perhaps most importantly, he had uncovered the truth of Rory's death. He finally understood the events that had led him, all those years ago, to that terrible scene on the beach. It was as if a gap had been plugged. Even with all the chaos happening around him, as he hobbled down that staircase Will felt soothed. Almost content.

Outside the keeper's hut, a small congregation greeted them. Hugh, Ian, Justin and the Cobbs were waiting, gathered around the door in a rough semicircle. Justin beamed, his phone poised as he stood ready to frantically photograph them emerging from the building.

Looking at the group, Lily's mother frowned. 'The police . . .'

'Will take you when they arrive,' said Hugh.

Confused, she looked towards the blue lights that were flashing in the Lane. Following her gaze, Will peered into the gloom and felt a look of realisation spread across his own face, as he saw two paramedics scurrying about the mangled police car.

'An ambulance . . .' She turned to Theo. 'Did you know?' He nodded, prompting her to give a small, sad smile. 'I suppose Jack was right about one thing. You are going to make a phenomenal actor.'

Lily put her arm around her shoulders, shielding her from the group, and Will turned away.

Nobody followed him. Nobody even questioned where he was going. He limped to the edge of the building site, passing a skip and a Portakabin, and peered through a gap between two of the fencing panels. Looking towards the beach, he quickly found the place he was looking for. The exact spot where he had stumbled on Rory's body.

He stared at it, oblivious to the conversation taking place behind him, and took a deep breath, feeling the cold air fill his lungs. Then, bracing himself, he closed his eyes.

There was nothing.

He didn't hear the sound of gulls. Didn't feel shale slipping beneath his feet or see the huddled mass of pale skin and damp clothes. There was only darkness. Perfect, gentle darkness.

For a while, he kept his eyes closed. Then, when he was certain that he was correct – that the memory wasn't going to resurface – he sighed, his breath steaming in front of him. His ribs ached and his body was numb with cold, but he didn't care.

For the first time in twelve years, a smile twitched of its own accord at the corners of his lips.

One year later

The crowd at the foot of the lighthouse was growing restless. Rain had been forecast, and the sizeable audience that had gathered – or as sizeable as an audience comprised solely of the residents of Hamlet could be – was shuffling nervously, umbrellas twitching as dark clouds massed overhead.

In the middle of it all, Will stood shoulder to shoulder with Theo and Lily. It was the first time he'd seen her since the events at Hamlet Hall, and he'd been more than a little surprised to find she wanted to stand with them. If he was honest, he was surprised she had come at all.

He supposed he shouldn't be so taken aback by her presence, though. After all, she was the one bankrolling the day's proceedings.

When Damien White's death was announced, speculation had been rife as to what would be done with the lighthouse. With White gone and the truth of Teddy's accident leaving Gwen's reputation in tatters, the most popular theory was that it would be left to rot, just as it had before.

In the end, the decision had been Lily's. It had taken a few months for Wendy White, as Will now knew her, to have her day in court. But when the trial came around, it had been short. The confession that Theo recorded was played for the jury, and Wendy quickly pleaded guilty to the murders of Carl and her husband. In the meantime, Lily had become the sole beneficiary of Damien White's will. A will that bequeathed her an undisclosed – although widely accepted to be exceptionally large – sum of money, a thriving property empire and, of course, the lighthouse.

It had been the *Hamlet Herald* that broke the news: the plans for a luxury home had been abandoned, and instead, the place was once again to be a memorial for Teddy Finn. Cobb Construction Ltd would carry out the work, accepting payment only for the necessary materials, and perhaps most dramatically of all, the project was to have Damien White's own daughter at the helm.

The spectators listened attentively to the Mayor, some dabbing their eyes as she spoke about what a fitting memorial the newly renovated lighthouse would be. Then, as Edward and Martha Finn cut the ceremonial ribbon, there came a polite round of applause. Nigel Cobb looked distinctly uncomfortable, standing at the front with the eyes of the crowd upon him. At his side, Sylvia beamed from beneath the brim of the largest hat Will had ever seen.

With the ceremony drawing to a close and a stiff January breeze rolling in from the water, the crowd began quickly to disperse. Justin, however, wasted no time in leaping forward to approach Edward and Martha.

Just as with Lily, it was the first time in nearly a year that Will had seen him, and he immediately noticed a difference in how the young reporter carried himself. There was less sense of a magpie searching desperately for a glittering story, and more of a self-assured swagger. Of course, it was clear where this change originated. Will knew all too well that the lanyard around his neck no longer bore the crest of the *Hamlet Herald*, but instead, the name of a national tabloid.

He had never read Justin's article, but he'd heard from those who had that it was sensational. An insider account of the murder of the country's most infamous property magnate, complete with a recorded confession from the killer herself for online readers. Just days after the *Herald* had run it, he'd been given his pick of three different jobs, and within a fortnight had left Hamlet for London. He'd barely looked back, apparently, only returning for the unveiling of the lighthouse so that he could write a follow-up to the story with which he'd made his name.

Just as they were turning away, Justin glanced over and locked eyes with Theo. Will tensed, but the pair of them shared an uneasy nod before Justin returned his attention to the Finns.

'You two seem on better ground,' said Lily.

Theo snorted gently. 'I suppose we are. A couple of weeks after it all happened, I had a call from the director I'd met in Bristol. Justin had been in touch, asking her to give me another shot. He told her we'd had a falling out and he'd written an overly harsh review just to spite me. She must have believed him, because she asked if I'd audition for a new show she was casting in Manchester.'

'And?'

Theo struggled to hold back a grin. 'And now I'm living in

Manchester. It's a supporting role. Not as big as the one I was hoping for in Bristol. But it's a start.'

Putting the lighthouse behind them, they made their way slowly down the hill. As they reached the harbour, they passed the building that had once been the Finns' shop.

'It's a gallery now,' said Will, noticing as Theo peered at a painting through the window. 'It was empty for a few months after Edward and Martha moved away, but it reopened just before the summer. The council runs it, I think. Showing work by local artists.'

'They moved away?' Lily repeated.

Will nodded. 'Only a few miles. But yes. After that night at Hamlet Hall, they sold up almost straight away.'

A small smile touched the corners of Lily's lips. 'Edward kept his promise, then. Good for him.' She looked around at the dispersing crowd. 'I guess I shouldn't be surprised that Gwen and Hugh didn't come.'

Will shook his head. 'Nobody's seen them in months. I don't think they've actually been into Hamlet since Gwen resigned from the tourist board.'

'How long did that take?'

'All of twenty-four hours. Once it came out that Teddy had climbed the lighthouse to impress her, I suppose she couldn't exactly stick around.'

They came to a stop at a gleaming Mini Cooper, parked neatly outside Hamlet Hall. Instinctively, Will tried to look into the restaurant, but there was nothing to see. The curtains were drawn, and across the oak doors, a large sign was plastered with the words *UNDER DEVELOPMENT*.

Will noticed that Ian hadn't returned for the ceremony either. He wasn't altogether surprised. Two months after the events that had unfolded within its walls, the *Herald* reported that he'd sold Hamlet Hall to a large hotel chain, which planned to convert the place into a luxury spa retreat. Ian had been so desperate to leave that the sale had supposedly been something of a bargain. By all accounts, he'd returned the money he stole from the Finns and then left Hamlet the moment an offer had been made. Will thought he might have heard about a new job in Exeter, but he couldn't be sure. Either way, it seemed Ian had no intention of coming back.

Looking at Hamlet Hall now, reduced to an empty shell, he couldn't help but feel deflated. Nor could he fail to see the irony of some other anonymous property developer descending on the place just weeks after Damien White's body had been removed. He wondered how much Hamlet Hall's new owners had been told about the fate of the last outsider to have set their sights on Hamlet Wick.

'Are you really going back to London already?' asked Theo, as Lily fetched a key to the Mini from her bag. 'You've been here barely an hour.'

She looked back at the lighthouse. 'It doesn't seem right to stay. After all the harm my family's done to this place . . . I needed to be here today. But I won't be coming back.'

For a fleeting moment, Will thought he saw a hint of disappointment in Theo's expression.

'And how are you? After . . . Well, after everything?'

'You mean after my mum murdered my dad?'

Theo began to shuffle uncomfortably. 'I suppose I wasn't sure if . . . Well, that is, if Mr White . . .'

'If he's still my dad?'

Theo said nothing this time.

'Rory shouldn't have died the way he did,' said Lily. 'But whatever he and my mum had was between them. For all his faults, my dad died in Hamlet Hall.'

'And what about your mum?'

'It's been tough. I've visited her a few times in prison, but I don't know how long it'll take to get back to where we were. If we ever *will* get back.' She hesitated. 'We have time, I guess. It'll be years before they even think about letting her out. Right now, with everything Dad's left me, I have plenty on my plate.'

She looked towards the lighthouse. 'I've been so frightened of the day I took over. Worried about how I could possibly walk in his shoes. But coming to this place, learning about the people he stepped on to build his empire . . . I've realised I don't need to. It isn't his, for me to watch over. It's mine. To run as I want. We aren't going to be as big as Dad would have wanted – we certainly aren't going to be as profitable – but we *are* going to start doing things right. Hamlet's just the beginning. All the people Dad screwed over; everyone he bullied and hurt . . . I'm going to be the one who makes amends.'

She shook her head, as if snapping from a daydream. 'I still can't believe she was there the entire time. Just across the hall. I keep thinking about that moment in the library, when Hugh went to the lounge to fetch the third clue. If I'd gone with him . . .' She sighed. 'Still, there's so much that makes sense now.'

'Like what?' asked Theo.

'Well, her phone for one thing. After the police arrived, I

went to Ian's office to call home and tell her what had happened. But when I tried her mobile, it went straight to voicemail. Didn't even ring. At the time, I assumed she must have turned it off for some reason. Now, I realise she was having the same problem that meant I needed to use Ian's phone in the first place. In Hamlet Wick, there isn't any bloody signal.'

Theo nodded. 'I'd be lying if I said it didn't explain some of what I saw too. Little things. So small I didn't think twice when they were happening.'

'Like my rucksack?' asked Will.

'That's one of them.' Seeing Lily's frown, Theo explained: 'I couldn't work it out at first – why she would think to hide the gun in there. How she would even *know* to. But after a little while, I remembered; when Will came to the lounge at the beginning of the interval, he was struggling with his inhaler, so your mum asked if he had a spare anywhere. He told us it was in Ian's office, in his rucksack.

'Once she'd decided she was going to put him in the firing line, it must have seemed too good an opportunity to miss. After she'd left the kitchen, it would only have taken a few seconds to slip into the office and drop off the gun.'

He grimaced. 'I should have seen it. Should have realised what was going on. Even when Fay first arrived, and she sent us all back inside Hamlet Hall – your mum was the first one in. She told me she was just feeling rattled by everything that was happening, but I get it now. The truth was that she couldn't risk you seeing her when Gwen brought you back from the beach. She wanted to make sure she was in the lounge, safely out of sight.

'The same thing happened when Jack found Carl's body, and

I still didn't see it. I went out into the hallway to find out what was happening, but she stayed put. I suppose she couldn't risk you being out there too and spotting her.'

Lily's eyes narrowed, but before she could reply, Will heard a voice calling out to them. Turning to face it, he saw Martha Finn hurrying down the hill. When she caught up with them, her eyes flickered to the key in Lily's hand. 'Are you leaving?'

Lily nodded. 'Heading back to London.'

For a few seconds, Martha didn't move. Then she threw her arms around Lily, pulling her tightly into a hug. 'Thank you,' she said. 'Thank you for what you've done here. For us. For Teddy. It . . .' She stepped away, tears in the corners of her eyes. 'Well, it means the world.'

Edward said nothing. He simply gave Lily a brisk nod, before putting his hand on his wife's shoulder. With one last smile, Martha let him guide her away.

Completely dumbfounded, Lily took a moment to collect herself. Clearing her throat, she turned back to Will and Theo. 'Well,' she said. 'Look after yourselves.'

She cast one last look around, taking in Hamlet Hall, the lighthouse and the beach. She might even have given a little sigh, although with the breeze that was still rolling in, Will couldn't be sure.

Without another word, she climbed into the Mini, started the engine and moved off. Will and Theo stood together, watching as she drove into the Lane. Once she had disappeared from view, they ambled towards Theo's own car, a battered old Ford Fiesta parked just a few yards away.

'Do you really need to go back today?' asked Will. 'We

could . . . I don't know. A Costa's opened on the high street. I thought we could catch up properly.'

Even after a year without a single flashback to the morning on the beach, it still seemed strange to Will that he of all people might invite someone for a coffee. From the expression on his face, Theo clearly thought so too.

'I'm sorry. I wanted to be here, but I can't stay. We have a performance tonight.'

Will nodded, trying to hide his disappointment.

'What'll you do now?' asked Theo.

'I'm not sure. I've been thinking about leaving too. Maybe applying for a university course somewhere. Although I've no idea what I'd study.' He shrugged. 'For the time being, it looks like I'm still here.'

Theo unlocked the Fiesta, but before he could climb into the driver's seat, Will caught his arm.

'Wait. Before you go. There's one last thing about that night which doesn't add up.' He took a deep breath. 'When did Wendy White get the gun?'

Theo looked pained.

'I'm just trying to understand,' Will added hurriedly. 'Carl came into the hallway while you and Lily were speaking, and he asked for PC Fay. I get why she killed him – she realised he was on to her. He was going to show Fay the bottle, tell her that she had given it to him and insisted he serve it to Mr White. But how did it get back to her that he'd caught on?'

At first, Theo didn't reply. He peered at Will, his eyes narrowing. 'I told her,' he said at last. 'When I went back into the lounge, I described what had happened out in the hallway.'

'And what about the gun? She had her own key to the Range Rover, but I've heard that Lily saw the gun in the glovebox when she and Mr White first parked up. When would Wendy have had the chance to fetch it?'

Theo sighed. 'I think she must have gone when Justin came to find me in the lounge. She convinced Jack to go out with her into the hallway, to give the two of us some privacy. When she came back, she said that Jack had gone to the loo for a few minutes. If Jack had left her alone, it wouldn't have taken long to run outside, fetch the gun from the glovebox and hurry back in.'

'And what sort of time do you think this happened?'

'It was a year ago, Will. I have no idea.' Theo frowned again. 'You know, you really shouldn't be thinking about this any more. You did it. You found out who murdered Rory. It's time to move on.'

With a tremendous effort, Will stopped himself from launching into another question. There was so much he still wanted to ask. So much that had been confined to the police reports. He'd even tried to get in touch with PC Fay, and see if she might be persuaded to share a few missing details, but he'd been surprised to learn from the officer who answered the phone that she'd since been dismissed. The officer wouldn't say why, exactly, although he seemed happy enough to drop his voice and whisper in an excitable tone that there had been allegations of misconduct.

Regardless, it was painfully clear that Theo wouldn't tell him anything further.

For a little while, Will stood outside Hamlet Hall and watched as Theo disappeared into the Lane. Once the car was out of sight, he reached into his coat pocket and drew out a small notebook. He flicked through the pages, breezing past a list of names, a hand-drawn floor plan of Hamlet Hall and several dozen lines of details and anecdotes.

Turning towards the back of the little book, he found a blank page and jotted down what Theo had just shared. Then he flicked forward to a page headed *Unanswered*, found the question about the gun and crossed it off.

It was a shame Theo hadn't remembered the exact timings, but perhaps it was for the best. Will knew that he had to mix up some of the details. After all, he wasn't going to make the same mistake twice.

He looked towards the beach and spent a moment watching the waves break on the shale.

No, he wasn't going to slip up in the same way he had at Hamlet Hall. He'd change the names of all involved. The location too. When it came to finding a publisher, he was even going to use a pseudonym. He was leaving nothing to chance this time.

Turning away from the beach, he tucked the notebook back into his coat. He was almost ready. Just a few more outstanding details and he'd start writing.

Tucking his hands into his pockets, he began to walk, feeling a little lighter with every step as he left Hamlet Hall behind.

Acknowledgements

The idea for this book first came to me while hunting a murderer through the streets of Reading.

Not a real murderer, I should add. This was, in essence, a real-life game of Cluedo. Actors waited beside local landmarks, ready to divulge vital information if you could track them down, while crafty clues had been hidden all over town. It was brilliant. But it got me thinking, in a way that my now-wife tells me is becoming increasingly morbid: What if someone was actually murdered here? What if, midway through this imaginary investigation, a real crime was committed?

And with that, I knew I had to write *The Murder Game*.

The next question, of course, was where to set it. I wanted a locked-room environment. Somewhere small. Claustrophobic. Maybe an old hotel? As the element of a lighthouse became key to the story I was plotting, I realised I also needed my location to be coastal. I've always loved being by the sea, so there was no shortage of candidates. But for this story, I wanted somewhere special. A place that's not only remote but also beautiful, and that seeps atmosphere.

It took me all of about three seconds to choose Exmoor, and it's at this point that I need to say my first thank you.

Readers of my books might wonder if I'm particularly drawn to the West Country, with several of *A Fatal Crossing*'s characters hailing from Somerset, while *The Murder Game*'s fictional setting of Hamlet Wick is in Devon. I can tell you that those readers would be absolutely right. More than that, I can tell you where this attachment to the West Country began. All through my teenage years, I would spend a week every summer with my mum, my brother, my step-dad and my step-siblings on Hindon Organic Farm. Nestled in the Exmoor hills, those weeks on the farm are among my fondest memories. It's hardly a surprise, then, that when I needed a coastal location for *The Murder Game*, I quickly chose Exmoor. In real life, I'll still leap at any opportunity to visit. It seems I'm exactly the same when it comes to writing, too.

So, thank you to that pocket of my family – in which I'm including Penny and Roger Webber, the owners of Hindon Farm – for instilling me with what I know will be a lifelong love for this remarkable place. From the rolling hills to the terrifying tales of the legendary Beast . . . Without those summers, there's a good chance *The Murder Game* would not exist as you see it today.

As always, thank you to my agent, Harry Illingworth, for all of your ongoing support. I struggle sometimes to get my head around everything that's happened since our first meeting in Caffè Nero. These last few years have been among the wildest and most rewarding of my life, and it's been a privilege to share them with you. I can't wait to see where this crazy journey takes us next.

Thank you to my editor, Emily Griffin, for your patience and wisdom. Not only would *The Murder Game* not exist without your incredible talent, but it wouldn't be half as good. It's a joy to have worked with you on this story, and of course, to know that I'll soon be doing so again on my third.

Thank you to Sam Rees-Williams, Laura O'Donnell and the many others at Century who have played a role in publicising both *A Fatal Crossing* and *The Murder Game*. You've done the most remarkable job of launching these stories into the world, and I'm so grateful to you for the many hours you've poured into them. Thank you also to Joanna Taylor for your editorial support.

Thank you to Amanda Maguire for sharing your invaluable knowledge of police procedure. Of course, it goes without saying that any errors a discerning reader might spot are entirely the result of my own oversight.

Finally, the biggest thank you of all goes to my wife, Hayley. Thank you for your patience, for the pep-talks, and above all for the limitless faith you've placed in me this past year. I can't imagine there are many people who, when their fiancé decides he's leaving his job to write a murder mystery, would not only accept it but actively encourage it. I couldn't do this without you, and I hope I'm making you proud.